DISCARDED BY THE
LA PORTE INDIANA
PUBLIC & COUNTY LIBRARY

SIGNATURE_____

SPECIAL MESSAGE TO READERS

This book is published under the auspices of

THE ULVERSCROFT FOUNDATION

(registered charity No. 264873 UK)

Established in 1972 to provide funds for research, diagnosis and treatment of eye diseases. Examples of contributions made are: —

A Children's Assessment Unit at Moorfield's Hospital, London.

•

Twin operating theatres at the Western Ophthalmic Hospital, London.

•

A Chair of Ophthalmology at the Royal Australian College of Ophthalmologists.

•

The Ulverscroft Children's Eye Unit at the Great Ormond Street Hospital For Sick Children, London.

You can help further the work of the Foundation by making a donation or leaving a legacy. Every contribution, no matter how small, is received with gratitude. Please write for details to:

**THE ULVERSCROFT FOUNDATION,
The Green, Bradgate Road, Anstey,
Leicester LE7 7FU, England.
Telephone: (0116) 236 4325**

**In Australia write to:
THE ULVERSCROFT FOUNDATION,
c/o The Royal Australian College of
Ophthalmologists,
27, Commonwealth Street, Sydney,
N.S.W. 2010.**

Grace Thompson was born in Barry, South Wales. She is a widow with a son and daughter, four grandsons and one granddaughter. After her children grew up, she qualified as a nursery nurse and worked with children in care and schools. Then, following six years in Berkshire watching her grandchildren grow up, she moved back to South Wales, and now spends her mornings writing and afternoons walking the cliffs and beaches of Mumbles and Gower with her Welsh collie.

Grace Thompson is the well-loved author of *Family Pride*, *Summer of Secrets*, *Missing the Moment*, and *The Homecoming*, as well as *Corner of a Small Town* and *The Weston Women*, the first two volumes of the Pendragon Island series.

UNLOCKING THE PAST
The third volume in the
Pendragon Island series.

The Griffiths live at the edge of the little
Welsh town of Pendragon Island, and at
the edge of convention. With poaching and
their 'deals', rationing is less of a problem
than to most. Basil is married to Eleri
and is trying to achieve respectability, but
brothers Frank and Ernie keep involving
him in dangerous situations. Their sister
Caroline is trapped in a marriage that
brings her close to despair as she and
her husband Barry are haunted by the
ghost of Barry's brother, the father of
Caroline's child. And Rhiannon Lewis
learns that love brings its problems . . .

Books by Grace Thompson
Published by The House of Ulverscroft:

GRACE THOMPSON

UNLOCKING THE PAST

Complete and Unabridged

ULVERSCROFT
Leicester

ABU - 3228

First published in Great Britain in 1997 by
Severn House Publishers Limited
Surrey

First Large Print Edition
published 1999
by arrangement with
Severn House Publishers Limited
Surrey

The right of Grace Thompson to be identified as
the author of this work has been asserted by her
in accordance with the
Copyright, Designs and Patents Act, 1988

All situations in this publication are fictitious and any
resemblance to living persons is purely coincidental.

Copyright © 1997 by Grace Thompson
All rights reserved

British Library CIP Data

Thompson, Grace
   Unlocking the past.—Large print ed.—
   Ulverscroft large print series: general fiction
   1. Domestic fiction
   2. Large type books
   I. Title
   823.9'14 [F]

   ISBN 0–7089–4128–1

Published by
F. A. Thorpe (Publishing) Ltd.
Anstey, Leicestershire
Set by Words & Graphics Ltd.
Anstey, Leicestershire
Printed and bound in Great Britain by
T. J. International Ltd., Padstow, Cornwall

This book is printed on acid-free paper

1

Caroline picked up the dress in which she had been married to Barry Martin. It had been an unorthodox wedding, as the couple had not intended to stay married. A divorce had been planned before the wedding date was fixed. But their feelings for each other had changed and now she and Barry were going to make the marriage a real one and the dress had greater significance. Perhaps she would wear it on the day she left her parents' house to live with him for the first time.

The flat above Temptations, the sweet shop in Sophie Street owned by Barry's mother, was empty and as Nia wouldn't charge them any rent, Barry thought they should live there for a while to enable him to concentrate on building up his business.

She held the dress up to the light to make sure there were no marks or serious creases. She would have to take in the seams a little as she had been expecting Joseph when she and Barry had dishonestly sworn they would stay together 'Til death us do part'. She hung the dress in the wardrobe and went downstairs where her mother was getting Joseph, her eighteen-month-old son, ready to go for a walk. She smiled contentedly. Little Joseph, the reason for marrying Barry Martin.

She watched her mother with great affection as Janet finished dressing the little boy. As Caroline had lived at home throughout the pregnancy and birth it meant Janet had been very involved in Joseph's welfare and now, with the plans to move out of the family home so imminent, Caroline knew that her mother was feeling an agony akin to bereavement.

Janet fastened the buttons on Joseph's coat, counting as she did so and praising the child as he joined in. Her face wore an expression of such love that Caroline felt a lump swell in her throat. She had a glimpse then of the lovely young woman her mother had once been, although Janet's hair had now turned to grey, held back in an untidy bun from which wisps fell to frame her face; her rosy, country-woman's face, which was lined now and showed so clearly her sixty-five years.

Janet picked up the child and kissed his smooth cheek and he wrapped his chubby arms around her neck to clutch her against him as he returned the kiss soundly.

'Nana's best boy,' Janet murmured.

As Janet put the little boy down and watched him scuttle away to find the toy he planned to take with him on his walk, Caroline saw her expression alter and a frown cross her face.

'Don't be sad about us leaving, Mam,' she said softly. 'I won't be far away, and I want you to be as happy about Barry and me as I am.'

'Happy for you? Of course I'm happy. Didn't I know that he wouldn't be able to stop himself falling in love with you? Married in name only, for heaven's sake! A beautiful girl like you? There isn't a man of flesh and blood who could fail to love you, Caroline, my lovely girl.'

Caroline Griffiths had realised she was carrying their child only months before Barry Martin's older brother, Joseph, was killed in a road accident. They had made plans to marry and for the shy Caroline her future looked perfect. Then a moment's stupidity had ended Joseph's life and Caroline couldn't face a future without him.

Barry had found her when she was overwhelmed by despair and contemplating suicide and agreed to marry her to give the child his rightful name of Martin. When Joseph Hywel Martin had been born, Barry had taken to the child as if he were his own.

His pride in his development and his charm and attractive looks — so like his dead father — had thrilled him more and more as time passed.

For a brief moment she relived the terror of the night when her life had changed so dramatically: hearing about the accident involving a van in which Joseph and Lewis-boy had been on the way back from Cardiff with two girls, the wealthy and outrageous Weston Girls. Then being told that both Lewis-boy Lewis and Joseph Martin were dead, leaving her carrying Joseph's child. Suicide had seemed the only way out.

Although it had not been a real marriage, Barry had enthusiastically taken on the role of father to little Joseph, and his affection for his nephew-cum-step-son gradually overflowed to include the child's mother. It was only recently that Caroline and Barry had accepted that their friendship was changing into something deeper, and now they had decided to make the marriage of convenience a real one and call off the divorce that had been their original intention.

Janet said little as the three of them walked along the lanes towards the outskirts of Pendragon Island. She pointed out the birds, who, in this lovely month of March were already pairing off and flying about with

4

beaks filled with materials for nest-building, and named the flowers and insects they discovered to an interested Joseph, but her replies to Caroline's remarks were brief and with even a hint of sadness.

'What are you thinking about, Mam?' Caroline asked. 'You seem miles away.'

'Not that far, only a few miles,' Janet replied. But although Caroline waited for further explanation, none came. Mam would tell her when she was ready.

★ ★ ★

Janet was thinking about her own parents and wishing they could have been there to enjoy little Joseph with her, but she hadn't seen her parents, her sister Marion or her brother Adrian, since she had run away from the miseries of her home to marry Hywel.

Since cutting off all contact with her family, she and Hywel had been so happy that she had rarely thought of the family she had left behind. With her own sons and daughter, life had been full, rich in laughter and contentment if not in material things. Hywel, and their boys, Basil and Frank had been joined by their orphaned cousin Ernie, who had been brought up as their brother. Her gentle and kindly daughter, Caroline, was the only one with a regular job, working in the town's wool and sewing shop.

Before Basil had married and settled down, her husband Hywel and the three boys had lived on their wits, rarely working, surviving on the crops they grew and the animals they kept, easing the family budget with odd-jobbing, poaching and petty thieving, something that Janet had learned to accept together with the rest of Hywel's carefree attitude to life.

Perhaps it was the fact of growing old, but thoughts had strayed more and more often to her family, wondering where and how they were. She hardly remembered her unkind brother and had even less recollection of her sister, Marion, who had left the family farm when Janet was very young. Curiosity about them grew and grew into a hesitant idea, which she shared with her daughter.

'Having your young Joseph and our Basil's little Ronnie has given me so much pleasure,' she began, 'that it's started me thinking of my own family, wishing they were the kind of people I could invite to share it. But Mam left when I was three, and apart from that gift when I married your father, I've never heard a word since. My father is dead. Mrs Phillips got in touch and told me that. There's only my brother, Adrian,

6

and I doubt if he's changed enough for me to enjoy his company!'

'Do you ever think about your sister, Mam?' Caroline coaxed.

Janet shrugged. 'I've wondered whether I could find her, but no, she's probably dead too. I've heard nothing of her since I was six years old. Eleven, that's all she was, poor little dab, when she ran away from my father's bad temper.' She opened the cutlery drawer and began setting the table for the evening meal, lips moving as she counted. 'Barry's coming, isn't he? That's eight and the two little ones, but our Frank and Ernie might be late. A law to themselves those two brothers of yours.'

'Auntie Marion. Strange to have an aunt I've never met. She could still be alive. Why don't you try again to find her?'

'I doubt she survived long. Sickly she was, and my father wouldn't make any allowances, insisted on her getting up for milking and doing a share of the heavy work like the rest of us. And *dear* brother, Adrian, snitching on her whenever she paused for a rest.' She sighed. 'We weren't born out of love, like you and the boys, and like little Joseph here. We were born to provide an unpaid workforce for Dad.'

'It wouldn't hurt to advertise for her, make a few enquiries.'

'It's all so long ago. Seventy she'd be, five years older than me, and I have tried from time to time and got nowhere.'

'Perhaps Uncle Adrian would know?'

'I'm not asking him! He wouldn't give anyone the muck off his boots! All I'd get from that one is the threat of a shotgun for trespassing. Worse than my father, Adrian is. Nasty bit of work. No, it's too late, best I lock up the past where it belongs and enjoy your Joseph and Basil's Ronnie all to myself.'

'Who did you say told you about your father's death?' Caroline asked.

'Mrs Phillips, the wife of a farm-worker who had once worked for him. She found out where I lived and wrote to me. Why?'

'She might be able to to tell you what happened to your sister.'

'Too long ago. She's probably gone too.'

Although she had firmly shrugged aside any idea of finding her sister, Janet found the idea, once revived, refused to go away. It wouldn't hurt to ask a few people. The farm where she had been born wasn't that far away, some fifty miles, no more. She was able to drive and the old van wasn't always needed by Hywel or the boys. She could tell the family she was going into Cardiff to buy a dress. The plan formed and grew almost of its own volition.

She could visit the village, chat to some of the elderly people who lived there, pick up some tenuous threads and check them out at her leisure. She quelled her growing excitement. Silly to build up her hopes. She'd been along that path before and it had come to nothing. A day spent asking about her family mustn't be important enough to end in disappointment. No, she would treat it as an outing to find a few of the people who might still remember her, nothing more.

But still that glimmer of hope remained, forming a vague picture of an elderly woman who would be her sister. She tried half-heartedly to push it away but it crept back and brought a *frisson* of excitement. So much would have happened in sixty-one years that listening to her sister's story would be like having a book read to her. And what a lot she would have to impart about her own unconventional and resourceful family!

* * *

Janet and Hywel Griffiths and their family lived in a small cottage a few fields away from the edge of the town of Pendragon

9

Island. They had a few acres of land and lived almost independently, growing food, keeping chickens and, from time to time throughout rationing, an illegal pig which they killed and cured in the smokehouse beyond the toolshed. A large toolshed-cum-garage had been joined to the house and was now a bedroom for their son Frank and his cousin, Ernie. Their other son, Basil was married to Eleri and lived in rooms in Trellis Street with their small son, Ronnie.

Although small, the cottage seemed capable of holding an inordinate number of people. With the windows wide open and light spilling out onto the yard, laughter echoing around the fields, it was a place that drew people to relax and have fun. Invitations were rarely necessary for a party to happen and regarding the celebration of Caroline and Barry's decision to start a home together, a party would automatically ensue. She made a list to remind herself to buy extra flour to make bread and hoped there would be some way to fill enough sandwiches. Hywel usually found something, bartering this for that, his shotgun and fishing lines being the starting point for acquiring off-ration butter and cheese and even an occasional joint of meat.

It didn't occur to her that no one would

come. Neither did it occur to her that Hywel's search for food to fill them all would fail.

★ ★ ★

Caroline knew she was making it difficult for everyone by refusing to decide on a date for moving in with Barry and beginning her new life. It was such a complicated and strange occasion to arrange. Not a wedding, not a house-move, not even a re-affirmation of their marriage vows. No ceremony and no excuse to dress up in splendid clothes or for people to bring gifts. How could even someone like her Mam make a celebration and a party out of that?

If it had been possible, Caroline would have chosen to just quietly move her belongings out of her parents' house and into the flat above Temptations sweet shop. It sounded so simple, but with the sweet shop run by Rhiannon Lewis, Barry's ex-fiancée, that was not possible. They had to mark the occasion in some way and give Rhiannon a chance to decide whether or not she could continue working at the shop with Barry and his family going in and out.

Before she could begin life as Barry's wife she had to talk to Rhiannon and, although she had tried to find or create an opportunity, she had so far failed. One Wednesday afternoon, as she and her mother finished a walk and reached home with a tired Joseph clutching some early primroses in his tight fist, she decided that she wouldn't leave it a moment longer.

'Mam, will you look after Joseph for an hour while I go and find Rhiannon? I can't let things drift on any longer and I can't decide on a date for moving out before talking to her.'

'Go on, you. Joseph and I will busy ourselves getting dinner. Now, let's see, Joseph, how many plates will we need?' She began counting the members of the family on her fingers helped by her grandson as Caroline kissed him and walked once more down the lane towards town.

★ ★ ★

In Temptations sweet shop on the corner of Sophie Street, Rhiannon Lewis was preparing to wash the shelves under the counter. It was a Wednesday afternoon and most of the town's shops were closed. She often used the opportunity to do the cleaning that was difficult to achieve while customers needed to be served. She had returned to the shop that day at two-thirty and, as usual, had run straight up to the flat to see whether Barry Martin was there. He wasn't and she washed his dishes and tidied the living room of the flat before going down to begin her pre-planned tasks.

She stopped in the doorway of the room above the shop and looked around to assure herself there was nothing else that needed doing. She knew she should no longer involve herself, even so trivially, in Barry's life, now he and Caroline had announced their intention to live together and make their marriage a real one, but the habit, begun so many weeks ago, was difficult to break.

The whole of Rhiannon's relationship with Barry Martin had been complicated. Most of her friends met someone, fell in love, became engaged then married; but for her things hadn't been that simple. She and Barry had fallen in love and that was followed by their engagement. But due to a misunderstanding the engagement had ended and, almost immediately, Barry had married Caroline Griffiths.

Then their engagement was on again when Barry had explained that the reason for his wedding was solely to support Caroline; to marry her and give his name to the unborn child of his brother Joseph, who had been killed at the same time as her own brother, Lewis-boy. The gesture had seemed so foolish, then noble, and now, with the engagement off once again and Barry telling her he would remain married to Caroline, so confusing, she didn't know how she felt or how she was expected to feel.

There was resentment, and some peevish anger towards Caroline. She had been let down and, worse, made to look foolish. That was hard to accept, with even her closest friends making jokes about the peculiar situation. She hadn't spoken to Caroline since the latest change in her relationship with Barry, and had wondered if she ever would. Then, the final insult. She had been told by Barry that he and his wife and her son were going to live in the flat above Temptations. It was so thoughtless of him, and somehow typical, she decided. He could at least have found somewhere further away so that he didn't have to walk through the shop every day, showing her and everyone else how happy he was.

She wondered how she would behave when she and Caroline did meet. Would she smile and pretend? Or act more in the style of her mother, the archetypal redhead, Dora, and rant and rave and tell her how much she hated her for ruining her life?

If she were truthful she couldn't say her life was ruined. She and Barry would never have been a perfect couple. In fact it was doubtful if they would have married even if Caroline's troubles hadn't intervened. There were many times when he forgot an arrangement, or was late, and each time he expected her to understand without complaint. What was worse, he had never made her feel adored. Adored was a word she used whenever she day-dreamed about the man she would marry. No, Barry had never adored her and that was what she wanted when she became a wife — an adoring husband.

Barry Martin was a carpenter by trade but he worked as a photographer, and was slowly building up a reputation for quality and reliability. He had bought an old garage and had converted it into a workroom with a reception and display area, but he continued to use the flat from time to time. It had once been intended to be Rhiannon's home, hers and Barry's, but walking through the rooms and looking around her now, the pain and disappointments had faded to the point where she could feel only the slightest tinge of regret.

She admitted to herself that the only pain really left was that of rejection. If only she had been the one who had faced facts and

15

told Barry goodbye. Then there would be nothing left but relief. But she hadn't, and the best way of dealing with the situation was with a façade of hurt pride. She couldn't make it too easy for Caroline and Barry!

The complications of her relationship with Barry and their on-off-on-off engagement, were exacerbated by the fact of her working for his mother in Temptations. And another thread in the tangled web was yet another connection between the two families. Her father, Lewis Lewis, had left her mother and was living with Nia Martin, Barry's mother. How could one small family create so many problems?

She was putting away the dusters, having cleaned one of the top shelves when she heard a knock at the door. At first she ignored it. There was often someone taking advantage of seeing her there and asking to be served with some sweets or a birthday card. The knocking was repeated and with a sigh that was also a smile, she pushed the blind aside and began to open the door. The smile faltered a little as she recognised Caroline. Her heart began to beat more fiercely.

'Hello, have you forgotten a birthday?' she asked, opening the door for her visitor to enter. She turned the key. 'Best I lock up

16

or there'll be a shopful before I turn round. You'd never believe the number of people who forget it's Wednesday!' She chattered on, aware of the incongruity of the two of them talking in Nia Martin's shop below the flat in which they had both planned to live with Nia's son Barry.

'I wanted to talk to you about Barry and me,' Caroline said in her quiet voice. 'I don't want to hurt you any more than I already have, and I wondered how you felt about us coming here to live?'

At once Rhiannon's resentment slipped away. Caroline was such a gentle, kindly young woman it was impossible to treat her with anything but friendliness. Plump and with a rosy face and warm, friendly brown eyes, and with a smile that could end wars, Janet and Hywel Griffiths's only daughter made a friend of everyone she met.

'I'll get used to you coming in and out, although Nia did wonder if it would be better to make the back door entrance easier to use, save you coming through the shop. For your sake, mind,' she added quickly, 'to get Joseph's pushchair in and out.'

'I think we should find somewhere else, you see.'

'There's no need on my account. Honestly. We're friends, aren't we? I don't think

17

that should change because you're marrying Barry, do you? He and I — well, it wouldn't have worked, I think we both knew that all the time.' As she spoke the words she knew with a sense of relief that she meant them.

It wasn't Rhiannon's discomfort Caroline was thinking of but her own. But she didn't explain. How could she tell anyone the real reason she was unhappy at the thought of living with Barry in the flat above his mother's shop?

'You really wouldn't mind seeing us in and out?'

'Friends we are. All of us. And I'll enjoy seeing little Joseph. I wish you well.' Shyly, she opened her arms and hugged Caroline's plump form and then said briskly. 'Now, when are you moving in? There's a bit of sorting to do, mind. Barry's terrible untidy, there's a mess of boxes and equipment to be shifted.'

'My brothers will help move it up to Barry's studio.'

'Full to busting that'll be,' Rhiannon said, laughing. 'Have you seen what's here? Perhaps you can get Basil to sell some of it.'

'That's an idea, sell anything our Basil can.'

'Are you having any sort of celebration?'

Rhiannon asked. 'Funny it'll be, a sort of wedding but without the ceremony and all the frills.'

'You know what Mam and Dad are like, they love filling the house with food then waiting for people to come and eat it. They don't need much of an excuse for a party and they aren't going to let this opportunity pass by. I hope you'll come. Your brother, Viv, will be there; he's bringing Joan Weston. And Eleri will be there with Basil, and — oh, you know, the usual crowd. My brothers and their friends are always about when there's food and drink to be had.'

'I'll be there,' Rhiannon promised.

'Thank you for being so understanding about all this. It would have been very unpleasant, if not impossible, for us to marry for real if you hadn't been so generous and kind.'

'I'm happy for you, I truly am,' Rhiannon said with an encouraging smile.

Rhiannon walked back home to number seven Sophie Street soon after Caroline left. Her mother, Dora, was in the kitchen cutting out circles of bread and toasting them to form the bases of savouries for the Rose Tree Cafe which she ran with Sian Heath-Weston, one of the once wealthy Weston family.

'You were a long time, love. Been cleaning

all this time? That Nia ought to pay you extra, takes advantage she does.'

'I've been talking to Caroline. She and Barry are going to live above the shop.'

'Wicked she is, that one. Stealing Barry from you and her looking as innocent as a new-born baby! Expecting before she was churched then walking off with someone else's fiancé! I hope you told her what you think of her!'

'I wished her all the best, Mam, and I meant it.'

Dora turned round to look at her daughter, her bright blue eyes glaring, then her expression softened and she said, 'Of course you did, love. Barry wasn't the man for you and we both know it. Him with a mother who stole Lewis from me. Pity they have to live above the shop, mind. You'd think he'd have more sense.' Rhiannon said nothing and Dora went on, 'What a pair, Barry and his mother. Her living blatant as a newly polished brass poker with your father, and Barry marrying Caroline when he was engaged to you.'

'They're having a party.'

'She's a Griffiths, isn't she? Of course they'll have a party. I often wonder how that old house of theirs stands up to the strain.' She frowned and queried, 'What sort of party for goodness sake? What'll they call it? Delayed Wedding party? Or Here We Are Again, party? Second Chance party? If our Viv is there Barry will take some ribbing. Married for more than eighteen months and only now persuading his wife to move in, that's what folk'll be saying.'

'Will you come, Mam?'

'Me, help celebrate Barry leaving you for Caroline? And besides, that Nia Martin will be there and wherever *she* is, so will your father be. Me sit and act social with those two? Fine party that'll be.'

'You'll cope.'

'And will you?' Dora asked more quietly. 'Can you sit there and watch Caroline and Barry kissing and cuddling, remembering it might have been you?'

'I'll take Jimmy Herbert with me.'

'Good idea.'

Rhiannon wasn't so sure. She was fond of Jimmy, who was a rep for a confectionary manufacturers, but she didn't want to marry him. When she announced her engagement she wanted to be absolutely sure this time. Taking him to the party would help her cope with the occasion, but might create misconceptions to bother her later.

'Yes, Mam, a good idea, but just to help me over the party, right?'

21

Dora nodded, then began to add small amounts of mashed sardine and wedges of tomatoes to the toasted rounds. 'D'you think three of these would be considered a meal?'

★ ★ ★

The party happened at the end of March 1954. Janet and Hywel rose early and began the preparation of food. Hywel, a burly man with grizzled hair, an untidy beard and very few teeth, helped his wife by filling the hot-water boiler and getting the fire underneath it burning well. He brought logs to replenish it and set them down in the wicker basket in the corner near the sink.

'Anything else I can do, love?' he asked.

'Come back early so you can bath before we eat,' Janet grinned. 'Don't want people to arrive and find you sitting in solitary splendour in the zinc bathtub!'

'Why not? Start the party off well, that would!'

'End it more like, the sight of you!' Janet teased. 'Don't be late!' she admonished as he kissed her and went out.

The joint of ham, given in exchange for a bucket of preserved eggs and a pair of working boots, had been cooked the day before and stood, covered in browned

22

breadcrumb, on the top shelf where dog and cats couldn't reach it. A huge fruit cake, which had been made with butter given by a local farmer in return for previous favours, stood on the table beside several loaves of bread.

With Frank and Ernie still in bed, and Caroline working in the wool shop in town, Janet organised some crayons to amuse baby Joseph and began to make sandwiches. Ham, fish, a paste made of tinned tomatoes and home-made cheese and, when those things ran out, meat paste, sandwich spread, and finally, for fear of not having enough, jam.

Making small cakes was a task undertaken with Joseph's help and pancakes too were piled up on the table to be heated up later. When the table offered no more space to be filled, Janet washed up and began to fill the bath.

First there were a few items to hang out on the clothes line and while she was doing this, with Joseph handing her the pegs, Frank came downstairs and began to strip off.

'Thanks, Mam,' he said trying the water with a big toe.

'Oh no you don't you lazy good-for-nothing.' Janet grabbed the yard brush made from birch twigs and threatened him, but Frank laughed, raising his hands in surrender.

'Only kiddin', Mam, honest! But can I have breakfast before you lock me out of the kitchen?'

'No, and you can look after Joseph for me. I won't be long.'

'All right, come on young niblo, we'll take a look at the garden, shall we? Leave the water, Mam, I'll use it after you.'

'Again? That's twice this week. You must be courting!'

Caroline returned from work at six o'clock and ran to greet her son before going upstairs to wash and dress in her new blue two-piece for the party. She felt apprehensive. What did people expect? Would there be innuendoes and suggestive remarks for her to cope with? She hoped Barry wouldn't be delayed, leaving her to manage alone.

When she went downstairs, carrying the water her mother had put in her room ready for her to wash, she heard his voice and sighed with relief. So long as Barry was beside her, she could cope with anything her brothers and their friends could do. There would be plenty to embarrass her but with Barry supporting her she would cope, and even enjoy it all.

Barry didn't have the kind of looks that turned heads; he had a heavy, powerful jaw that made him look pugnacious at times, especially when he was deep in thought, although he was the calmest of men. But to Caroline he was one of the most attractive men she had known. Good looking in a very different way from his brother, Joseph, but nevertheless creating a strong magnetism, gradually born into love. Twenty-five years old, he was tall and had an air of authority about him. Now, as she stood at the bottom of the stairs and studied him, she saw he was wearing his best suit and a dazzlingly white shirt. His shoes were polished so they looked like glass and he looked well-scrubbed, the light picking up a shine on his freshly shaved skin.

He was so different from her brothers, who seemed to believe that clean and smart was synonymous with being a sissy! Frank and Ernie, the inseparables, were dressed in denim trousers as worn by most working men, and 'cowboy' shirts. Barry always looked neat. Standing among the men of her family, it made him appear to be in control, someone who would automatically take charge of a situation, while Frank and Ernie would be the type to hover and wait for orders.

Perhaps it had been his army years, although that hadn't changed her brothers overmuch; any training they had suffered was soon diluted once they had returned home.

She took a deep breath and walked into the room, still carrying the bowl of soapy water, which Janet immediately relieved her of, allowing her to greet Barry with a shy kiss.

'Here comes the bride,' Frank sang.

'All dressed in blue,' Ernie continued.

'Barry's waited ages, cos,'

'He didn't know what to do!'

'Pack it up you two,' Hywel growled, but everyone was laughing, including Caroline, and his disapproval softened into a smile.

* * *

By eight o'clock the room was so full that there didn't seem to be room for another soul, but still they came. Rhiannon and Jimmy Herbert arrived with Dora at eight-thirty, and they found a place to sit by squashing themselves in between two guests fortunate enough to find room on the couch, until the guests gave up and moved somewhere else. There was a murmur of greeting and Dora looked up to see

Nia squeezing through the throng towards the kitchen. Alarmed, Dora whispered to Rhiannon,

'I knew we shouldn't have come! Sitting here while Caroline canoodles with your ex-fiancé is bad enough, but now *she* turns up, that Nia Martin, with *my* ex — your father — in tow!'

'Dad isn't coming, Mam. I asked him and he said he wouldn't. He'll see Caroline and Barry tomorrow at the flat.'

'What's she come for, then? To rub it in that she stole my husband?'

'Nia's here because Barry's her son. Be fair, Mam, you could hardly expect her to stay away.'

'We shouldn't have come.' Dora's eyes looked threateningly bright.

Rhiannon hugged her. 'Don't be upset, Mam. Our Dad is living with Barry's mother and there's nothing that will change that.'

'Where's Viv? He ought to be here. And where's Basil and our Eleri? Is she bringing the baby?'

Rhiannon hoped so. There was nothing more likely to soothe her mother's tense nerves than Basil and Eleri Griffiths's five-month-old baby son, Ronnie. Being in the same room as the woman who had taken her husband from her was an ordeal for

Dora. Rhiannon knew that, although Nia and her mother had spoken to each other and managed to remain civilised, and Dora was trying desperately hard to accept the situation, it was at times like this, when Dora was outside the family circle to which her husband now belonged, that were hardest for her to bear.

'If it's too much for you, Mam, we'll leave,' Rhiannon promised. 'Jimmy will take us home whenever you say.'

'I'll be all right,' Dora muttered. 'But where's our Viv got to? He said he'd be here.'

* * *

Dora and Lewis Lewis had had three children, but only two now survived. Viv, who worked for the Weston family's wallpaper and paint shop, and Rhiannon, who ran Temptations for Nia. Her eldest child, Lewis-boy, was dead. He had died at the same time as Nia's son, Joseph.

Losing her eldest son, then immediately finding out about the affair between her husband and Nia Martin, had sent Dora into a deep depression, but she had survived and now ran a cafe in partnership with Sian Heath-Weston, one of the Weston family. Having to face Lewis's mistress at celebrations like this, where her daughter was watching her own ex-fiancé with his wife, was doubly difficult. Nia Martin and her son had messed up her life and that of her daughter. Staying calm was almost impossible. She was quick-tempered and her feelings were so outraged, both for herself and her daughter, she knew an explosion of rage could come at any moment. She should have refused to come. What had she been thinking of, coming here? But if Rhiannon could face it, then she had no alternative but to do the same. She glanced at the clock. Only nine o'clock. God, how time could drag. Hours to go before she could leave with dignity.

When her son Viv arrived with Joan Weston, and Jack Weston with his shy little fiancée, Victoria Jones, things livened up and Dora was able to sit back and watch the fun created by the young people, aided and abetted by Hywel.

Basil Griffiths, tall, gangly and more than a little drunk, was trying to dance with his diminutive mother. Bent almost double and picking her up to show off some intricate steps of his own invention, he forced everyone to lift their feet out of the way for fear of being trampled by his size tens.

'Better than a cabaret, that Basil when he

gets going,' Dora chuckled.

Basil Griffiths had married the widow of Lewis-boy and was proud of the fact that he had worked regularly ever since. He had worked as a nightwatchman in a furniture factory for a while but now held the same position for a firm making building and gardening tools. The goods were mostly for export as the country struggled to begin paying off its war-time debts and rebuild trade with other countries. Only a few of the items manufactured were allowed to reach the home market and most of those were seconds.

Janet watched anxiously to see how Barry acted towards Caroline as she attended to the food. So far the celebratory couple had hardly spoken and had certainly not shown by a touch or even a glance that they were in love. She crossed her fingers and shared a look with Hywel, who guessed her concern and hugged her tightly.

'They'll be fine, love,' he whispered. 'Stop worrying, now this minute, or I'll get up and sing a song!'

Janet tried to do as he said by concentrating on the comfort of her guests as the food disappeared, drink flowed and the party became divided between the somnolent older members and the livelier and more outrageous actions of the young ones. Once assured that the food wouldn't run out, she sang a sentimental Irish song, to which Frank and Ernie added their own verse, Hywel was persuaded to do a sword dance between the pokers, and when it was time to leave, everyone agreed that it had been fun.

'The Griffithses certainly know how to give a party,' Dora admitted.

'There's nothing like a good laugh to drive away sorrows,' Jimmy Herbert said, in a maudlin voice. 'Lovely it is,' he said, almost in tears, 'to have a good laugh.' He staggered and looked around him in a bemused way, and with Rhiannon one side of him and Dora the other, he forced himself upright and moved forward.

The tall, and extremely skinny, Basil gathered his family around him and set off home smiling inanely and walking like a double-jointed ostrich, assuring them at intervals that they needn't worry, he'd look after them and see them safe home.

'Another man to rely on,' sighed Dora with a weary smile.

* * *

Caroline was aware of her heart beating in a frighteningly heavy way. The party was over and the excuses all used up. Now she was Mrs Barry Martin. But there was still a feeling of disbelief, still that sense of estrangement, as if she were taking part in a pageant rather than truly being Barry's wife and all that implied. Worries about sharing Barry's bed had increased until the thought was more a punishment than a joy.

She sat in her mother's kitchen trying to calm herself and watched Barry, waiting for some sign, wanting a romantic gesture, a murmur of encouragement to tell her everything was going to be all right. But he treated her no differently from when they had made their vows, falsely, for the sake of her then unborn child. In fact he had hardly spoken to her throughout the evening. Doubts and fears swelled up and threatened to overflow into a panic that would make her want to grab Joseph and run without stopping until she had left Barry far behind and could hide in a place where she and Joseph would never be found.

The drive back to her mother-in-law's house in Chestnut Road was undertaken in silence.

2

After the party for Caroline and Barry, Hywel eventually went to bed as the sun was coming up at seven o'clock on Sunday morning. Janet had decided it was hardly worth undressing, and stayed up. The last of the guests had not left until almost five o'clock, having found their second wind at three. The place was a shambles with abandoned glasses and bottles and plates perched everywhere, many with forgotten remnants of food; some of which having been found and discarded a second time by the dog and cats.

Frank and Ernie had gone to bed at a quarter-to-five, only to find their beds occupied by exhausted guests whom they had been unable to wake. They were now sprawled inelegantly on the floor near the still glowing fire, heads together, stockinged feet resting on the brass fender. Asleep on Frank's foot was a hen.

Janet sighed, lit the boiler for hot water to wash the dishes, and settled the kettle on the fire to make tea. The house had seen many parties and this was the first time in many years that her daughter Caroline hadn't been there to help sort out the aftermath.

By nine o'clock the hens had been fed, the fire revived and the washing-up finished. At ten she kicked Frank and Ernie into action and washed the slate floor and shook the mats. When Hywel came down at eleven the place looked as though the party had been nothing more than a dream.

'Go to bed,' Hywel urged.

'They'll want breakfast,' she hesitated, glancing at the prostrate figures of Frank and Ernie, now asleep on the couch.

'I'll get something to eat for them two, and whoever else surfaces.' He looked at the bowl of freshly gathered eggs. 'Boilt eggs and toast it'll be. Whatever time they wake they'll be convinced it's breakfast time!' He always pronounced it 'boilt' and every time it made her smile.

'I'm thinking of Caroline. I'm going to miss her so much.'

'She'll be here every day, you daft 'aporth! Minding little Joseph aren't you? How'll he get here unless she brings him?'

'I'll see her, but it won't be the same.'

'Not sorry she's married, are you?'

'Of course I'm not. But that doesn't mean I won't miss her.'

'Me too an' all,' he said ungrammatically,

around a wide yawn. 'She makes better roast potatoes than you!'

She threw the tea-cloth at him and, smiling contentedly, went up to bed.

★ ★ ★

Caroline didn't go straight to bed after the party either. The first official day of their marriage and she stayed up, unpacking the items she had been given, washing a few of Joseph's clothes, then standing watching the day begin, in her mother-in-law's tree-filled garden.

Nia had suggested they stayed the first night with her before setting off for their honeymoon the following day. A night's sleep was better than setting off after the party, and to miss the party would have been impossible.

Barry had gone into the bedroom prepared for them by Nia and, collapsing on the bed, had fallen asleep within seconds. Caroline had stood for a moment, looking down at him, loving him but unable to resist comparing him with his brother, whom she had once planned to marry. Joseph had been so different from Barry. Smaller, darker and with such a glow of happiness and fun that people said he lit up a room when he entered.

She left the room after covering Barry with an eiderdown, and went softly downstairs. When Nia woke at seven and padded down to make herself a cup of tea, Caroline smiled and handed her one freshly made.

'I'd have brought it up but I didn't know how soon you would wake,' she smiled.

'Have you been up long, dear?' Nia asked.

'Yes, well, I — '

'You haven't slept at all, have you?'

'It hardly seems worth it. I'd have preferred to stay and help Mam clear up, but I couldn't, could I?'

'No, dear.' Nia poured a third cup of tea and handed it to her. 'Take this and wake Barry. Little Joseph will be awake soon, and I want you all to have a good breakfast before you set off for Aberystwyth.'

★ ★ ★

They travelled to their 'honeymoon' destination, with Joseph, in Barry's van. It was another silent journey, Joseph sleeping much of the way, and Caroline untypically subdued. Barry said little, wondering if Caroline was regretting their decision to stay married. Afraid of the answer, it wasn't a question he wanted to ask.

The hotel was away from the sea-front,

but within an easy walk of it and as soon as they had settled into their room they put an excited Joseph into the pushchair and walked to the beach. It was very cold and they were all three muffled up in scarves. The grey skies made Constitution Hill look uninviting, but they strolled along the front and around the castle ruins before heading back to the town to find somewhere to have a cup of tea.

They drove through the surrounding countryside during the afternoon and the mood of quiet contemplation continued, although both Caroline and Barry made an effort to encourage the child to see and enjoy the different sights. Back at their hotel, when it was time to put Joseph to sleep, they sat watching him for a while, each unable to judge the mood of the other. Caroline was achingly tired, not having slept the previous night, but somehow it was impossible to suggest an early night, the connotations of that phrase were making her uneasy.

Barry solved the dilemma by going down to the bar for a nightcap.

'Go to bed, love,' he said, kissing her cheek. 'You're dead on your feet. I'll have a few drinks and sit there for a while. You need a good night's sleep and I expect you'll be well gone by the time I come back.'

She undressed and slid beneath the cold sheets, not expecting to relax in the strange room with Barry about to return and share her bed. But when Barry looked in half an hour later she was fast asleep. He stared down at her, a worried frown on his face, then slipped in beside her. They slept, straight as two pokers. Not touching each other, unmoving, as though encased in ice.

During the following two days as they explored the area, Barry tried to bring up the subject. Longing to know how she felt but afraid of what Caroline would say, he ended each attempt by turning the disjointed, stumbling words into a discussion of his plans for his photography business.

He suggested that, as she was continuing to work at the wool-shop, they should use her wages for housekeeping while his earnings would be ploughed back into the business. She agreed willingly, as if glad to be included in his future ambitions. Making plans for the future was a safe subject and one to which they returned each time the conversation touched a more personal zone. Hedging around their emotions was a relief to them both, although every time they got into bed they were dragged down with disappointment that another day had passed without bringing them closer.

★ ★ ★

Janet was pleased with the success of the party. Frank and Ernie had managed not to pick a fight with anyone and for the Griffithses that was a success. Sunday lunch was quiet, conversation desultory, in fact Frank kept dropping off to sleep; once falling forward to land with his face on his plate.

'Come on, shake yourselves,' Hywel said when the meal was finished. 'We've got work to do.'

Frank and Ernie groaned but Hywel insisted. 'You promised, mind. We've got to get all the surplus out of that flat so Caroline and Barry can move in when they get back from Aber.'

'Give me another hour,' Ernie pleaded.

'Another cup of tea?' suggested Frank, but Hywel pushed them towards the door. 'We don't know when they'll be back, so today it is. Come on, shift yourselves.'

'They won't be back today.'

'Can't we do it tomorrow?'

'All right, don't push, our Dad.'

Janet chuckled as the voices drifted away towards the van.

* * *

Frank was tall and lanky like his brother, Basil. He often wore a lugubrious expression so that, again like his brother, he was called upon to act as mourner when the funeral director needed an extra man. He earned his living in a variety of ways, mostly petty thieving and poaching, although he had never been as skilled at taking the occasional bird or rabbit as Basil, who, Hywel said, was capable of coaxing a wildcat to treat him like a brother.

If asked to state his favourite pastime he would have said fighting, and in this he had a willing partner in his cousin, Ernie. The pair of them were frequently in court accused of causing a disturbance, and they were both proud of their record. Hywel was a regular in court too, although he always insisted he was trying to break up a fight and not start one. Janet bathed their wounds unsympathetically, and philosophically refilled the first-aid box for the next time.

Ernie was one of Hywel's nephews. When his mother and father died, Ernie had been taken in by the family and treated the same as Frank, Basil and Caroline. He and Frank were very close, although Janet suspected it was Frank who was the instigator of their various escapades and Ernie the follower. He wasn't tall and skinny like Frank and Basil, following instead, Hywel's family's stocky build. To Janet's constant dismay, neither boy had yet brought home a serious girl-friend.

They worked willingly once Hywel had started them off by explaining what was needed. All the photography equipment was to go up to Barry's studio and the flat put in order ready for the honeymooners' return. It was five o'clock when they finished and as they were walking out through Temptations sweet shop, Ernie's hand wandered towards the blocks of chocolate. He picked up two and handed one to Frank.

'That will be one shilling please!' Rhiannon's voice ringing through the quiet shop made Ernie drop the chocolate and turn around in alarm.

'*Two* shillings, for your cheek!' Hywel echoed, holding out a grubby hand and glowering at Ernie. 'Stealing from your brother-in-law's Mam! You're a disgrace.'

'What are you doing here?' Rhiannon demanded.

'Emptying the flat ready for when our

Caroline and Barry get back. Sorry we startled you. Ernie! Hand over the money!'

A sheepish Ernie handed a half a crown to Rhiannon who looked at it and said,

'You'll have to come back for your change, the till's locked.'

They shuffled out with Ernie and Hywel repeating their apologies and Frank chuckling at his cousin's discomfiture.

'You needn't look so innocent, Frank Griffiths,' Rhiannon said. 'You were about to take one of the bars yourself!'

'Keep the two and sixpence, and there's sorry we are,' Hywel muttered.

Rhiannon watched them walk to the van and smiled as Hywel aimed a swipe at Ernie before getting in and driving off, leaving both boys to walk. Frank gave the bar of chocolate to young Gwyn Bevan who was delivering papers, and looked at Rhiannon for approval.

Making sure the shop door was locked, Rhiannon went up to the flat. It had been emptied of all the surplus but it still didn't look welcoming. She placed the card and the flowers she had brought on the kitchen table and then took a duster and put the final touches to the rooms. It wasn't perfect, but she knew that Caroline would soon make the sparsely furnished rooms into a home, as she had once planned to do herself.

She went back down the stairs and through the shop without looking back. All that was behind her and as she closed and locked the door she knew all traces of regret had gone. But, what now?

She wanted to continue running Temptations. She was coping with the embarrassment of working for Nia, with whom her father now lived, and would soon accept having Barry and Caroline living in the flat that would have been hers. The job was one that interested her and her plans to expand the business had been a success. She was happy in her work but there was a need for something more, a social life so long abandoned on account of Barry, had to be revived. Jimmy Herbert was kind and very good company, but she knew that he did not hold the key to her future, and she was guilty of using him. It was time to let him go, fade from his life gently but firmly and start anew. This would be difficult, as he was a rep, calling on her for orders of sweets and chocolates.

She walked towards the docks and crossed them to visit the sandy bay. The Pleasure Beach appealed even in the winter months, but in a different way from the rowdy, overcrowded, kiss-me-quick, happy days of summer. The out-of-season emptiness showed its other side, the natural beauty of the wide stretch of sand unmarked by people and their possessions. And the bleak headlands, hardly changed from the glorious, muted shades of autumn, coming down to touch the protruding feet of the cliffs and the white frills of the sea's edge.

Behind her, the shuttered cafés and fairground amusements were somnolent, their façades slightly battered by the storms of the past months, like sleeping giants about to wake up and clean up, to change the solitude once more into a trippers' paradise.

On the way home she stopped to talk to Mr Windsor, the owner of a garage where her father usually bought his petrol and brought his repairs and maintenance. Her reason for calling was to ask him if he would consider talking to Charlie Bevan, recently out of prison for robbery.

'He needs someone to give him a chance, Mr Windsor,' she explained. 'I don't think he'll let you down, he's that determined to make a home for his son. With old Maggie Wilpin dead there'd be no one to look after Gwyn if he went inside again, you see.'

Mr Windsor looked doubtful but agreed to talk to the young man. 'No promises, mind,' he said wagging a finger at Rhiannon's smiling face. 'I'll talk to him and see what I think of *his* promises.'

★ ★ ★

Caroline and Barry stayed three nights at Aberystwyth, but they didn't consummate their marriage. Caroline became tense every time Barry even kissed her and he was afraid of sending her deeper into the shell she had grown around herself. He wondered whether, at moments approaching tenderness, his bride was thinking about his brother who had died. Every time he thought of taking her in his arms, the look in her eyes was like a barrier keeping him at bay. They both used young Joseph as an excuse, bringing the little boy into their bed to lie between them.

They returned to the flat above the sweet-shop as Rhiannon was closing for the half-day on Wednesday. She was shy of meeting Barry's gaze and felt her colour rise. They were back from honeymoon where Caroline would have done with Barry what she, Rhiannon, had dreamed of doing for so long. But she kissed Caroline and welcomed her home. She didn't stay, just delivered the takings to the bank then hurried home.

She had the house to herself. Her mother, Dora, was working at The Rose Tree Cafe over near the lake and wouldn't be home until six-thirty. Her brother, Viv, was still at Weston's Wallpaper and Paint Shop. He would be home, starving hungry, in less than an hour. But for a while at least she had time to sit and think.

Her wages were generous. Nia appreciated how much effort she had put into increasing the trade in the small corner shop and paid her accordingly. She hadn't used much of it, paying her share of the household expenses and putting the rest into the Post Office. She had quite a few pounds there and wondered if she might use it for a holiday. Butlins was supposed to be good fun, but she would have to find someone to go with her. Fun never came to someone on their own, it had to be shared, expanded by another's contribution. That sombre observation made her thoughts return to Barry and the wedding that had once been so certain.

She wondered how Caroline would cope with living in the flat with only Joseph for company after the lively home of her parents where a day never passed without someone calling in. She was going to continue working at the wool shop in town, taking Joseph to her parents each morning, but the evenings were sure to be strange for her, sitting on her own while Barry went out on one of his many party and dance appointments.

Gathering together the ingredients for an omelette, using off-ration duck eggs and left-over vegetables, she waited for her brother to come home. She didn't have to wait long. She heard him whistling before she had beaten the eggs.

'Rhiannon?' Viv called as he banged the door shut behind him. 'It's me and I'm starving.'

Rhiannon said the last words with him, and promised an omelette in five minutes.

As usual, Viv was in a hurry to be out. 'Joan and I are off to Cardiff,' he explained between mouthfuls of the delicious, fluffy food. 'Pictures I expect. Or the theatre.'

'Why go to Cardiff for pictures? Plenty of choice here in Pendragon, surely.'

'Shops,' was the succinct explanation. 'Joan wants to look at dresses and stuff for the wedding.'

'It isn't until August. It's a bit early isn't it?'

'Can you imagine Joan waiting to spend money, when she can spend it today?'

'She won't be buying, though?'

'She might, if she sees something she likes. Not her wedding dress of course. Her mother will go with her to choose that and I mustn't see it, must I?'

'It's all weddings at the moment,' Rhiannon sighed, sitting down to begin her meal. 'You and Joan Weston, Jack Weston and Victoria Jones. Both unbelievable a few months ago. How Gladys and Arfon Weston have had to swallow their pride. Their grandson, Jack, marrying their ex-servant, and their granddaughter marrying you, a mere employee. I never thought I'd see the day!'

'I'm a partner in the firm, remember.'

'Another unbelievable happening!'

'And there's Barry marrying Caroline for real. Now there's a surprise.' He looked at his sister as he spoke, to gauge her reaction, and saw to his relief that she was smiling. 'Are you and Jimmy — you know?'

'No, we're not. I like him, Viv, but I can't imagine spending the rest of my life with him. I — I have to start letting him know that.'

'Fresh start, eh?'

When Viv had gone to meet Joan, and the vegetables were prepared for the evening meal, Rhiannon put on a coat and set off for a walk. The weather was cold, with a sneaky wind slanting through the houses and slicing through her clothes to chill her. As she passed the shop on the corner she automatically glanced across to make sure all was well, and from the window of the flat above, she saw the curtains move and a hand wave. Caroline, sitting there all alone. She stopped and gestured, inviting her to walk with her.

The window opened and Caroline thanked her but explained there was so much to do.

'Perhaps next week?' Rhiannon suggested and she walked on towards the docks. Whatever the circumstances of her marriage, Rhiannon sensed the young woman needed a friend.

* * *

Jack Weston's real surname was Heath, but his grandmother, Gladys Weston, who had produced only twin daughters, had insisted they carried on the family name, intent as she was on founding a dynasty. Jack had let her down twice; first by being unable to achieve greatness in college and career, choosing and enjoying the post of teacher in the local school, then by falling in love with Victoria Jones, daughter of a local drunk, who had worked for her as a servant.

Jack had been saddened by the plight of Victoria's family when he had called at the home in Goldings Street after her drunken father had drowned. Mrs Jones, expecting her seventh child, was desperately trying to

49

survive on what she earned washing and ironing clothes for other people, plus the little that Victoria earned with his grandmother.

Steve Jones had taken most of his family's possessions and sold them for money to spend on drink and, with Basil Griffiths helping, Jack had managed to buy back enough to make them comfortable. Now they had a piano, on which Mrs Jones was hoping to give piano lessons, two of Victoria's brothers were working and things were looking up. Amidst all this he had realised that there was no one in the world who could make him truly happy except the quiet, capable and loving Victoria.

After school closed on that Wednesday, he went straight to number seventeen and swept her into his arms. Today they had decided to make plans for the wedding. To his dismay, Victoria looked fit to burst into tears.

'Victoria? What's happened?' he asked, glancing at Mrs Jones with a questioning frown.

'Victoria went to see your grandmother this morning, Jack. She sent around a note inviting her to call,' Mrs Jones explained.

'Inviting? Demanding more like.' He looked at Victoria and said, 'You should have waited for me, love. You know how she loves to organise people.'

'She's determined to make me into the kind of wife she considers you need,' Victoria said and she smiled. 'I think she's begun to realise I'm a lost cause.'

'Lost cause? Nonsense, you *are* the kind of wife I need.' He kissed her cheek then went into the neat kitchen and gathered together decorating materials. He had started work on the tiny back bedroom which was occupied by the three smallest Joneses, determined to completely transform the drab house before he started thinking about the place he and Victoria would call home.

At seven o'clock, after they had eaten, he took out notebook and fountain pen and began making lists.

'First of all a house,' he said. 'Where shall we look first?'

They spent the next hour discussing the pros and cons of each road in the town, settling finally for an area around Sophie Street. Gethyn Street that followed Trellis Street and ran behind Sophie Street was a quiet spot that would suit them quite well. It was near the shops and the school, and close to Goldings Street, where Victoria's family lived.

When it came to the plans for the actual wedding, he sensed apprehension in his bride-to-be. Her face stiffened and there

51

was a slight pulling away from him, and he at once feared the worse. She had had second thoughts, she wanted to call the whole thing off.

Trying to keep his voice calm, he asked, 'What is it, Victoria, something worrying you? Tell me and I promise we'll get it sorted, you and me, we can solve any problem in the world, so long as we're together.' Aware of her mother not far away he leaned forward and touched his lips against her soft cheek and whispered, 'I love you.'

'I love you too,' she whispered back.

'But?'

'I want to be married to you, Jack, but I don't want to marry you.'

'What on earth does that mean?' he laughed.

'The wedding is beginning to grow into a nightmare. Your mother is sweet about everything, and your cousins, Joan and Megan are trying to be nice, but your Grandmother is 'training me up to Weston standards', *and* insisting on a huge wedding with half of Pendragon Island being invited. I hoped, what with Joan and Viv's date so near ours, she might concentrate on them and leave us alone,' she said wistfully.

'Leave Joan and Megan to me, and as for

Grandmother, I don't think they have the money for anything grand. Don't worry, she talks in thousands but it's thousands they no longer have. We'll have a happy day with just the family there and a few friends.'

'Just the family! Oh, Jack, if only we could run away and come back married and settle into our life without all this fuss.'

'It'll be fine, you'll have a day to remember and I promise you won't be unhappy for even a moment.'

As he walked to The Railwayman's to meet Viv Lewis and Basil Griffiths and the others, he was wondering on the best way to make sure that promise was kept. Glady Weston, his grandmother was a very determined woman and he was afraid that having no money was not enough to prevent her making his wedding the event of the year.

He would have to get Megan and Joan on his side. If they would help Victoria to choose the clothes for the wedding and help dress the younger members of the Jones clan, he would willingly foot the bill. But more important than dresses and suits, having Megan and Joan as supporting friends would increase Victoria's confidence and reduce her fear of being made to look foolish.

He was unaware that he was not the

only one to worry. Victoria's mother was concerned for her daughter marrying into a family for whom she had once worked. The habit of being subservient might refuse to go away. Apologising and constantly saying sorry for the slightest error of etiquette-according-to-Gladys, could easily get on Jack's nerves and irritability was a grinding tool that might soon wear holes in their happiness and, eventually, their love.

Without Jack's unwavering support Victoria would always be at a loss at social functions, although, she admitted to herself, Jack himself seems more at home in the bar of The Railwayman's with Viv Lewis and the Griffiths boys than in his grandmother's parlour. Perhaps, she allowed herself to hope, perhaps it would be all right. She took a cup of tea up to Victoria the following morning, kissed her and said,

'Whatever problems you find or create for yourself, dear, remember that Jack loves you for what you are now. What I mean is, don't try desperately to change. If he wanted someone who'll grow up into another Gladys Weston, heaven forbid, he would have chosen someone very different from you. He loves you, the real you, very much.'

★ ★ ★

The three Griffiths boys were there when Jack reached the pub and, as he walked in, Frank went to the bar and bought him a pint. He sat down next to Viv Lewis and at once started talking about Victoria.

'D'you think you could persuade Joan to give Victoria some time, Viv? I think she's finding taking on the Westons a bit daunting.'

'I'm not surprised, with Gladys in matriarchal control! Why does your mother allow your grandmother to organise your wedding? Shouldn't it be her talking to Victoria?'

'I know that, my mother knows that, but you try telling my grandmother!'

'Best thing Victoria can do is say yes to everything Gladys suggests, then do what she wants, so quick the old girl can't change it!'

'Victoria isn't up to those tricks. She needs a friend to talk to.'

'If she needs help with her frock she'd be better off seeing Megan rather than Joan. She works in Gwennie Woodlas's gown shop now.'

'It isn't dress sense she lacks, it's a friend, Viv. Are you being deliberately obtuse or have you had too much of the brown nectar?'

'Oh, I know what you're on about, boy. Changing from staff to relation isn't easy, I know that. God'elp, don't I just! I'm marrying one of the Weston Girls, remember. I know what a handful your Grandma Gladys can be. Yes, I'll have a word with Joan, get her to boost Victoria's confidence a bit.'

Basil, the only Griffiths who had ever stayed in the same job for more than a month, was a nightwatchman, having been in regular employment ever since he proposed to Eleri Lewis, the widow of Viv's older brother, Lewis-boy. Now, as he gathered his foodbag, and stood to leave, he said, 'I'll ask my Eleri to call, shall I? She isn't one of the God-don't-I-fancy-myself-Westons, but she knows Victoria and will enjoy a chat now and then.'

'Thanks,' Jack said warmly. 'The more friends she has the better.'

Ernie Griffiths was quieter than usual. He and Frank and Viv usually kept up a supply of remarks about the people around them or swopped jokes, but tonight he sipped his beer and seemed, to the observant Basil, to be watching the door. Frank noticed it too.

'Expecting someone gorgeous to walk in, Ernie?' Frank teased.

'Yes, he'll have to peel his eyeballs off the

56

paintwork if he doesn't blink soon!' Basil added.

'I'm off girls, they cost too much money,' Ernie muttered.

Basil had only stayed an hour before leaving to begin his night-shift at the factory. As Basil drained his glass, Ernie glanced into the corner where four people were playing darts, then stood up, preparing to follow Basil out.

'Where are we going?' Frank asked, beginning to rise with him. 'Hang on, I'll come with you.'

'No, it's all right, I just need some fresh air. I'll meet you back home.' Without giving Frank a chance to follow him, Ernie darted out ahead of Basil and disappeared around the corner. Out of sight, he hared up the road, then, cutting through a lane, turned back on himself and walked sedately across the wasteland that was all to see of Phillips Street, destroyed by two war-time bombs.

He and Frank were such teases, tormenting their friends once they had found a girlfriend, that, having made a date with Helen Gunner, he was trying to keep her existence a secret.

So far they had only met for a brief hour when her parents were in The Railwayman's Arms. The secret had to be kept from them too, as no self-respecting mother would allow her daughter to be seen with one of the dreadful Griffithses.

As dates go it was unexciting, but to Ernie it was one of the highlights of his life. They walked and stopped at convenient places to kiss primly and shyly, then walked some more. They made another date before he saw her to her door, he stole a final and very brief kiss and ran home as if his heart was on fire.

* * *

Janet Griffiths was worried about Caroline. She had a strong feeling that all was not well with the marriage. She saw her daughter every day and on most days Barry came too, either to bring Joseph to her while Caroline worked, or to collect him to take him back to the flat in Sophie Street.

One Wednesday lunchtime when Caroline came to take her son home, she persuaded her to stay and eat lunch with them. Leaving Hywel and the boys to eat theirs in the living room, she took two steaming plates of rabbit stew into the kitchen.

'There's something I want to tell you,' Janet began. 'I wrote to that Mrs Phillips who told me when my father died, and asked her if she could give me any ideas on where to look for my sister.' She took a letter out of her apron pocket and handed it to Caroline. 'That's her reply. The address is a place where Marion once worked. They might know something. Will you come with me, love? It isn't far. We could go this afternoon.'

Once the arrangements had been made and they had set off in the old van with which Hywel and the boys made what money they needed, Janet glanced at her subdued daughter and said,

'I've confided in you, love. Isn't it time you confided in me?' To her alarm, Caroline burst into tears.

Janet stopped the van in the gateway of a field and hugged her, talking soothingly, patting her shoulder as if she were a child.

'I've made the most awful mistake, Mam. Barry doesn't love me. He still wishes he was married to Rhiannon.'

'What a lot of nonsense. I only had to look at his face to see how he cared for you. Plain as plain it was, even before he realised it himself.'

'We go through each day in our separate lives, share the same small rooms but I might as well have stayed with you and Dad.'

'You mean you haven't — ?'

59

'He's done it all for Joseph. He doesn't love me at all.'

'And you?' Janet asked softly, 'Do you love him or are you still in love with the other Joseph, the baby's father?'

'I'll always love Joseph Martin. I don't think that will ever change. Barry is different but I really felt a love for him, Mam. But sharing a home, just the two of us, it seemed to bring everything back. I keep imagining living there with Joseph, waiting for Joseph to come in and eat the food I've prepared. It was where Joseph and I were going to live, remember.'

'D'you know, foolish old woman that I am, I hadn't remembered. What a stupid woman I am not to have realised it was a mistake.'

'The whole thing was a mistake. Marrying Barry so the baby would have his father's name was a mistake and everything we've done since has made it worse.'

'You have to talk to Barry, make him understand that the flat is filled with ghosts. You can't be a wife to him in the very place, the very room, where you had planned to live with his brother. He'll understand and see that you have to get out and find a place of your own. His mother will too, I'm sure. Come on love, all it takes is honest talk and that's not so hard is it?'

Honesty is relative, Caroline thought sadly. She wasn't honest enough to tell her mother that the room where she slept with Barry was the room in which her child, Barry's brother Joseph's child, had been conceived. How could she tell Barry that?

Hugging her daughter again and surreptitiously drying her own tears, Janet said,

'We'll leave the visit for today. We can go next week, things will be better when you're more cheerful. You'll have talked to Barry by then and sorted everything out, won't you, love? It'll be that easy once you start you'll wonder why you didn't do it before.'

3

Hywel Griffiths was arrested at the end of March. It was an amicable affair, with Farmer Booker and the local constable escorting him to the police station to charge him, and at the same time discussing the best way to cook pheasant.

An appearance at court and a fine was hardly surprising and was not worth more than a brief few lines in the local paper alongside those habitual drunks that received a regular mention. For Hywel it was a turning point. He had no intention of giving up taking the occasional pheasant or rabbit for the pot, but the fines made it an expensive food and Farmer Booker was becoming more sophisticated and more determined in his campaign to stop poachers making a living from his land.

'Janet? Are you there?' he called when he went into the cottage, looking far from his usual happy self. A scowl creased his face and his dark eyes glowered with something akin to fury. He was not pleased with the day's happenings so far. His rare lack of humour was due in part to his uncomfortable attire.

A court appearance necessitated looking respectable, and today Hywel had abandoned his misshapen denim trousers, which even after suffering the indignity of being scrubbed and hung out to dry still carried the imprint of his legs, and had dressed 'tidy'. He wore a pair of pin-striped trousers, a long overcoat that had belonged to his father, and a trilby hat, that had seen better days, which he wore tilted rakishly across one eye. He didn't possess any shoes but his boots had been scrubbed clean of mud and polished in the army manner with spit and polish and a lot of elbow grease until the toe caps shone like a calm sea in sunlight.

He was not a tall man like his sons, but he was strongly built and now, with shoulders squeezed into the coat and threatening to pop the seams in protest at the restraint, he looked dangerous.

'Hywel? What on earth has happened?' Janet asked as she hurried forward to relieve him of his coat, tugging to free it from the wide and well-padded shoulders of her irate husband. 'Come on, I'll get you a drink of cider, calm you down.'

'I don't want to calm down. I want to stay angry,' he said, kicking off the heavy boots and feeling under the table with his feet for his slippers. 'D'you know, them rabbits,

63

them measly rabbits, cost me more than if I'd bought them legal, in the shop? Miserable sod, old Booker. I think he's in cohorts with that damned magistrate. That fine is the last I'm paying.'

'What will you do?' she asked as she handed him a glass of foaming cider from the barrel in the kitchen. 'Don't tell me, you're going to find a job!'

'Yes I am. And as well as chickens I'm going to keep geese, ducks and goats.'

'How will that prevent fines?'

'Every time I'm up there accused of stealing a wild rabbit from old Booker, the magistrate points out that I must be guilty as I have no other means of support. He natters on about not paying taxes and being a drain on the purses of decent people and slaps the biggest fine he can on me. I'm going to show that I'm gainfully employed and with eggs and milk, cheese and meat to sell, I might even pay tax! I'll prove that I've no need to pinch his miserable rabbits and pheasants. I'll plead not guilty.' His face lit up and he added, 'Perhaps I'll be able to summon Booker for defamation of character!'

'I don't think that would work, Hywel,' Janet laughed. 'They'd only have to look at your record.' With a sigh she added, 'Yours and Basil's and Frank's and Ernie's.'

'Perhaps not, but I can threaten him though.'

'You'll have him shaking in his shoes, love!'

'You're laughing at me.'

'Guilty!'

Hywel began searching the house and garden for things to sell to make the money to buy a few goats. He had been given the idea after talking to a woman at the court. She had a child who couldn't tolerate cow's milk and had to travel a long distance each day to buy milk from a goat-keeper in a village almost five miles away. The idea instantly appealed. He took her name and promised to get in touch if he heard of a goat-keeper nearer. He had reasoned that there must be others who would like the milk and cheese, beside one little boy. Although he wasn't sure he'd try it himself.

'Eat anything, they will,' he said enthusiastically and incorrectly, to Janet. 'We'll soon persuade locals to bring their leftover food for them. They did it for pigs during the war didn't they? Well, they can do it now for my little war against the magistrates and farmer John Booker!' It all sounded so simple, Janet thought with a sigh.

By the end of the following day, Hywel had filled the van with implements no longer

65

needed, or which they could do without for a while, and set off to sell them. His son Basil was with him. There was no one like Basil for finding what was wanted or knowing of a place where that same something was needed. Their destination was an estate of prefabs where every tenant was determined to outdo their neighbours by setting out the garden and filling it with flowers ready for the summer display.

Two old lawn mowers that Frank had persuaded to work, three rainwater butts, one complete with a tap that wouldn't turn but looked good, an eclectic assortment of tools, some with the stamp of the local council only partly erased, plus several buckets containing shrubs, all rattled behind them as they set off to persuade someone they had just what he needed. They also had a dozen bottles of homemade wine. Hywel was loath to part with these but money was needed fast before his enthusiasm waned or Janet thought of more reasons for not increasing their animal population.

★ ★ ★

Watching Hywel starting to clear the ground to build housing for the goats was a diversion, but Janet's mind was rarely free of worry about her daughter. Caroline continued to bring the little boy each morning and either she or Barry would collect him each afternoon, and on the surface everything looked fine. But Janet looked into Caroline's eyes and saw the truth. Her lovely daughter was deeply unhappy.

★ ★ ★

Barry had never undressed in front of his wife, the unease she felt was contagious, and made him in some inexplicable way ashamed of his body. Did Caroline look at him, taller and a lot heavier than his dead brother and with more than a hint of fat around his middle, and grieve more desperately for Joseph who had been smaller, and darker and altogether more attractive? Joseph had been so handsome, and a lot more fun than the sober-sides he, Barry, had always been.

As the weeks passed, his confidence in himself, as well as the state of the marriage, slipped lower and lower. Caroline found him gross, she hadn't said so, but he too looked into her eyes and saw the truth. He was big and ugly and boring, compared with his trim, light-hearted brother. How could he have believed he could compete with Joseph even now, more than two years after his death?

Yet he had to make something out of the mess. He couldn't face the derision both in jest and in malicious gossip that would result in Caroline leaving him and returning to her parents. The humiliation would kill him. He would have to leave the town and start again somewhere else, and even then he would be trailing his empty marriage and pending divorce behind him. That capricious offer of help he had made when Caroline had been so desperately in need of a friend was ruining his life.

In all these considerations he hardly thought that the problem was as great for Caroline.

'Caroline, I haven't any appointments this afternoon,' he said one morning as his sad wife was getting Joseph ready to go to her mother's. 'As it's Wednesday, your half-day, I thought we could take Joseph to the park or to the beach. Shall I collect him and meet you outside the shop at one? I'll bring a picnic, he'd like that.'

'Oh, Barry, I'm sorry, I've arranged to go somewhere with Mam.' She looked at him, her dark eyes trying to assess whether he was disappointed or pleased. 'Why didn't you tell me sooner? She's borrowed the van and made arrangements for food and everything.' She frowned. 'But perhaps I can ask her to change it until next week. I'll talk to her when I take Joseph, shall I?'

'No, you go with your Mam. I should spend the time finishing off some prints anyway. I've got some new mounts I want to experiment with too. Go, love, we'll try again in a week or two, when it's warmer.' In a small corner of his mind he admitted to relief that he didn't have to spend hours pretending to be a happily married man and a proud father. Although his feelings for Joseph were no pretence. He loved the little boy, who warmed him with his undemanding love.

Caroline wondered whether to tell him about her mother's search for her missing sister or whether that would be breaking her mother's confidence, although there was no conceivable reason for secrecy. But he didn't ask where they were going. She sighed. He didn't ask because he wasn't sufficiently interested.

They both felt the marriage slip another notch.

* * *

Although it was early April and the weather was far from warm, Janet had prepared a salad for Hywel and the boys' midday meal.

69

'They'll grumble for sure but we won't be there to hear them,' she chuckled as she and Caroline climbed into the van.

'I'm hungry, Nanna,' Joseph said pleadingly and stuck a thumb into his mouth.

'Eat your thumb and you get no picnic,' Janet said and the thumb was swiftly removed.

They stopped only a mile or two outside the town, at a place where they could park on the cliff and look down over the sea. Below them was a sandy beach with jagged rocks at each end spreading curved, protective arms. On the brown and rusty-red surfaces, greenery struggled bravely to survive.

The hardy samphire that smelled a little like lavender and was once used as a vegetable, made attractive mounds that softened the harsh angles of the rocks. Wild spinach and thrift clung defiantly, spreading their roots down through cracks and finding moisture enough to survive. Under their feet, thyme crept leisurely and imperceptibly along the ground, colonising any space and offering a delicious scent to those who touched its leaves as they passed by.

The sky was blue but the wind was cold, whipping the turquoise and jade coloured water into tips that Joseph told them looked like a birthday cake. It made Janet shiver at the thought of paddling in it, as some foolhardy youngsters were doing. The shrieks of their laughter soared up to reach them on their high vantage point.

'Coward that I am, I think we'll eat our picnic in the car,' she said, catching hold of Joseph's hand and hurrying him along.

'Mam, I want to come back home,' Caroline whispered when they had eaten their fill and Joseph had dropped off to sleep in her arms.

'And welcome you'd be. Me and your dad would love to have you back, but not yet. It wouldn't be right to give up on your marriage before you've given it a real try.'

'It'll never come right. I thought I loved him enough but, well, the truth is, I look at him and all I see is a man who isn't Joseph.'

'Joseph is gone, love. There's no future for you or for little Joseph if you insist on looking over your shoulder to what was once there. Playing fanciful games, imagining that somehow everything will change, and Joseph will walk back into your life and laugh and tell you it was all one of his practical jokes, is wrong and very foolish. You have to accept that it's over. You have to look forward, love.'

'It's hard. On Barry as well as me. He

71

tries to please me but he isn't sure either. I can sense that, and his hesitation adds to my own and we're drifting further and further apart. Today he said he'd take an afternoon off and we'd go for a picnic but I couldn't face it.'

'What couldn't you face? A pleasant afternoon out with Barry? You and Barry have always got on well.'

'We still would if we hadn't been stupid enough to try and make this parody of a marriage into a reality.'

'Come on, let's go and indulge ourselves in a real wallow in the past, and try and find my sister.' Janet smiled as she stepped outside and with the starting handle, cranked the engine into reluctant life. Then she laughed. 'Hark at me telling you not to look back and at the same time talking about finding a sister I lost sixty years ago!'

★ ★ ★

Rhiannon closed the shop at one o'clock and at two-thirty was back there, keeping the blinds down while she tackled some cleaning. As usual, a few customers knocked on the door and pleaded for her to serve them with a forgotten card or a few sweets for the pictures. One of these was the paper-boy,

Gwyn Bevan. He held out a shilling piece and asked for a Lovell's nougat wafer and some Poor Ben's aniseed gums.

Trying not to sound suspicious, Rhiannon asked him where he'd got the money from.

'My paper round, Miss. Dad lets me keep it and I'm saving for a bike, but Dad's taking me to the pictures today and I'm buying the sweets.'

'That's smashing, Gwyn. I hope you enjoy it. Dad not working yet?'

'Yes, he's got a job, Miss. Works in a garage he does, and he's learning to drive so he can deliver cars back after repairs.'

'Windsor's was it?' she asked.

'Yes, Miss. He said he'd train our dad to be a top mechanic in no time.'

So, Rhiannon smiled to herself, Mr Windsor had kept his promise. 'There's pleased I am. Well done you for keeping the paper round all winter. Easier in the summer, eh?'

'I did it for Gran, but now I'm doing it for me,' he grinned. 'It'll be great to have a bike.'

Gwyn Bevan, who was a small thirteen-year-old, had been living in Sophie Street, opposite the Lewises, since he was a tiny baby; sharing the shabby, bomb-damaged house, after his mother had left him and his father in the care of Maggie Wilpin, his mother's grandmother.

Maggie Wilpin had cared for the boy as well as she could during the several times his father, Charlie, had been in prison. She had died soon after Charlie had been released in January, and now he and his son seemed to be trying very hard to make a life for themselves. Charlie's most recent imprisonment had been for breaking into and stealing from Temptations Sweet Shop and Rhiannon felt guilty at being the cause of his arrest.

Another knock at the door and Rhiannon sighed. 'I don't know why I bother to come in and do some work, there's never a minute passes without an interruption.'

'Sorry, Miss.'

'Oh, it's all right, I don't really mind. Enjoy the pictures.'

The newcomer was Gertie Thomas who kept the shop on the opposite corner, selling groceries and vegetables.

'Sorry to my heart to bother you, lovely girl, but seeing you're serving Gwyn, can I have a card for our Florrie? Sick real bad she is, and her with a birthday tomorrow and me forgetting to send.'

Rhiannon served Gertie with a card then locked up and went home. Today was not

the day to get things done, she might as
well go for a walk. Perhaps she'd go and
see Eleri and ask Basil to look out for a
good secondhand bike for young Gwyn.

* * *

Janet drove up to the cottage in the middle of
the row on the village street. Number twelve,
the letter had said. A Mrs Grant. She left
Caroline and Joseph in the van and knocked
on the door. Superstitiously, she crossed her
fingers and hoped the old lady's memory was
clearer than her windows.

It was some time before the door opened
to reveal a small, white-haired lady wearing
what looked like a dozen layers of clothing
ending with a wrap-over apron.

'I'm sorry to bother you,' Janet began,
stooping to speak to the sharp-faced occupier.
'I wondered whether you can help me. I'm
looking for my sister.'

'Nobody lives here except me and my son!'
the woman's voice was sharp and unfriendly.

'She used to work for you, many years ago
and I expect you've forgotten all about her,'
Janet persevered.

'I never forget a thing.'

'Oh, good. Then would you have an idea
where I might find Marion Williams.'

'Marion who?'

'Marion Williams. She lived at Hayes Brook Farm, but I believe she worked for you many years ago.'

The frown on the old woman's face deepened as she thought back. 'Marion? Would that be a little bit of a thing, scrawny and with eyes like a scared rabbit? She was here when the children were small but she's gone this long time. Lived in Spring Cottage after she left me, but I haven't seen her for years.'

'You really remember her? It must be over fifty years,' Janet marvelled.

'Not such an achievement, she was the only servant I ever had. I was ill, see, after the second child and I couldn't do the housework. But I didn't think her name was Williams mind. Jolly? Colly? Something more like that. It's no use, I can't remember. Perhaps it *was* Williams? No, I don't think so — still, I suppose at eighty-two I'm entitled to get something wrong.'

'You don't know where she might be now, I suppose?'

'You suppose right. Never seen nor heard of her in years, but you could try Spring Cottage.'

After thanking her for her help, Janet returned to the van. 'I forgot to ask directions.

I wonder where the post office is?' she said to Caroline. 'We have to find Spring Cottage.'

To their dismay Wedensday was half-day closing in that village as well as in Pendragon Island. A knock at a door resulted in another elderly lady asking how she could help. On asking for Spring Cottage, they were directed through the village, up a narrow lane and into a muddy turn-off about a mile further on.

They reached the muddy lane without mishap but it was obvious that the van would not be able to cope with the thick mud and deep, water-filled craters of the dark, tunnel-like track.

'What can we do?' Caroline asked. 'We'd need a tractor to get up there.'

'I've got wellingtons in the back. You stay here and I'll go and see how far the worst of it is. If someone lives up there it has to be navigable, surely.'

'No, Mam, we'll go together. Come on, I'll wear Dad's boots and we can carry Joseph between us.'

They set off, laughing like children as their feet squelched in and out of the mud and once or twice they screamed as their feet slipped and they were in danger of landing full length in the thick, glutinous mess.

It wasn't very far but the lane twisted

and turned so each time it straightened out they still looked to be a long way from the end. Branches met overhead and hid the spring sunshine. Beside them they could hear the chuckling of a small stream, hidden from sight by a rich variety of wild flowers including Jack-by-the-hedge and Herb Robert with its red stems and its distinctive scent, and garlic and the first leaves of hedge parsley and a dozen others, so it smelled fresh and clean in spite of the thick mud oozing around their boots.

Once they were out through the last of the gloom, there were fields ahead of them and beyond, a headland rising up. In the distance the wheeling gulls and the chug-chug-chug of a ship's engine told them that the sea was just out of sight.

Forgetting the search for a moment, they plodded on and up until the sea was spread before them, sparkling in the afternoon sun with the sails of a few boats gliding across making use of the slight breeze to tack lazily home.

'Wales is a land filled with delights,' Janet announced, 'with a surprise around every corner.'

There was no time to seek a way down to the beach, which was rocky from what they could see, but they promised themselves they would come again, prepared with food and the accoutrements of a day out, and explore.

As they turned back to the tunnelled path Janet frowned. 'We haven't seen a cottage, have we? We'd better look around a bit before we go back to the van. It has to be here somewhere.'

The overgrown path seemed to lead nowhere else but the way they had come, but they still went left and right of it in the hope of finding the route to Spring Cottage.

Hidden by the undergrowth of many years, they discovered rusted machinery and household implements. A wheelbarrow, bed springs, numerous buckets and a kettle colonised by a community of woodlice. Joseph shouted in delight when he picked up a toy car, which he insisted on taking him with him 'for Barry to mend.'

The sound of water led them to a stand of trees, bent over and distorted over the years of their growth by the gales from the sea. There, beside the spring that had obviously given it its name, was a ruined house. The name, Spring Cottage, was still visible on the drunken door, but it was a ruin, its roof partly open to the skies.

They stopped for a drink of the clear, ice-cold water and returned to the van.

'The trail ends here,' Janet said briskly.

'Ah well, it was worth a try.'

'Sorry, Mam. It must be a disappointment.'

'Not really. I didn't expect anything more than a dead end. I'd be foolish to hope for more, wouldn't I? It was fun though, for Joseph as well as you and me. An excuse for a lovely day out. I think we should come here again.'

They were getting into the van, scrubbing the worst of the mud from their boots in the grass when a man came along with a dog beside him.

'Been to look at the view?' he asked. 'Not many go that way now, so it's very overgrown.'

'We were looking for Spring Cottage. My sister lived there many years ago, but it's a ruin now.'

'Lost her have you?'

'Lost touch more years ago than I like to count.' Janet lifted Joseph into the van and added, 'Too long to have a hope of finding her again. She'd be seventy, if she's still alive.'

'If she lived round here why don't you put a notice in the post office? Someone might remember. There are plenty of old dears long past that age.'

'What a good idea. Oh, I can't, at least, not today, it's closed.'

'Give me your name and I'll do it for you. Cost you threepence mind.'

Expecting to lose the money and have the advertisement forgotten, Janet nevertheless wrote a message on an old envelope and handed it, with the coins, to the man. He tucked it in his pocket, whistled for the dog, and walked on.

'That's sure to be a waste of money but it was worth risking threepence,' she explained to Caroline. 'Don't tell your father, he'll call me all sorts of a fool.'

'Forget all about it. That's best.'

They said little on the journey back until they reached the outskirts of the town, then as they turned down the lane that led to the back of the cottage, Janet said, 'About you coming back, love. Will you leave it for another month or so, see what happens? I know you're unhappy, and that worries me. But if you abandon it all without giving yourselves a chance you might regret it for years to come. My old mother-in-law used to say it's lonely not having someone to share the good as well as the bad.'

'Better alone than unhappy together.'

'Does it have to be one or the other? Barry isn't unkind and certainly not uncaring, is he?'

'No.'

Janet noted that the word was elongated, a hint that the answer was not completely truthful perhaps.

As the van stopped and the engine fell silent, Janet looked out at the lighted house in front of them. Hywel came out and was silhouetted against the glow from within. Barry stepped out and stood beside him. Janet patted her daughter's arm and said softly, 'It's nice to look across and see someone who's looking at you, knowing they care.'

'When I look across at Barry, his eyes are staring far away from mine.'

'Love is worth a bit of a fight though, even when the battle seems to have been lost, love.'

'Is that another of your mother-in-law's wise sayings, Mam?' Caroline laughed.

'All right, I admit it. I made that one up too!' Seeing Caroline laugh was worth putting up with a bit of teasing.

★ ★ ★

In the overcrowded terraced cottage in Goldings Street, Jack Weston was pleading gently with Victoria.

'If we're to be married in August, we have to make plans.'

'I go to see your mother with all the best intentions, Jack, but once she and your grandmother start discussing colours and seating arrangements and etiquette, and the rights and wrongs of every little thing, my mind closes up and I leave them to it. Then they ask me a question and I pull myself out of a daydream of a quiet wedding with just a few friends and ask them to repeat what they were saying, and they're convinced you're marrying an idiot!'

Jack laughed but he could see that Victoria was genuinely worried, and said so.

'Worried?' she exclaimed. 'More than worried, Jack. I find it all terrifying.'

'We can't have this. There must be a better way of handling what should be the happiest day of our lives.'

'Perhaps I should go and talk to your cousin, Megan? She might help me with the dresses. Hers and Joan's and mine.'

'Good idea. We could go now.'

Mrs Jones was upstairs getting the younger children to bed. They could hear her soft voice telling a story which was punctuated by laughter. The older boys were out in the street playing football in the light from the solitary street lamp, the thump of the ball against the house a reminder that they were due to come in for the night.

It was apparent that his bride-to-be was not enthused with the idea of visiting his cousins, but he gently persuaded her.

'They're all round at Grandmother's this evening. We were all invited to dinner but I declined for both of us. I hope you didn't mind, but I couldn't face it.'

'It wasn't that you couldn't face it with me there, was it?'

'You know it isn't!'

'I do try to fit in but it's hard for me not to get up and start clearing the dishes,' she laughed, and he joined in, hugging her and telling her how happy she made him.

After a clear April day the night was crisp with frost and they ran through the empty spaces where Philips Street had stood, and up onto the main road. Still walking briskly, they stopped twice to shelter in a shop doorway and enjoy a kiss. When they went into Arfon and Gladys Weston's big house overlooking the docks, they were rosy-faced and with eyes that were bright with love.

For Victoria the worst was always the first few moments. Once she had deposited her coat and found somewhere to sit, she relaxed a little, confident that Jack wouldn't leave her to the mercy of his grandmother's carefully veiled put-downs.

The conversation began between herself

and Jack telling the others what they wanted for the wedding day but from then on, the words flew around the room, ideas offered by Gladys, picked up and rearranged by Jack's mother and aunt, and his cousins Joan and Megan, before being presented to her again. Only for her to glance at Jack and for them both to shake their heads.

When they left two hours later nothing had been decided and the only progress was that Victoria had arranged to meet Joan and her mother Sally and the formidable Gladys, in Gwennie Woodlas's shop on the following day.

'I wish,' Victoria said with deep dismay, 'that they would allow my mother to arrange a quiet wedding.'

'The Westons? *Gladys* Weston? Can you imagine Grandmother arranging a quiet anything? There's not a chance. We'll just have to grin and bear it, love.'

'Then let's make it sooner than August and get it over with.'

'August is when the school closes. I don't want us to bring it forward, rush it, fit it in over a weekend.' He was thinking more about his plan to get a house bought and ready for them to return to after their honeymoon, but that was to be a surprise and couldn't be included in the general discussion. 'No,' he smiled, 'we'll go along with it all and stamp on anything too outrageous.'

'All right. There doesn't seem to be an alternative, does there?'

'I have *some* good news. I didn't want to tell the family in case they try to get involved in that, too, but on Saturday we are going to look at that house we saw for sale. It's going for eight hundred pounds and I think we can afford it.'

'And we'll look at it together? Just the two of us?'

'Just the two of us,' he smiled.

'And furnish it together?'

'Just you and me, with Basil's help no doubt.'

'You are wonderful, Jack.'

'And so are you.'

The house was in Gethyn Street leading on from Trellis Street where Jack's parents now lived. A turning off Brown Street, it ran behind Sophie Street, convenient for shops, the school where he worked and not far from Victoria's mother.

Before Jack went home, they walked down Goldings Street, across Brown Street and along Gethyn Street to take another look at it, then they both went home, to dream their dreams.

4

Frank and Ernie Griffiths were more like twins than cousins although Frank was in fact, at twenty, two years younger than Ernie. Ernie had arrived on the Griffithses doorstep one dark winter night, carried in the arms of a policeman. His mother and father had been killed and there was no other family to give a home to the child who was then only five years old. Janet and Hywel had shared the merest glance before taking the boy and promising him a place in their family. Since then, Ernie and Frank, who was then only three years old, had been inseparable.

Janet had not found it easy. Ernie was a disrupting influence and having him as a close friend brought out the worst in Frank. Ernie led the younger boy into every imaginable trouble. One of their earliest escapades was stealing washing from the gardens of the houses in the town and hanging it on someone else's line. Missing school the following day, they had spent happy hours watching from the hedges and fences as irate neighbours lost, then found their possessions, and accused each other of theft and a wide variety of deviant habits.

As the boys grew up their roles changed and it was Frank who had ideas and planned their various forays into petty crime, and Ernie who willingly followed.

Stealing came naturally to them and from small beginnings, like a few sweets from Temptations during the time Nia's mother ran it, they followed a steady and varied course: taking friends' toys, and small, often unwanted items, graduating to items they could sell. At a time of shortages there were people only too willing to buy without asking questions about ownership. One of their favourite scams was catching cats and dogs and holding them for a few days before returning them to their owners, and bashfully accepting a reward.

Their career reached a high spot when they stole a sheep, which they took to a distant market and tried to sell. This was when they were twelve and ten years old, by which time the police knew them well.

Frank, being tall and, like his brother Basil, unbelievably thin, looked so solemn and so full of remorse he usually achieved a light sentence while Ernie, who was sharper and argumentative, invariably caused the magistrate to increase his punishment. At present, they were in court on a charge of driving a van without consent and without insurance.

Frank was all for pleading guilty and looking ashamed, but Ernie insisted on telling the court he had mistaken the van for their own. The Griffithses van and the one the boys had 'borrowed' were ten years different in age and several layers of amaturish paint more scruffy. They each had a heavy fine.

* * *

They were fishing on a sandy bay using two beach rods each hoping for a late cod or an early bass, thinking about their latest fine. Both looked utterly fed up.

'We've got to earn some money fast, Ernie, if we're to pay it off without our Dad finding out,' Frank sighed as he pulled his line out of the water and examined the chewed up lug-worm. 'And catching fish to sell to the fish shop isn't the way to do it.'

'You're right. Hours we've been hanging about here and we haven't caught a damned thing,' Ernie frowned. Then he suggested, 'Time we went out with the van I think. Our Dad'll lend it us, won't he?'

'Unless he's still mad about the crunch we gave it last time. What did you have in mind?'

'For a start off, there's manure up at the farm going for practically nothing and the allotment holders are starting to dig.'

Abandoning the fish and throwing the bait into the waves, they walked back home and pleaded with Hywel to lend them the van. Promising to clean it after use, which they assured him was 'only a few bricks and things,' they set off for the allotments. It took less than an hour to take orders for barrow loads of manure and only three more to collect and deliver the stuff, making a profit of a little over three pounds.

'Put it straight in the kitty to pay the fine, is it?' Frank said.

'Dad isn't expecting the van back just yet. I saw a load of sawn tree trunks just inside the gate of the wood waiting to be collected. Just begging to be 'lifted' it is. What say we fill the van with that? We might make another pound or two?'

At seven o'clock, tired and filthy, the two of them walked into Janet's kitchen and were spun around by her small hand on their shoulder to walk straight back out again to wash at the pump and take off their smelly clothes.

'And wash out that van!' Hywel demanded. 'Bricks you told me. Since when did bricks smell like sh — '

Janet 'shushed' him just in time and reminded him that Joseph was still there.

'Still no sign of your Barry, love,' Janet said as she took the drowsy little boy from her daughter to give her arms a rest. 'I wonder what's keeping him?'

'Can you give us a lift home, Dad?' Caroline asked. 'It's way past Joseph's bed time and he's ready to drop.'

The van smelled far from sweet but with the back doors tied open and the windows down, they suffered the cold night air and survived the ride to Sophie Street. The lights of the flat were on and Caroline frowned. 'It looks like Barry's home. He can't have forgotten he was collecting us, can he?'

'No, of course not,' her father said. 'As if he'd do that. Though he might be working on something and forgotten the time,' he conceded.

'Yes, he does do that sometimes.' Caroline sighed, and Hywel hugged her.

'Lucky you are to have a man who works for you as hard as your Barry does.'

'Yes,' she said, but she didn't sound convinced.

Barry was full of remorse for forgetting he had promised to collect Caroline and Joseph, he didn't try to cover up his neglect with a lie and Hywel teased him about his memory.

'He has a good memory really, Dad,' Caroline said softly. 'I've never known him forget an appointment where work is concerned. It's just that work takes other things out of his mind.'

'Come on, that makes me sound like a terrible husband,' Barry laughed. 'You and Joseph aren't 'other things', for heaven's sake!'

'Of course we aren't,' she smiled stiffly. 'Now, come on, Joseph, let's get you to bed, shall we? Or you'll never be up in the morning.'

Hywel left a few moments later more than a little concerned.

'What's the matter with Barry, forgetting he had to collect our Caroline and the baby!' he stormed as he entered the kitchen where Janet was wiping hens' eggs and placing them in a basket. 'Sitting there reading, he was. Tried to hide the book, but I saw it. Where did he think they were? Did he care?'

Janet put the last egg down with care then told Hywel all that Caroline had confided to her.

'I don't think they should be living there, in the flat she was planning to live in with Joseph. If they had a proper home, or gone anywhere else but that place they'd have stood a better chance.'

'What's that got to do with him forgetting his wife and son?' Hywel threw off his boots and wiggled his feet around searching under his chair for his slippers. 'If I came home and you weren't here, I'd wonder why. Find out where you were.'

'Seems to me they're drifting further and further apart, Hywel.'

'And we thought everything would be perfect once they had started life as a real married couple.'

'Perhaps it still could,' she mused, 'in the right place.'

'There must be somewhere for them to rent. Both working they could afford somewhere decent. Why didn't he think things out and give our Caroline a proper home?' He stood up and looked out at the extension to the house formed by the shed, where Frank and Ernie slept. 'Pity we can't get rid of them two buggers and let our Caroline and Barry use the shed.'

'You couldn't expect anyone except our Frank and our Ernie to sleep in a place like that! Besides, that would be coming home to Mam, and that isn't a solution either.'

'I saw Jack Weston and that Victoria Jones today,' Hywel said a while later. 'Getting married in August, soon after Viv Lewis and Joan Weston. Pity 'elp the girl. Imagine getting yourself related to Gladys Weston! Looking at a house in Gethyn Street they were, the end bit that wasn't knocked down.'

'They could hardly be looking at the bit that *was* knocked down you idiot!' She laughed and he joined in as the door opened and Frank and Ernie came in.

'You two are always laughing,' Ernie said. 'What's your secret? How have you stayed happy together all these years?'

'We live how we want to live, we listen to each other and not other people, and, we love each other,' Hywel surprised himself by stating.

Janet stood to put the kettle over the fire and kissed him as she went passed. 'I'd have said the same,' she said smiling.

'Why are you asking about wedded bliss, our Ernie?' Frank asked suspiciously. 'Not seen a girl you fancy have you?'

'Don't be stupid!'

Ernie turned away, afraid Frank would see the lie on his face. He had met Helen Gunner several times without any of his family knowing and he was beginning to think it was time he confessed. But not yet. He had to tell Mam and Dad and Caroline first, so they would help him cope with Frank's teasing.

★ ★ ★

Frank was suspicious that Ernie was up to something but he hadn't considered a girlfriend, apart from in jest. He suspected he was involved in something planned by Percy Flemming.

Percy was a man few could call friend. A solitary man, rarely seen in The Railwayman's or any other public house, who spent most of his time at home, with his common-law wife and their daughters. Outwardly respectable, he worked as an assistant gardener in a local hospital but it was rumoured that his real income derived from burglaries. Although he had been questioned many times, he had never been found guilty. Frank hoped that Ernie had not become involved, because if something went wrong and someone were caught, it would not be Percy Flemming.

The reason Frank was suspicious, was partly due to Ernie's evasive attitude towards him, when they had always shared every thought. And partly because Ernie had borrowed the van a few times without explaining why he needed it. Once, Frank had been walking home from The Railwayman's alone, Ernie having left early and without giving him the chance of following him. He waved as the van approached, expecting a lift, but if Ernie saw him he pretended not to, increasing his speed along the dark lane and out of sight. Later that evening, when Frank had complained, Ernie had denied being the driver.

With Ernie uncharacteristically secretive, Frank suspected the worst and thought his cousin was doing deals without sharing with him. When he saw Ernie handing Janet an extra five pounds for 'extras', his suspicions increased. Quick to rouse to anger, he saw this as traitorous and picked a fight. As they fought often and without the necessity of a reason, Ernie had no idea of Frank's growing mistrust.

★ ★ ★

The night was moonlit and so still and silent, the watcher could almost feel a tingle as if the woodland around him were a stage set, waiting for its actors. The oak tree with its crown of new growth showed not a quiver of a leaf, the grasses at its feet didn't stir to reveal the presence of even the smallest creature. Shadows were black and solid, not the gentle promise of shade offered in daylight hours but ominous places where danger might lurk.

The hand on his shoulder was the lightest touch but made his blood chill, his heart race, his body prepare for flight or fight. Then he calmed as Ernie's voice whispered,

'Hello, Frank.'

'I didn't hear you come!'

'I've been watching you this ages.'

'Well, you can go now. I'm only waiting for a sight of the badgers. Beautiful sight they are, nine of them now the youngsters have joined in the nightly rambles.'

'Sorry I disturbed you, then. They won't come now.'

'Go on you, I'll wait a bit longer,' Frank said.

Ernie faded into the quiet night but he didn't go far. He slid into the thicket of evergreens and waited. Frank was up to something, he was sure of it. He was afraid it might include Percy and if so, Frank could be in serious trouble. Percy Flemming was not a man to trust, he thought, echoing those of Frank.

A mile away, upwind of the thicket, the badgers set out on their search for food. Sniffing the air, they chose a route that would take them away from the men.

★ ★ ★

With the cafe to run in partnership with Sian Weston, Dora's life had begun to settle into a pleasant hum of activity: the days spent at The Rose Tree Cafe and the evenings attending to household chores and watching the comings and goings of her son and daughter. At the weekends, when Viv and Rhiannon were occupied with their social life, whizzing in and out of the house between exciting dates, she found plenty to do keeping the books up to date and starting on the season's gardening tasks.

This weekend she planned to dig over where the potatoes were to go, and also to fill the bottom of the bean trench with the manure she had bought from the Griffiths boys. There was enough to stop her dwelling on how life had once been, but not enough to exhaust her and stop the depression that hovered darkly around the edge of her emotions from creeping in and threatening to spoil things.

The telephone rang and she picked it up to hear Sian Weston's rather sharp voice asking her to call.

'Anything about the cafe is it?' she asked. 'Shall I bring the books?'

'No, it's about this wedding.'

'Which one, your Jack and Victoria or my Viv and your high-falutin' niece, Joan?'

'Your Viv and Joan. My mother is furious, of course, but the young people want us to cater.'

Dora laughed. 'We did it before, didn't we? Your mother's posh Christmas do?' Her mind was thinking fast, ideas coming and being rejected and being replaced by others. 'We could manage, with a bit of help, and still have time to get ourselves dressed up posh and be a part of the ceremony.'

'Bring your note book,' Sian sighed. 'Between its pages there has to be something to please them all.'

★ ★ ★

'It was our Jack's idea, would you believe,' Sian began when Dora stepped into the small terraced house in Trellis Street. 'Joan and Viv agreed enthusiastically. I think my Jack and Victoria hope that if Joan's wedding is less extravagant, then they can have one even smaller.' She frowned and added, 'I think young Victoria is finding my mother a bit powerful and she wants to tone everything down. Jack is a bit concerned, to be honest.'

'She's every prospective bride's nightmare, your mother!' Dora stated in her forthright

99

way. 'You're the mother-in-law but there's Gladys Weston taking over, as usual, and behaving like she's in charge.'

'I'm afraid she is in charge, and I confess it's my fault,' Sian sighed. 'Mother has always been a strong-minded woman and for most of our lives Sally and I have been content to let her take over. Both of our husbands were given easy, well-paid jobs in Daddy's firm, and her generosity to our children made us accept all the rest without a thought.'

'Until it all blew up in your faces.' Dora put the kettle on the gas stove and reached for the teapot, completely at home in the house of the woman who had once treated her like a sub-species of humanity. 'Funny how we've all had a change in our lives, isn't it? You Westons losing your money and me losing my Lewis to that Nia Martin. And our Rhiannon losing Barry to Caroline Griffiths. It's as if someone was shuffling the cards, gently meddling with the suits, then suddenly threw them up in the air, just for the hell of it.'

'I miss having money to buy what I fancy, I'll admit that,' Sian said. 'But for the rest, well, I think I'm happier than I've ever been, us running the cafe, and Islwyn — my dear husband, once director of Weston's

Wallpaper and Paint, and now working in the Fortune cafe — cooking chips.' They both laughed then at the incongruity of it, Sian wiped her eyes and reached for the teacups. 'Come on, Dora, let's start working out a menu for Joan and Viv's wedding that will enable us to impress everyone and still give us time to join the jollifications!'

'It's all right for Joan. She's a Weston and used to getting her own way. It's young Victoria I'm sorry for. Marrying your Jack, and your mother constantly reminding the poor girl that she once worked for her as a maid of all work.'

'Jack is aware of the problem and he's very caring. I think they'll be all right, in spite of the unlikeliness of the partnership. He really loves her. She's a lucky girl.'

'I hope she stays lucky,' Dora sighed. 'I thought Lewis loved me once, and now look at us!'

* * *

Victoria and Jack, the subjects of their discussion, were entering the middle house of three in Gethyn Street. The three properties had once formed part of a long terrace but a landmine had resulted in a lot of repairs and two houses being demolished. What remained were two terraces and a lot of empty space in which buddlea and rosebay willow herb flourished, and children played.

Jack grasped Victoria's hand as they entered number nineteen, invited in for another guided tour. Mrs Toplas showed them the two living rooms, the kitchen, the yard, the two bedrooms, and the box-room that would one day be their bathroom, with great pride. She seemed to have learnt her patter by rote, hardly taking a breath, and spelling out all the advantages as if this were their first visit.

'Now,' she said when the tour was completed. 'Sit down and I'll make you a cup of tea. In the kitchen I'll be if you have any questions.'

'Well?' Jack looked at Victoria, a quizzical eye-brow raised. 'D'you think we could be happy here?'

After giving a huge sigh, Victoria whispered, 'I wish we could move in today!'

'You're still worried about the wedding?'

'Terrified.'

'I don't want you to feel terrified. I want you to enjoy our special day.'

'Wouldn't it be nice if we could be married by special licence and tell everyone afterwards?'

'I'm proud to be marrying you, love. I

don't want it to be a hole-in-the-corner affair.' He frowned, a thoughtful expression on his lean face. Then he smiled and gave her a quick hug before Mrs Toplas came bustling in with a neatly laid tray. 'Wait until August,' he whispered, 'and we'll do it properly, but in a way you'll enjoy. I promise. Go along with everything Grandmother suggests and trust me.'

Later that evening, when Jack had walked Victoria back to her home, he went to find Viv.

'How do I persuade Grandmother Gladys that Victoria and I want to plan and arrange our own wedding?' he asked.

'Register office, then make a bolt for it. There's something of the Welsh Dragon about our Gladys, mind, and she'll be breathing fire, so when you come back make sure you're wearing fireproof suits!'

'At least your wedding comes first and so close to ours that it's taking some of the preassure off.'

'Glad to oblige, mate,' Viv grinned then he added more seriously, 'Mind you, Jack, you ought to listen to Victoria. It's her special day and although you're able to ignore most of your grandmother's excesses, Victoria can't. Make it a day she'll enjoy, eh?'

'I've just promised to do exactly that, Viv,' Jack replied thoughtfully.

* * *

Hywel had not really meant it when he told his family they were going to keep goats. The energetic clearing of land and uprooting trees to make way for them had been a necessary task to disipate his anger. But a coincidental meeting with a man with goats for sale made the idle thought into reality.

He was driving the van from Pendragon Island to a small village about three miles away to collect some hardcore for a local builder who needed to fill in the foundations of a new house. The weather was cold and there was the threat of rain in the air.

He turned on the wipers and watched as they did little more than scratch the dust on the windscreen. After suffering the poor visibility for about a mile, he stopped and took out a cloth to clean the glass. Looking over a hedge near where he parked was the solemn face of a goat. Stretching up to see if there were others, he saw a man in a very large floppy hat bending over in a corner of the field.

'Keeping goats difficult, is it?' he called.

'Want to buy a couple?' was the eager response.

After a long conversation, during which the old man described the endless joys of owning a goat and Hywel's quest for information failed to achieve any useful result, Hywel abandoned the collection of hardcore for the day and travelled home with two nanny goats and one kid in the back of the van.

★ ★ ★

'But where will we keep them?' Janet asked as the noisy and anxious cargo was unloaded. 'You should have finished making a place for them before you bought them.'

'No trouble. Where's Frank and Ernie? There's a couple of rolls of chicken wire behind the shed, a few stakes and they'll be settled until morning. We'll knock up a proper pen in a couple of days.'

Three goats who are unhappy can make a lot of noise and these were really unhappy goats. One wanted milking and the others were just cold and miserable. Janet tied up the nanny without a kid and tried to take her mind back to her childhood when milking was a part of every day. But that was a herd of cows. Did they differ from goats?

Tying the creature's head and talking

soothingly seemed to be a good start, but each time she managed to get the milk flowing in rhythmical squirts into the pail, the goat panicked and kicked it over. Frank tried and was kicked in the shoulder as the goat twisted away from the pail.

Tethering as a temporary arrangement seemed a simple idea, but finding ground firm enough to hold a stake against the unhappy tugging of the nanny with a kid was no easy task. Besides, dogs could roam in and terrify the captive creatures.

Frank came in, asked if Ernie was home and looked around for supper but was sent out with some urgency to find some fencing. The fencing seemed a good idea to everyone but the goats. It was dark and they were ready to settle for the night, instead they had been dragged into a van and dumped among maniacs. They struggled against every effort of Janet and the rest to confine them.

★ ★ ★

Ernie had been out with Helen. He had given Frank the slip again and had taken Helen for a walk in a part of town where he was unlikely to meet anyone he knew, stopping occasionally to steal a kiss.

'Isn't it time we told our parents we're

meeting?' Helen said with a sigh.

'I want to, I really do,' Ernie said. 'But I need a little more time to talk to them. I want everything to be perfect when we tell them.' He couldn't explain that he was afraid of the ribbing they would both get, afraid she would walk away and not come back if Frank and Viv started on at her with their jokes and innuendoes. He had to take the worst of it himself before she was introduced to their so-called wit. He dawdled home wondering how to introduce the subject.

When he reached the cottage at about eleven-thirty, expecting the house to be dark and quiet, he was alarmed to see every light on. Extra oil lamps were hung on the white-washed walls of every shed and outbuilding. The shadows created were three and four-fold as each light came from a different angle and created a different shape. All the shapes moved in a frantic way and, besides the dancing shadows, there was noise.

Ernie stared in horror and was convinced his whole family was being murdered and the shadows were of devils cavorting and dancing around the area of carnage and devastation. The shadows were of huge animals. Or were they? They were definitely part animal. He had clearly seen a horned head.

He closed his eyes, willing the terrifying

sight to disappear, but when he reopened them the images were still there. Devil-worshipping maniacs were abroad! And they had killed his family! Without stopping to investigate further he ran back down to the town and woke the constable.

The scene was the same when he returned with reinforcements but the constable, who refused to believe in devils, swiftly deduced the cause of the chaos. He convinced Ernie that the 'devils' were his family plus chickens squawking in fright and some very irate goats.

The policeman surprised them all by grabbing the distressed animals firmly one in each hand and guiding them into the back kitchen. The two adults trotted with him obediently, the kid following without further fuss.

After thanking the constable, and locking the door, and making sure everything edible was well out of reach, they all staggered, exhausted, to their beds.

★ ★ ★

The builder for whom Hywel was collecting hardcore was at roof height on two of his houses when, overnight, the roofing timbers vanished. If he wondered about the smart pen and goat house boasted about by the Griffithses a few days later, he didn't say.

* * *

The advertisement which Janet had paid for, requesting information about her sister, Marion, resulted surprisingly in three replies. Two were obviously mistaken in that they described women who were the wrong age, but the third told of the young woman who had worked for Mrs Grant in the village and then left to marry the son of the local policeman, whose name she had forgotten.

Janet showed Hywel then waited for her daughter to return from work to see whether she thought it worth another trip to the village. Caroline read the letter and her eyes sparkled in a way Janet hadn't seen for weeks.

'Mam, this is something we can work on. We'll have her married name!' For a while, the letter explained, the young woman had lived in Spring Cottage alone, but when she had married the policeman's son they had moved on and no one knew where they went.

A few days later they had learned that the name of the policeman was Jolly. 'That old Mrs Grant remembered well,' Janet said.

109

'Didn't she say Colly or Jolly?'

On the following Wednesday, Janet told Hywel she needed the van, but, with the hardcore still a four-trips-a-day job, Hywel had to refuse.

'I can take you there and pick you up on the next trip,' he offered and this was arranged, but it was Frank who actually drove them. With a picnic basket tucked into the cab between three adults of assorted shapes and sizes, plus a child and his teddy, they set off.

The lady who had written was a disappointment. All the information she had was in the letter and much of that had been passed on to her by an aunt.

Frank returned to them after loading the van and delivering the hardcore, then he stayed to share their picnic. The lane was still as muddy but with Frank carrying Joseph and the picnic shared between Janet and Caroline the journey was easy. They stopped short of the cliffs as the day was cold, and ate in the shelter of the abandoned cottage.

While Frank and Caroline walked to look over the sea, Janet and Joseph explored as much as they dared of the house. The stairs were sound and the roof over the two bedrooms kept out most of the weather, although mosses and lichen grew on the walls making weird patterns in the damp wallpaper and peeling paint.

In one of the bedrooms, Janet picked up a scrap of paper held between two pieces of glass from which the frame had fallen. It had been nibbled at the edges by some beetles or bugs, but just visible was a photograph of a young man. Janet's heart began to race with excitement. Could this be the man her sister had married? Was this stranger her brother-in-law?

★ ★ ★

So far, Ernie hadn't taken Helen Gunner through the town. He had kept to the backstreets or met her on the bus and went to Cardiff where they were less likely to be seen. Their only foray through the streets of Pendragon Island were no further than the smaller cafes at the edge of the town and, with great daring, to the cinema, where he led her in during the performance and squashed her into the back row, hoping not to be recognised.

'Come on, Ernie, you must be ashamed of me,' she pouted one evening when they walked home via the back lanes to her home in Trap Lane. 'If you aren't, why don't we ever go where there are people? And when are you going to meet my family and me yours?'

'Tomorrow we'll go down the Vale and have a pint or two in a pub. We'll talk to people and have a laugh. Right?'

'There you go again! Out of town, in case we're seen!'

'No, we'll meet my brother there. You can play darts can't you? We'll have a game and a laugh.'

'Ha-blooming-ha.'

* * *

Frank continued to wonder what Ernie did on the increasing number of times he gave him the slip.

'It can't be a girl, Viv. He'd tell me if he'd found himself a girl, for sure. Tell each other everything, we do.' Then he frowned as that niggling doubt returned. 'I think our Ernie could be earning money without telling me. I hope he isn't mixed up with that Percy Flemming. A girl, or money. It has to be one or the other.'

Sitting in the bar of The Railwayman's, Viv and Jack discussed it and came to the conclusion that Ernie was seeing a girl but a girl of the kind he wouldn't take home to meet his mother. Molly Bondo, was the name that came to their mind. Molly had introduced many young men to the joys of love, but Frank wasn't sure. The idea of earning money seemed more likely.

His suspicions seemed to be confirmed one night as he was walking home across the fields. Once again Ernie had gone out without telling him he was going and he was angry at having to walk across the fields alone once again.

The van, their van, passed him as he reached the stile and he saw clearly that there was only one person in the cab: Ernie.

★ ★ ★

Hywel heard the disturbance and ran out, the light from the kitchen, where the goats still slept, silhouetting him in the doorway. Frank and Ernie were rolling on the floor, fighting so intensely that they didn't hear him call. Hywel took one of the planks of wood from the pile made ready to build the goats their house and waved it wildly around. When he had heard two satisfyingly loud clunks of wood against bone, which he hoped meant one blow for each head, he went in and locked the door.

The following Sunday, Ernie, bearing two lumps on his head, one each side, walked

113

sedately into the house with Helen Gunner, who had been invited for tea.

As always, few invitations had been issued, but Janet expected news of the visit to be broadcast and for many others, uninvited, to turn up. The television, one of the first in the town, was relegated to the shed, and sawn lengths of tree trunks were dragged in to serve as extra seating. Caroline came early to help with the food and to Janet's relief, Barry was with her.

'He didn't forget this arrangement,' Caroline whispered. 'I think he's aware of how he hurt me last time and he won't do it again.'

'Good on him,' Janet smiled.

Rhiannon came with Jimmy Herbert, followed by her brother, Viv, and Joan Weston. Rhiannon was subdued, allowing the lively fun and games, the teasing and the laughter to swirl around her without feeling its touch. She had decided to tell Jimmy she wouldn't see him again, except as a friend. He could hardly vanish from her life as he was a rep, selling sweets for Bottomleys, and he called at the shop regularly to take orders.

She sat and watched as Helen was introduced and teased, the girl giving back as good as she got and making friends of them all without the slightest awkwardness. She only watched, refusing to be drawn into

114

the discussion, as Viv and Joan answered questions about their wedding plans. She admired Eleri and Basil's little Ronnie, and was genuinely thrilled to be told that Ronnie was to have a brother or sister around Christmas. All the time she felt as if the activity around her was something apart. 'It's like I'm looking through a window and watching strangers talking without understanding what they say,' she confided to Eleri. 'I'm so tense, wondering how I'm going to tell Jimmy goodbye, how he will take it. And half of me doesn't want to finish with him for fear of being alone and never being a part of a family like this.'

'I know I shouldn't say this, Rhiannon, but I'm so happy with Basil I wake each morning and marvel at my luck. I loved your brother, Lewis-boy, you know I did, but he would never have made me as happy as Basil does.' She looked across at her long, lanky husband, standing beside his diminutive mother and, catching his eye, smiled so serenely, Rhiannon felt a lump swell in her throat.

'Basil adores you, doesn't he?' she whispered. 'It must be wonderful to be adored.'

'And I adore him. What I'm saying is, don't settle for second-best. Wait for the one-and-only.'

When Nia arrived with Rhiannon's father she was carrying an armful of clothes.

'They're yours, Barry. I thought you might need them and they're no use stuck in a wardrobe in Chestnut Road.'

Barry took the clothes from her and held them against himself one at a time to decide whether or not he wanted them. Shirts and trousers and a couple of jackets. Caroline came over to help him. He put one jacket across him and saw at once that it was obviously too small.

'Oh, sorry,' Nia said with a painful expression on her face. Her eyes filled with sudden tears as she explained, 'That's one of Joseph's. I thought they'd all gone.'

Barry took it and handed it to his mother, embarrassment making him want to leave. It reminded him how big and awkward he was compared to his brother and he couldn't look at Caroline. He concentrated instead on little Joseph, who would probably grow up as perfect as his father had been. At least he wouldn't have a memory of his true father to compare unfavourably with him.

Janet busied herself with food, loading the table with a variety of food few households could manage to gather at one time, but while she worked at making sure everyone had what they needed, she watched Barry

116

and Caroline. She didn't like what she saw. Barry was attentive all right, but in the role of father to little Joseph and not as a husband to her shy, gentle daughter.

When Ernie had taken his girlfriend home and the others had drifted into that semi-sleep state where the party was over but no one believed it, Janet spoke to Hywel.

'I can see why Caroline is unhappy, can't you? Barry is happiest when he's boasting about our Joseph, his clever step-son. When little Joseph's not around, our Caroline doesn't exist.'

'Seems our lovely daughter was right, love. Barry stayed married to her for the child's sake. There's no love in him for Caroline, nor ever will be.'

5

Making a home for the goats was not as easy as Hywel had anticipated. A quickly tacked-up three-sided box and a few rolls of wire was a serious undertaking by him, but to the goats it was a joke. For his first effort at confining them, he hammered in a few posts to which he attached chicken wire about two-feet-six inches high. This the goats jumped immediately, turning to look at him with an expression on their faces that showed they thought it a game.

The housing was another problem. No temporary lean-to for these cheerful characters. When it rained, they ran for shelter as fast as greyhounds. Having no second coat they felt miserable when wet and were determined not to let it happen. As the first spots touched them they made for the kitchen by the shortest route and there they stayed until it stopped. The back-kitchen was given up to them and they spent the nights there, while Janet used the main kitchen for everything, crowding in the washing bath and the table on which she cleaned and washed vegetables as well as the vegetables themselves. Even the rickety chair on which they cleaned shoes was found a corner, and trying to cook a meal with all the other activities carrying on around her made Janet wish she hadn't agreed to their keeping goats. Although, come to think of it, she didn't think she had anyway!

One of the goats, which Hywel had name Ermintrude, took a great liking for Frank and whenever he was around the goat followed him, even trying to squeeze past 'sentinel' Janet and trot after him up the stairs.

'Whoever thinks that country life is peaceful ought to try living here for a few days!' Janet sighed one morning.

The enclosure finally succeeded — at least temporarily — when Hywel put up a solid six-foot wire enclosure supported by metal posts and thick, twisted-wire supports. But, as he had spent so much time building abortive fencing there was still no shelter, so their occupation of the kitchen continued, as did Ermintrude's adoration of Frank. She looked towards the lane each evening, listening for his footsteps, seeming to be aware of his imminent arrival long before the family.

★ ★ ★

Frank walked disconsolately along the lane towards his home, his two-miles-an-hour, long-legged movement evidence of the previous hour spent in the mourning procession of a local man. His dark suit and white shirt, the highly polished black shoes, all looked out of place on him. His hair, which he always wore extra long, was normally pushed carelessly back, but now it hung, neatly parted, down over his ears.

The reason for the gloomy expression was not sadness for the recently departed but disappointment over the disloyalty of Ernie. He might have used the family van once or twice to impress Helen Gunner, but on the two occasions he had seen him driving it, Ernie had been alone. No, Ernie was up to something. He was making money somehow without dealing him in.

April was coming to its end and celandines and violets carpeted the woods close by. Catkins still hung on the hazels and the hedgerows were splendidly decorated with blackthorn blossom, a few brave hawthorn hinting at the delight to come. But although the signs of spring were all around, the air was crisp with the threat of snow. Daffy snow, Janet called it. Frank idly wondered, during the biting chill of evening, whether he could lock Ernie out and make him sleep in the back-kitchen with those goats. At times like these he remembered that Ernie was a cousin and not a brother and he spitefully wanted to remind him.

A pheasant got up in the field beside which he walked and he raised his arms grasping an imaginary gun, and shouted the thwack of a cartridge that probably would have missed anyway. Basil was the expert with a gun, Frank's favourite tool was a ferret plus small nets. He wondered idly whether it would be worth going out and bagging a few rabbits. They would earn him money for a pint or two. He kicked at the grass verge and growled out an explosion of anger. He needed to get his hands on big money. What with the fine still to pay and his contribution to the household overdue, life was becoming a worry. 'Damn Ernie,' he shouted aloud.

'What's up with you, then?' a voice asked.

'Nothing to do with you, Percy Flemming!' Frank replied. He had been startled at the man's silent approach. 'And don't creep up on me like that or you'll get a nasty shock!'

'Creep up? Damn me, boy, I called you from the corner of the wood and there's you lost to the world, standing there pretending you could hit that poor pheasant.'

Percy Flemming was a man in his early

121

forties. He had been married twice and lost each of his wives to other men. No one knew how he survived financially on his low wages as assistant gardener at a local hospital, although most suspected it was not honestly. He paid for the upkeep of two illegitimate daughters plus the woman with whom he now lived, Claire Wheel, and their two girls. Claire was a friend of Molly Bondo, a local prostitute, and had shared her occupation before Percy had set her up in a small house near the centre of the town and kept her 'decent'. His daughters seemed to lack nothing.

Frank looked at Percy now, smartly dressed in good quality clothes, looking more the country gent than a man who, by all accounts, lived mainly on his wits. Perhaps he could pick up some tips on making money. Percy certainly never seemed short of cash.

'I need money desperate, Percy,' he admitted with an exaggeration of his normal lugubrious expression. 'There's the fine, see, and I have to pay Mam and Dad for my keep, and with only our Dad's van to earn money with, I'm out of ideas.'

'Would a hundred pounds sort you out?' Percy said quietly, after looking at Frank thoughtfully for a long moment. 'For a night's work and a still tongue afterwards, I'll give you fifty pounds. There's another fifty in a month's time if you want it and you manage to keep your mouth shut.'

'What do I do?'

'I have to be convinced you can keep your mouth shut. Not a word to anyone, specially that Ernie. A few pints and he'd gab non-stop.'

'I wouldn't tell Ernie!' He looked outraged at the suggestion and Percy nodded knowingly.

'Quarrelled have you? Now there's a pity. When you make it up you'll share every last thing. I know you two of old.'

'You have my word, Percy. I won't tell a soul. Ever. Now, what d'you want me to do?' Whatever the job he would do it. Fifty pounds! He could settle his fine and wouldn't Ernie be narked over that! And he could give Mam a tenner. He doubted whether she'd ever seen a ten pound note. Was there such a thing? Or would he hand it to her in a fan of twenty ten-shilling notes? That would be fun. He smiled as he imagined her face. The smile faded when he saw the doubt on Percy's face.

'You can trust me,' he assured him. 'I want this so bad I'll do anything.' He had to convince Percy. He had to get one over on Ernie.

Percy stared at him again, as if assessing the risks, then he nodded. 'Right then, you're in.'

Frank went home in a more cheerful state of mind. It was much later before he wondered exactly what Percy had let him 'in' for. He tried to reassure himself that the stories about Percy were exaggerated. It couldn't be anything terrible, Percy wouldn't get him into real trouble. Although, a hundred pounds was a lot of money and might involve a lot of risk. He shrugged the uneasy thought away. A hundred pounds! The fan of notes swam before his eyes in a dazzling array. Whatever the risk, he was *in*, and in he would stay.

* * *

In Trap Lane, Ernie and Helen were near the gate of Helen's house, using the tall privet hedge as a screen to hide their goodnight kisses. After a few hurried words confirming their plan to meet later in the week, he reluctantly walked away. Helen watched him go, then turned to walk up the short path to her front door. As she put out a hand to push her key into the lock, the door was wrenched back on its hinges and her mother stood there and demanded how long she had been meeting one of the dreadful Griffithses.

'Oh Mam, they aren't that bad, just a bit different, that's all.'

'Different? I'll say they're different. Thieves they are the lot of them. You don't see him again, d'you understand?'

'Sorry, Mam, but Ernie and I like each other a lot. I like all of the Griffithses, they're good fun. I have no intention of ending our friendship.'

'Friendship? Is that all it is?'

'For the moment,' Helen said, glaring at her mother. There was a look in Helen's eyes that Gloria Gunner recognised of old. It had appeared the time they had tried to make her stay at school and she had been determined to leave. And again when she had asked to go to London with two friends to visit the relation of one of them and they thought her too young. Without another word being spoken, Gloria knew that to argue now would only entrench them in a battle of wills, which she would almost certainly lose.

'Your father and I insist that you bring him here so we can judge him for ourselves,' she said finally. If she made sure to pull out all the stops and prepare a grand meal with serviettes and an array of cutlery, Ernie was sure to be ill at ease. That would show Helen

125

how unsuitable he was. Better than trying to make her point with words. A little subtle action was called for here.

* * *

Dora and Sian met at seven Sophie Street to complete a menu that would please Gladys Weston, a daunting task but one which they were determined to achieve.

'Your Viv doesn't like us doing the catering for his wedding any more than my mother does,' Sian admitted when they took out their lists and compared notes.

'All the more reason for getting it right,' Dora said firmly. 'Thank goodness rationing will be finished by then.'

'D'you think it will? I can hardly believe it after so long.'

'Joints of ham and pork will be easily dealt with the day before, and we can do some large flans too.'

'Oh yes. They add to the table displays, don't they?' Sian ticked away at her list. 'Then there'll only be the vegetables and salads to do on the day, that shouldn't be difficult, so long as we start early.'

'We need to be at the hall by seven, if we can get the key.'

'Mother's talking about vol-au-vents for

a starter,' Sian said, referring again to her list.

'Unless she wants to roll up her sleeves and make them, she'll have soup and like it,' Dora said.

They made a diary of things to do and then went to look at Gomer Hall to make sure they had a clear picture of the kitchen facilities and how they would set out the tables.

The hall was rather shabby having been untouched throughout the war and the years following. Being empty, it was easy to see the worn decorations, the peeling and chipped paint. It was a dirty cream and a gingery brown on which an attempt had been made to brighten it with borders of stencilled green leaves and flowers.

'My mother will have a fit!' Sian exclaimed. 'A Weston wedding in a place like this!'

'Once the tables are set and flowers add their colour she won't notice the walls. When we've finished, every eye will be drawn to the tables, I promise you,' Dora assured her friend.

'I've never been here before, have you?' Sian said when they stepped through the double doors.

'Yes, years ago, when Lewis and I enjoyed dancing. It seems strange to remember those

127

times now our Rhiannon and Viv come here and do the same.'

'Not quite the same,' Sian chuckled as they went through the foyer and into the main hall. 'Rock 'n roll, jitterbugging and jive doesn't have the same ring as the slow foxtrot and the Viennese waltz.'

'They don't allow much of that carry-on,' Dora said with a grin and she pointed to a notice hanging in the corner of the hall: 'Jitterbuggers keep to the corners.'

* * *

Despite their rather prim image, the dance classes at Gomer Hall were very popular. Basil and Eleri went whenever they could arrange for Janet and Hywel or Dora to look after Ronnie. Rhiannon was usually there with Jimmy Herbert, Viv and Joan, Frank and Ernie, plus several other friends. Basil's work as nightwatchman meant he had to leave before nine, but if Eleri stayed on, she would be seen safely home by Frank or Viv when the class ended at ten o'clock. Basil didn't mind her staying. With their second child due around Christmas, he wanted Eleri to have fun while she could.

He knew she missed Rhiannon, having lived with the Lewises throughout her first marriage, and after Lewis-boy's death, right up to her marriage to him fourteen months ago. They were as much like sisters as Ernie was like his and Frank's brother.

When they walked into the over-full hall one evening, he saw Rhiannon and at once guessed she was upset.

'Better go and see what's up, love,' he said to Eleri, nodding in the direction of Rhiannon. 'Had a fall-out with young Jimmy I expect.'

'I've just told Jimmy I don't want to go out with him any more,' Rhiannon confided when she and Eleri were alone in the cloakroom.

'I thought you liked him?'

'I do, but not enough. I don't want us to drift into an engagement and a marriage in a casual way. I like him very much, but I don't want to spend my life with him.'

'Are you going to stay, or go home? I'll come with you, shall I?'

'I want to run away and hide, but I won't. If I mean what I told him, that I want to build a life on my own, then I have to stay don't I? I have to feel able to come to the dance class without him. I have to accept that I'm no longer one of a couple.'

'Come on, I'll get Basil to whizz you around the floor a few times, that should shake the blues away. Worse than riding a bad-tempered donkey it is, dancing with my Basil.'

Rhiannon smiled. Basil's dancing was enthusiastic rather than stylish. She wiped her eyes, added more make-up and followed Eleri back into the throng. Eleri whispered a word or two to her husband and he came over to Rhiannon. Bending his long, lanky frame into a suitable pose, he began to dance and make her laugh, assuring her without needing to put it into words that whatever happened, she was among friends.

Basil left just before nine and Rhiannon sat with Eleri for the last hour, between dances. She danced once with Jimmy, who put no pressure on her to reconsider, twice with Frank. When the last waltz was announced, she ran quickly into the cloakroom. She didn't want to sit and watch other couples dancing, looking into each other's eyes, thinking about the slow walk home with their arms around each other, unaware of the cold night air. Slowly, she dressed ready for the solitary walk home.

With Viv and Joan, she went first to Eleri's flat in Trellis Street where Janet and Hywel were sitting beside a low fire and listening to the radio. Refusing their offer to walk her the short distance back to Sophie Street, she left them and hurried down Brown Street.

It was dark and in the light from the street lamps there was a suspicion of sleet falling. She hardly noticed the cold, she was on the very edge of tears, wanting to turn around and run to where Jimmy parked his car in the hope of seeing him, and begging him to forget what she had said earlier. She stopped on the dark, cold street and wondered if it represented her future, cold and empty. Had she been a fool?

She might still catch him, the hall wouldn't yet have emptied and he might have stopped outside to talk. With a stifled sob she turned as she reached Temptations on the corner. 'Jimmy,' she whispered. 'Please be there.' She began to walk back to the hall.

From the corner, where Temptations stood, someone called to her. She gulped down the sadness that choked in her throat and brushed away tears that filled her eyes. Who could it be? She didn't want to see a soul. A second call, and she turned to recognise a man and a boy with a dog on a lead. Charlie and Gwyn Bevan.

'Rhiannon, have you seen our pup?' Gwyn called. 'Our Dad got her for me. Great, isn't she?'

'Oh, Gwyn she's beautiful.' He stopped for them to approach her and smiled at Charlie Bevan. 'Good idea for him to have a pet.

Our Mam was talking about getting one, but she never did. Now we're all out all day it wouldn't be fair.'

'I'll take him to show her, shall I?' the excited boy suggested.

'Thanks, she'll like that.' Rhiannon picked up the little dog and buried her face in the silky fur. 'I wish we had a pet, they're company when you're lonely aren't they?' Tears slipped then as the word lonely reminded her of her parting from Jimmy.

'Go home and give Polly a drink of milk then put her in her bed,' Charlie said to his son. 'I'll be there now in a minute.'

'Is anything wrong, Miss Lewis?' Charlie asked after his son had scampered across the road. 'Can I help?'

'Thanks, but I'm all right. I've just — ' she hesitated, how could she tell a virtual stranger? Then, because he *was* almost a stranger and knew none of the facts, it all came out. She told him that she had parted from her boyfriend and that she now wished she could run back and ask him to forget her words. 'But I know that giving things another chance would be wrong. Ending it and facing the world on my own is hard but I know it's the right thing to do, for Jimmy and for me,' she finished.

'Sometimes the hardest things to do turn

out to be the most important decisions of your life,' was all he said. He took her arm and guided her to the door of number seven. He didn't ask for explanations, but walked her to her door and saw her safely inside. 'Come and see the pup tomorrow if you have time,' he said when they parted. 'That son of mine loves showing her off.'

Rhiannon leaned against the inside of the door. The house was silent. Dora was probably in bed and Viv wasn't yet back from walking Joan home to Glebe Lane. Without putting on a light, she crept upstairs, scrubbed off her make-up and got into bed. It was done and, thanks to Charlie Bevan, she hadn't run after Jimmy and started it up again.

★ ★ ★

On Saturdays, Weston's Wallpaper and Paint Store was always busy. Viv left the upstairs office where he dealt with the paperwork and phone calls, to help with sales. Since they now stocked carpets and a few small items of furniture, business was increasing faster than ever. He had always made it a policy to deal with the customers whenever he could, not wanting to be the sort of manager who sits in isolation, cut off from the comments of

133

the people who buy.

Taking over the running of the business after old man Arfon's son-in-law had been sacked, Viv had worked many extra hours to re-build the business. Now, with Joan, Arfon's grand-daughter, beside him, Viv thought he could never be happier. Joan, who with her twin, Megan, had once been notorious for rudeness and outrageous behaviour, now listened patiently to the needs of those who called for advice, helped them choose wallpaper and carpets, and, to her own surprise, took a pride in what she did.

One of their earliest customers that Saturday morning was Jack, Joan's cousin and one of Viv's closest friends.

'Oh, here he is, one of the big spenders,' Viv teased. 'Why do I think you're on the scrounge? Battered old tins of paint, slightly damaged wallpaper rolls? Is that it, Jack?'

'Yes and this time it's for us. Victoria and me! We're buying a house in Gethyn Street. What d'you think of that then? So besides being cheap, it has to please Victoria, right?'

'Bring her in when we close for lunch and we'll see what we've got.'

'Oh, I can't. Not lunchtime. Got something on,' Jack said evasively. 'Will half-five do?'

'Five-thirty it is.'

'Just as well, really,' Viv said to Joan when Jack had gone. 'I want to get those orders written out when the shop's shut.'

'What about lunch?'

'I'll nip out and buy a pie at The Railwayman's.'

It was late when Viv entered the pub and he was relieved when the barman nodded to his thumbs-up gesture, and served him with a pie and a pint. He didn't sit in his usual spot where he met with Basil, Ernie, Jack and the others, but found a quiet corner behind the door. Taking out a newspaper he began to read the latest on the Mau-Mau problem in Kenya, and the Vietnam War where the seige of Dien Bien Phu was being fought, and was glad he didn't wear a uniform. He had been failed on medical grounds. A damaged knee that didn't bother him but was enough to prevent his being called up to do National Service.

As it was almost time for lunchtime stop-tap, the bar slowly emptied. Looking up from his paper he was surprised to see he was one of only three people left. One of them was Barry Martin. What was he doing there on a Saturday lunchtime, he wondered? With a wife working just down the road he should be having lunch with her, or looking after their little boy.

'What you doing drinking alone, Barry?' he called. 'Caroline fed up with you already, is she?'

'I've got an appointment in a few minutes,' Barry replied, leaving his beer and hurrying out. Viv frowned. The way Barry scuttled out it seemed all was not well in the Martins' love-nest.

The lights were switched off, towels thrown across the pumps, and the only other man there drained his glass and left.

Stretching, Viv prepared to leave. Then he heard Jack's voice and it was coming from behind the bar. Whatever was he up to? Pressing himself into the shadows, he grinned and waited.

The landlord threw off one of the towels and began explaining to Jack the trick of pulling a good foaming pint.

'What's this then? Left school at last have you?'

'Viv. Silly sod! You gave me a fright. No, I haven't been sacked, I haven't resigned, just curious to know how a pint is pulled. That's all.'

'All right, I don't want to know if you don't want to tell. Part-time job is it?'

'I'm going to work in the bar but not for pay. Right? I told you, I'm curious that's all.'

'Working for nothing? There's got to be more to it than that,' Viv retorted as he went out.

'Well there isn't!' Jack shouted after him. 'So mind your business! Right?'

* * *

That same lunchtime, Helen Gunner was pushing away the lunch her mother had prepared and glaring at the tablecloth.

'I'm sorry, Helen,' her mother was saying, 'but your father and I have discussed it and we have no intention of going to meet the Griffithses. We know enough about them to be sure they aren't our sort.'

'And to know that we don't want you mixed up with them either!' Helen's father, Wilfred, added. Wilfred told Gloria not to invite Ernie but to ignore the situation, convinced that their daughter would soon tire of such a boorish companion. Gloria wasn't so sure, in fact she had rather looked forward to embarrassing Ernie with her superior knowledge of etiquette. Now, watching her daughter's face with its combination of anger, determination and pride, she wondered again if they were being wise.

Making a big fuss of putting her untouched meal in the kitchen and putting on her coat,

Helen left to return to work in the large grocery shop on the main road. She knew that eating no breakfast and leaving her midday meal, giving the impression that she had eaten nothing since the previous day would worry her parents. She smiled as she bought two sticky buns and went into the park to eat them. She wasn't worried about their refusal to meet Ernie and visit his family. Mam was a bit above herself but she'd come round. It was the Griffithses she was more concerned for — how would they cope with Mam?

* * *

One Sunday morning early in May, Rhiannon was putting the small joint of meat consisting of three small chops, into the oven for lunch when there was a knock at the door. She opened it to see Charlie and Gwyn, who had the struggling puppy in his arms. She invited them in and called Dora.

'Mam, come and see your visitors.'

'Three pounds seven and fourpence half-penny,' her mother muttered before putting down the pen and coming out of the kitchen.

'Hello Charlie, Gwyn. And who is this then?'

'Polly,' she was told.

She took the puppy and admired her while the boy stood proudly by. Charlie glanced at Rhiannon and asked quietly,

'Feeling better?'

'Thanks, I'm all right.'

Dora went into the kitchen and found some treats for both Gwyn and Polly. Charlie shuffled his feet as if undecided whether or not to speak. 'Things can change so suddenly you'd never believe,' he said. 'I was beginning to think I'd never escape the mess I'd made of my life, but then I was offered a job.'

'At the Windsor garage, Gwyn told me. That's wonderful.'

'Dogsbody in a garage — it isn't much, but it's a beginning. I'm quite a good mechanic and I hope that once they've learnt to trust me, 'train me up' as Mr Windsor puts it, I'll be able to progress to better things.'

'I'm sure you will,' Rhiannon said, smiling.

'It's the boy, see. He's the reason I have to succeed.'

They listened to the laughter coming from the kitchen and Rhiannon said, 'What better reason could you have than a son, specially one like your Gwyn? He tried so hard to care for old Maggie, didn't he? Now he needs someone to spoil *him* a bit.'

'Maggie left some money you know. Only

a few pounds plus the rent. She'd saved enough to pay the rent on the house for six months and although I've been tempted to borrow from it, I haven't. She knew how important it would be to have the security of a roof over our heads, if I'm to succeed and stay on the straight. It's still there and I take strictly the right amount every week. Now I have a job I'll try to keep it in reserve. Perhaps buy a headstone one day, eh?'

'Maggie was a wise old woman and I think she'd prefer you to spend it on things for the living.'

Gwyn came several times after that to show them the pup and occasionally, when Rhiannon opened the door as he was leaving, she saw Charlie standing at his front door, waiting for his son to return. They would smile and wave to each other and Rhiannon found her smile remained for a long time afterwards.

Charlie had been working at the Windsor Garage for a few weeks when Rhiannon passed on a Wednesday afternoon and saw him there. He was working on a big blue van. 'Overhauling the engine and making sure it's giving its best,' he explained. 'I told you I'd be given proper work to do once they knew how good I was,' he grinned, his teeth white in his grease-stained face.

'I'm off for a walk,' she explained. 'Perhaps I can take Polly when she's old enough?'

A car squealed to a stop and the driver pressed the horn irritably. Charlie frowned and Rhiannon looked curiously around. 'It's my father,' she said. 'What's upset him I wonder?'

'Get in, Rhiannon,' Lewis Lewis demanded, as she walked over to see what he wanted.

'I'm going through the fields to Tremanor for a walk, hoping to pick some bluebells, I don't want a lift home,' she said with a laugh.

'I said get in, or I'll drag you in!'

'Dad? What's the matter?' she slid into the passenger seat and was jerked back as he accelerated away.

'*He's* the matter. That criminal you were talking to and smiling at. That's what!'

'Charlie Bevan? I was only asking how the job's going, Dad. What's wrong with that?'

'Keep away from him. I'm warning you, Rhiannon. Keep away from him or I'll speak to him and make sure he stays away from you! Right?'

She sat back in the seat and stared into her lap, counting the flowers in the pattern on her dress. She felt like a child caught in some misdemeanour by an unpleasant schoolteacher. He pulled up outside the house and turned to her.

'You and Jimmy, you aren't seeing each other any more?'

'That's right, Dad.'

'Is that Charlie Bevan the reason?'

'Of course not! I've hardly spoken to him.'

'Not what I've heard. Calls often doesn't he?'

'His son does, Gwyn brings the puppy for Mam to see.'

'Oh, well keep clear of him. He's trouble. Been in and out of prison more times than I can remember.'

'I know. But he's trying hard to leave that behind him. He deserves a bit of encouragement, doesn't he?'

'Not if its coming from you he doesn't!'

She stood at the door, her hand on the key, not wanting to go inside, but neither wanting to return to the walk she had planned. Turning round, she went to see Eleri and Basil and baby Ronnie.

It was a while before she realised that all the time she had been with Eleri she had been talking or thinking about Charlie Bevan. Her father's reaction had made her realise that he was only a few years older than herself, and also that he was far from unattractive.

Approaching Sophie Street once more, she glanced up at the window of the flat above Temptations. The curtains moved and Caroline waved. Barry's van wasn't parked nearby, Caroline was on her own again. It seemed impossible that Barry had an appointment every Wednesday afternoon. He had to be avoiding Caroline on her half-day, instead of welcoming the extra hours in her and Joseph's company.

She waved a beckoning arm and, when the window was opened, called, 'Come and have a cup of tea with me. Dad's just messed up my walk, Mam's out and I'd be glad of your company.'

'Are you sure?' Caroline hesitated. She was still embarrassed, meeting Rhiannon, aware of how she had taken Barry from her.

They talked mostly about young Joseph, and Eleri and Basil's baby Ronnie. Laughing at the funny things children do and avoiding mentioning Barry. But although Caroline gave a good imitation of a happy wife and mother, Rhiannon was more and more convinced that Caroline was lonely. Barry was neglecting her.

Caroline's face was always ready to smile but today there was a strained look around her jaw and a haunting sadness in the lovely brown eyes that made Rhiannon want to hug her and offer words of comfort. Unable to comment, she bent once again to play with Joseph.

'Did you know Mam is trying to find her long-lost sister?' Caroline said as Rhiannon poured more tea. 'Lost for over sixty years, mind, but she's realised she could still be alive, and is having one last try.'

'How exciting. I don't know where you'd start on something like that.'

'There's a village called Cwrt y Celyn, and Auntie Marion worked there for a while when she was very young. She married the local policeman, so we know her married name. We even found the house where they lived, but it's derelict and the trail's gone cold from there on.'

'I know Cwrt y Celyn. Gertie Thomas in the corner shop lived there. She might know something.' They discussed the possibilities for a while and decided to call and see Gertie later, when they had drunk their fill of tea.

'You miss them, don't you?' Rhiannon dared to say. 'Your Mam and Dad, your brothers and the lively house where half the village congregates?'

Caroline didn't trust her voice, she only nodded. Rhiannon decided that next time she saw Eleri she would suggest she called on her sister-in-law each Wednesday, to ease the long hours of Barry's absence.

On Wednesdays when the shop closed at one o'clock, Gertie often went into Cardiff. This afternoon she hadn't and was already regretting it. The hours alone behind the shop dragged on her half-day too, and again on Sundays, now she didn't have old Maggie Wilpin to gossip to. So hearing the knock on the door and seeing Caroline, Joseph and Rhiannon there, gave her great pleasure. Over-full of tea as they were, she insisted on making more while they explained the reason for their visit.

'I remember the farm and the frightening old man who lived there. Was he your grandfather, Caroline? Well I never did! Thank the good Lord you didn't take after him, then!'

'D'you remember my mother living there? And her brother, Adrian?'

'Pig of a man. Worse than your grandfather he was.'

'And the sister?'

Gertie wrinkled up her face in heavy concentration but finally shook her head. 'Never remember no sister.'

'Marion, her name was,' Caroline coaxed. 'Older than Mam. She ran away when she was eleven.'

'Best for her, poor dab.'

Gertie's face had a faraway look as she remembered the atmosphere of secrecy and rumours of violence surrounding the family but no amount of hinting could rouse the girl called Marion from Gertie's memories.

'I can see the farm, and I can picture too the old man and his son, but until this very minute I didn't realise that the little girl who lived there and who was never allowed out to play, was your mam. Funny old world, isn't it?' she smiled as if the remark were newly minted.

When Caroline went to her parents' house the following morning to deliver Joseph into their care, she mentioned the conversation with Gertie to her mother. It was a surprise to Janet that Gertie Thomas, whom she had known ever since she and Hywel had married and come to live at the cottage, had been born in the same village as herself.

'Say something more original than, 'it's a funny old world', Mam,' Caroline pleaded.

'My old mother-in-law used to say that coincidences are more common than brown eggs, and the unlikely happens more often than we think,' Janet said.

'Almost as bad,' Caroline teased.

'As soon as I find a minute I'll go down and have a good chin-wag,' Janet promised. But any hope of Gertie helping her in the

146

search for Marion was already quashed. If Gertie remembered her father and brother and herself, yet had no recollection of Marion, it was unlikely such a memory would return. She sighed. It was all so long ago.

6

Frank met Percy Flemming one evening without telling anyone where he was going. It wasn't difficult. Ernie was off meeting that Helen Gunner, or doing a deal of his own. Whatever Ernie was at, he wasn't giving a thought to what he, Frank, was doing. It hurt. Close friends they'd always been. He nodded a vague cheerio to his mother and went out. Mam and Dad would presume he was going to The Railwayman's, so they hadn't bothered to ask. The place Percy had chosen was a bit cloak-and-dagger he thought, with slight irritation. A corner of a field in which Farmer Booker sometimes kept his young steers.

He walked up the lane almost silently in his rubber-soled 'daps' and after he had gone a few yards, he realised that someone was following him. If this was Percy having a bit of fun at his expense he'd be very sorry. He stopped and melted into the soft branches of a fir tree. The footsteps came on and he clenched his teeth. 'Get ready for a shock, Percy Flemming,' he muttered. The footsteps continued to draw near but in the gloom of the evening, there didn't appear to be anyone there.

His heart leapt into his mouth and he tensed himself for flight. As he was about to burst out of cover he recognised the unmistakable scent of goat.

'Ermintrude!' he whispered. 'Scared me half to death, you did!'

The goat who seemed to think she was a dog, had broken out once again and followed him. It had taken the goats less than three days before they found a way out of the enclosure Hywel had made. The next attempt had been cleared in a few hours. They seemed to treat it like a game, the challenge of outwitting Hywel was great fun. Frank greeted the friendly creature and was rewarded with an exuberant welcome as the goat danced around him in delight. He found a piece of string in his pocket and tied up this newest member of the family, and sat to wait for Percy with a silly grin on his face.

'I didn't expect you to bring a friend,' Percy chuckled a few moments later.

They walked back in the direction of the Griffithes house as Percy presented Frank with his plan, or as much of it as he was willing to tell.

'It's a factory storeroom,' he said, 'where they keep the orders ready for dispatch. I've got everything set up, the dates when the contents will be worth taking, when there'll be money held to pay wages too. And I have a driver standing by as well as someone to take the goods off my hands.'

Frank felt his knees weaken. It sounded very high-risk stuff, a long way from pinching one of Booker's pheasants. 'What d'you want me to do, then?'

'I want you to open the gates and dispose of the watchman.'

'Don't talk daft, man! How am I to get rid of a nightwatchman?'

'Put him to sleep or distract him. Do it any way you like, but make sure he isn't around to blow the whistle on us when we go in.'

'I won't hit anyone, mind! I couldn't. Our Basil's a nightwatchman.'

There was a pause. 'I know.'

'When is this to happen?'

'I'll tell you where and when on the night, you'll have details when we're on the way and not before. Not a word, right?' Percy began to walk away and Frank called after him.

'I'm not sure, Percy — '

Percy darted back and held the tall man by the front of his jacket and glared up at him. 'You're in, boy, and there's no way you can

150

change your mind, right?'

'All right. But is that all you're saying? I still don't know what you want me to do!'

'Unlock the gates, that padlock chain looks easy to snap, then make sure the watchman isn't watching. That isn't difficult, is it? And,' he added, 'leave your friend home.' As the night swallowed him up, Frank heard him laughing.

This was out of his league, Frank knew that much. He had been satisfied with selling a few rabbits and pheasants, and 'lifting' an item when the opportunity arose to make a few shillings. But this was serious thieving. The smell of prison seemed to surround him as he walked home through the clear night. Mam and Dad had supported him throughout his various brushes with the law, but would they help him through this if it all went wrong? But in spite of his fears the thought of having fifty pounds in his hand was intoxicating. That, and the thought of getting one over Ernie.

After returning the goat to her pen, he set off again. Walking across the fields to The Railwayman's, he thought about his attitude towards Ernie and his girlfriend, Helen. A part of his resentment was the fear of being on his own. All his life he'd had a willing partner with Ernie, whatever he had planned. He had never been without company either, never without someone to listen when things were good, or console him when his plans weren't going smoothly.

There had been girlfriends in the past, but they had never been important enough to separate him from Ernie, in fact the choice of girls to take out was decided by whether or not there were two of them. Now it seemed likely to change and Frank wasn't ready for it.

He walked into the bar and stared in amazement. There, behind the counter, pulling a pint like an expert, was Jack Weston.

'No, I haven't been sacked and no, it isn't a part-time job,' Jack pre-empted him. 'I was curious, that's all. I wanted to find out how to pull a pint. Right?'

Frank chuckled. It sounded as though Jack had been called to explain himself time and again. Serve him right, larking about on the wrong side of the counter. He found himself a seat beside Viv and Basil, called for a pint and snapped his fingers at Jack for service. Jack's response was another gesture, even less polite.

'Want to earn some money?' Jack called across during a lull in serving.

'Don't be daft, when do I not?' Frank replied. 'But you aren't getting me behind no bar, mind. Disorientated completely I'd be, behind there.'

'I'm buying a house. We need someone to do a bit of decorating.'

Frank groaned. Wallpapering he could do without. 'If there's one thing I hate, it's wallpapering,' he began, but he hesitated. It might be a good idea to accept. If he had money it was a wise move to have some way of accounting for it. 'All right, I'll come and see you at the weekend.'

Ernie came in just before stop-tap and they walked home together across the fields.

'Jack wants me to do some decorating,' Frank said.

'I'm in if you want help,' Ernie said. 'I need a bit of extra money.'

'I guessed as much, you going off and doing deals on your own. You haven't started gambling have you?'

'No, and I haven't been doing deals without counting you in, either!'

'That's what you tell me! Using that Helen Gunner as a cover, even bringing her to the house to meet Mam.'

Normally a fight would have ensued, but Ernie shook his head and replied, 'I haven't, Frank. I guessed that's what's been eating you. I wouldn't do anything without telling you. When you saw me in the van, Helen was with me. I made her duck down out of sight, afraid of leg-pulling.'

'Bet you've never been invited to her house!'

'They wouldn't have me,' Ernie said and as Frank began to laugh, he joined in.

Frank believed him and was ashamed of his lack of trust. For a moment he was tempted to tell him about the deal he was doing with Percy Flemming, but he didn't. Getting on the wrong side of Percy wasn't recommended. 'Serious is it, you and this Helen?' he asked.

'It could be. I feel different about her. But it won't stop us being mates, will it? I mean, we've both known that one day things would change. But you and me, we'll always be a partnership. I wouldn't like that to change, Frank.'

'Of course it won't. We'll still work together on anything that crops up, won't we?' They walked the rest of the way in silence, Ernie thinking about Helen, and Frank thinking about Percy Flemming and wishing he could get out of his involvement.

★ ★ ★

Caroline felt all hope of a true marriage slipping away. And worse, having once mentioned it to her mother and been told to try harder, she felt unable to bring up the subject again. Once being a part of a loving family, and living in a house where loneliness was impossible, moving to Sophie Street and spending hours alone at the flat was hard to take. Barry was always out on photography appointments and Joseph went to bed at seven. The flat was more like a prison than a home. Wednesdays, like today, were worse. She looked ahead and was threatened by a life of unhappiness.

She looked out of the window and saw Rhiannon closing her front door. She knew she would look up as she passed and, seeing her, would wave. If only she would stop and spend a part of her half-day with her. She didn't feel able to ask. Once having been engaged to Barry, Rhiannon could hardly be expected to forget her role in ending it and become a close friend. She watched as the girl approached and was already smiling as Rhiannon looked up. On impulse she opened the window and called, 'Time for a cup of tea, Rhiannon? I'd be glad of your company.' To her relief, Rhiannon stopped and unlocked the shop door.

Caroline was in the kitchen filling the kettle

when Rhiannon's footsteps came lightly up the stairs.

'I was going for a walk, why don't you come?' she announced. 'After the tea of course!'

'Joseph would like that, if you're sure you want company,' Caroline hesitated.

'We could go to the beach if you like. It's not cold.' Then she changed her mind. 'I've got a better idea, let's go to the lake and have a cup of tea in The Rose Tree Cafe with Mam.'

Dora was pleased to see them, and as usual, went first to talk to the little boy. She found them a table in the corner and served them with a set afternoon tea. The cafe was busy, as the sun had shown itself and encouraged people out for a walk along the lakeside and to the beach where the wind always blew and brought colour to cheeks, and an appetite that had them looking for tea and cakes.

Walking back to Sophie Street, Caroline felt happier, more relaxed and when she went into the flat she began to prepare a meal with a lighter heart: one of the hated Wednesdays was almost over. She could cope well enough with evenings, there was plenty to do after a day at work, and the hours soon passed, even though she found them lonely and quiet. But the days when the wool shop closed at lunchtime, and meant five more hours to kill, were dismal.

Perhaps she ought to plan something similar on every half-day? Wednesdays were becoming more and more a dread. A little housework and some cooking then watching the clock and wondering how many hours before Barry would come in. Then excitement when he arrived which soon degenerated into dismay at his silence and lack of interest. Leaving her mother after picking up Joseph, and walking home to the emptiness of her own home on Wednesdays was more and more daunting. Using the half-day to give herself a small treat would stop the spiral of dread.

The meal was ready for six o'clock but there was no sign of Barry. She put the meal on top of a saucepan of water and put it to simmer on the cooker. The gravy would soon shrivel and dry up around the edges, but she admitted to herself that she didn't particularly care. Barry could have left a message if he'd known he'd be late.

★ ★ ★

Barry was in The Railwayman's. He was sitting at the bar and, as it was too soon for any of the others to arrive, he was talking to Jack.

'How's business?' Jack asked him.

'Bad. No parties, no special need for portraits, and there seems to be a lull in weddings at the moment,' Barry said dejectedly. 'It'll pick up again later, for sure. Something about tax back if you marry before the end of the tax year gave me a rash of weddings up to the beginning of April, now there doesn't seem to be anyone out there with plans to wed.'

'There's Victoria and me, and Joan and Viv. Both in August.'

'Very fat that'll keep me, won't it?'

'*Us*, Barry. You don't say 'me' anymore. You have Caroline, you should be saying *us*. I take great pleasure in thinking about Victoria and saying, 'us'.'

'Caroline's my wife, but it doesn't seem like we are 'us', Jack.'

'I thought you'd decided to make it work?'

'That was the plan. But I think she still loves my brother.'

'Of course she doesn't! See it in her eyes we could that it's you she wants. What went wrong?'

'Apart from getting drunk and passing out on the day we'd decided to call our wedding day, you mean?'

'That can't have done irreparable harm!' Jack laughed.

'She didn't come to bed the night we came back home to the flat. I woke up during the night and she wasn't there. I went down and she was washing the floor. Can you believe that? She stayed up and did some washing and then she unpacked the rest of her things and stacked them in the cupboards, and scrubbed the kitchen floor. Not very flattering, Jack, coming second in importance to a kitchen floor.'

Jack looked thoughtful. 'Coming from such a lively family as the Griffithses, Caroline's surprisingly shy. I think she depended on you to do all the running. If you showed even the slightest indifference she'd convince herself you were only marrying her for the child's sake. She has very little confidence. A bit like Victoria. She'd been my grandmother's maid, for heaven's sake. And my grandmother is Gladys Weston! How's that for a handicap?

'I had to make Victoria believe I really loved her and wanted to marry her, and did she take some convincing! Still does. Like thistledown, our plans are. One puff of disapproval from my family and she wants to run away and hide. I'd never give up on her, though. And I'll never stop reminding myself how much she needs my reassurance.'

159

'You think that's what it is with Caroline?'

'It won't do any harm to let her know you love her, will it?'

'You're getting sentimental, aren't you?' Barry was about to tease but something in Jack's expression stopped him. He added quietly, 'She might put me down.'

'So what? She won't make it a public announcement will she? No one else would know. But somehow I don't think she will.'

The bar was filling up and Barry sat in the corner, his thoughts in turmoil. He imagined scenes where Caroline welcomed his advances, running towards him with her arms wide and welcoming, her brown eyes filled with love, and then those scenes were replaced by others in which she stared at him coldly and turned away. Perhaps he had left it too late?

He left before Viv and Basil appeared. Driving the van home slowly, Jack's words kept repeating themselves in his head. He wanted to see Caroline, but was afraid of disappointment. As he drove down Trellis Street he paused at the junction where a right hand turn would take him down Brown Street to the corner where Temptations stood. Instead of taking the turn, he drove on, along Gethyn Street through the quieter area of the town and out onto the common a few miles beyond. There, he stopped the van and sat staring out into the semi-dark and tried to think out what to say to his wife who wasn't his wife at all. Imagining his words and her responses gave him moments of alternate distress and joy and gradually he forgot the sad and the bad possibilities and imagined only the good and optimistic. He still sat there as his thoughts became vague and he slept.

* * *

Caroline put Joseph to bed and at ten-thirty, took the shrivelled dinner off the saucepan and lifted the lid of the bin. As she stood there poised, with the plate held in a tea-towel in one hand and a knife in the other, she heard Barry's key in the lock. She tilted the plate and scraped the contents into the bin. As Barry entered the kitchen she gave him a sad look and dropped the lid.

'I hope you've eaten,' she said in her quiet way.

'No, but I'm not hungry.'

'You haven't been on a job,' she said, standing in front of the sink and looking down at the plate with its border of burnt-on food.

'I was talking to Jack, then I went for a drive.'

'Joseph was disappointed. Again.' The final word, although spoken softly, seemed like a slap.

'I'm sorry.'

'Are you, Barry? I'll tell Joseph shall I? Tell him you're sorry? D'you think that will make him feel better?'

Barry stared at her in confusion. Caroline was never like this, quietly angry and with such an expression of hurt in her dark, luminous eyes. This wasn't how he had imagined it at all. He was going to walk in and explain and she would melt into his arms.

'I want to tell you something,' he said. 'It's important.'

'I'm going to bed.' She dropped the sizzling plate into a bowl of water, hearing it crack, and left the room, squeezing past him without touching him.

Barry stood for a long time in the doorway of the kitchen, undecided about what to do. He knew he should do something, but what? Follow her to their bedroom and get in beside her? Or walk out and spend the night in an hotel? Either alternative seemed fraught with dangerous possibilities. Getting in beside her and being told to go

162

away would be an impossible situation from which to extricate himself; leaving the flat even more so. He was tired and desperately saddened by the expression on Caroline's face. She didn't want him, she never had. Tonight she had accepted the fact she never would. He sat down on a fireside chair and stared at the ashes until sleep brought escape.

He was out of the flat before Caroline woke in the morning. She came into the kitchen to make a pot of tea and, putting two cups and saucers on the tray and adding a small beaker for Joseph, she walked into the living room. A note was propped up against a vase of flowers.

'I will be out all day, but I'll collect you and Joseph from your mother's at six.
We have to sort this out.
Barry.'

Caroline went to a call box and phoned the wool shop to say she was ill and wouldn't be in. Then, catching a bus, she went to the end of town and walked over the fields to her parents' house. She walked in, talking to Joseph about the goats and how he would be able to see them later, and was startled to see Barry there talking to her father.

'Gone and spoilt the surprise, haven't you,' Hywel said.

'Surprise? What surprise?'

'I've asked your Mam and Dad to look after Joseph for us so we can go out,' Barry said, bending down, avoiding her eyes by concentrating on removing Joseph's coat and hat.

'I can't go out this evening, Barry,' Caroline said. 'I've just phoned to say I wouldn't be in work today. They'd think it odd if I was ill only until half-past-five.'

'What's the matter, love?' Janet asked.

'Just tired and a bit headachy, nothing much, Mam.' Aware of Barry standing there watching her and not showing concern, she added, 'Don't worry, Barry, I'll be all right.'

'Oh, good, I was, er, just going to ask.'

Barry left straightaway and Caroline went back to the flat a few hours later, leaving her parents very troubled.

She walked through the shop to get to the flat, thankful it was closed for lunch, and on the kitchen table was a huge bunch of flowers. The note was simple, it said, 'From Barry'.

Not 'With love'. No message at all, really. Then it hit her like a cold shower. Barry was going to tell her it was over, that the marriage hadn't a hope and never would

164

have. He had tried and failed. If it had been a reconciliatory move he would have written more than, 'From Barry'. He had something important to say and it was surely going to be, 'Goodbye'.

In a frenzy, she gathered a few clothes for herself and for Joseph and before Rhiannon returned to open for the afternoon she was gone, in a taxi, back to her mother's house, and this time she intended to stay.

★ ★ ★

Rhiannon saw Barry come in and rush out again but didn't think about it as he was often late for appointments, having spent too long at a previous one. It was when he came back several times and left looking more and more distraught that she ventured to ask if there was anything wrong.

'It's Caroline, you haven't seen her have you?'

'Not today. She leaves before I get here at nine. Why? Isn't she at work?'

'No. She wasn't well this morning and was taking the day off, but I tried the shop anyway. Where can she be?'

'Visiting a friend? Have you tried Eleri? They meet when they have a spare hour.'

'I've tried everywhere and everyone, except

her parents. Janet is in Cardiff for the day so she won't be there.' He went up the stairs and Rhiannon followed him into the flat and made them both a cup of tea.

Barry was distraught. He was remembering the time when Caroline had walked into the sea. Leaving the tea untouched he hurried out, intending to try some of the more lonely beaches in the area with dread in his heart. He was afraid for the child too, and pictured the sadness on Caroline's face the previous evening. It couldn't happen again could it? If it did it would definitely be down to him.

As these thoughts filled his mind, he ran unseeing through the shop door and bumped into Gertie Thomas and it was she who told them about the taxi.

'Suitcases she had, mind. Three of them. And some carrier bags with some of Joseph's toys sticking out of the top. Going on holiday is she? There's lucky for some.'

'Yes,' Rhiannon said. 'She's having a little holiday and Barry's joining her later.'

'Oh, I see. I did wonder, like — '

Barry went to the cottage a little later on Rhiannon's advice, and found Caroline there, with Frank and Ernie busily sorting out the smallest bedroom to accommodate her and the little boy. When he walked in, Frank said 'watcha,' and sidled out, giving Ernie the nod to do the same.

'What are you doing here, Caroline?' Barry asked, picking up Joseph and cuddling him.

'This is where I'm staying, Barry. I can't pretend any longer.'

He presumed that she meant pretend to love him and he flinched. 'I see. Will you come back while we discuss it? I don't mean now, this moment. Stay with your Mam for a few days, Gertie Thomas thinks you're having a holiday anyway, then come back and we'll try to sort everything out for the best.'

'We can talk here. I never want to set foot inside that flat again.'

'I see,' he said again.

'I doubt it,' she said exuding sadness in a sigh. 'Now I'd like you to go. I want to settle Joseph down before he goes to bed.'

'I'll stay and put him to bed if you like?'

'Best we stay with the usual routine,' she replied. 'It's always me who reads his story and puts him to bed.'

'You mean I'm never there.'

Caroline didn't reply and as he walked out of the house she didn't once turn to look at him. She didn't want him to see the tears welling up in her eyes.

★ ★ ★

167

Rhiannon saw Barry come back just as she was locking the shop door.

'Have you found her?' she asked. He nodded his head and she could see from the expression on his face that something was far from right. 'Barry? Can I do anything?'

'No, it's all right. She's visiting her mother for a few days.'

A knock, and a face at the window distracted her from more questions and she opened the door to see Gwyn Bevan standing there.

'Our Dad says, have you got a shilling for two sixpences in case the gas goes when he's cooking our porridge in the morning?'

She had the shop money sealed up in the bank bag, so she opened her purse and handed him the coins he needed. 'How's the puppy?' she asked.

'Come and see. You can feed him, if you like.'

She walked through the doorway where old Maggie Wilpin had spent so many lonely hours waiting for Charlie to come out of prison, and into the living room. She was surprised by how clean and neat it was. There was very little furniture, just a couple of old armchairs and, on the floor, a rather worn mat, but a card table near the window was set for two, with a piece of cake and an apple on two side plates, and plates of chips and a small portion of fatty bacon ready to eat.

'Sorry, I didn't mean to interrupt your tea,' she said as Charlie came into the room. 'Gwyn invited me in to see the puppy.'

'Some puppy,' Charlie laughed. 'Cop hold of something solid, and I'll open the door and let her loose.'

She felt a draught of cold air as he opened the back door and whistled. Polly burst in like a tornado, her body twisting and turning as she wriggled with delight. She had grown since Gwyn had last brought her to see them. The excited creature greeted them all in a contortion of back-flops and somersaults. Then, suddenly smelling the food, she made a dive at the fragile table and was caught by Rhiannon as she was about to reach the nearest plate.

'She's had Dad's supper twice,' Gwyn said with a hint of pride. 'She's that quick you'd never believe.'

Charlie grinned wryly at Rhiannon and whispered, 'Biggest mistake of my life having that great lolloping thing, but it's good for the boy.'

Apologising for the interruption, Rhiannon left them to enjoy their chips and walked across the road to number seven. She glanced up at the flat above Temptations and saw that the light was on. Barry was on his own, and Caroline was back with her mother, or so it seemed.

★ ★ ★

When Janet returned from Cardiff she was disappointed to learn that her daughter was back home.

'I didn't think you'd give up so easily, Caroline, love,' she said sadly. 'After the unusual start to your marriage there're bound to be a few bumpy moments.'

'He was going to tell me it's over, Mam. I just got in first, that's all.'

'What made you think the flowers were to tell you he wanted to end it?' Janet asked when Caroline had explained.

'Isn't it obvious?'

'Not to me, love. Wasn't he here, arranging to take you out?'

'He was going to say goodbye.' Refusing to be convinced she had made a mistake, Caroline told them she would settle into her mother's house and try to pretend the wedding had never taken place. She was still Miss Griffiths whose fiancé had been killed before they could marry, she told her parents.

'You can't be Miss Griffiths,' Hywel teased. 'Your Joseph can't have a different name from his mam, now can he?'

For the first time since she was a child, Caroline burst into tears.

★ ★ ★

When Charlie Bevan told Rhiannon he was looking for a bicycle for his son, Rhiannon had thought at once of Basil. Even though he had a regular job, Basil still had his eyes open for who had what for sale and who would be glad of a bargain. She had done nothing about it because of her father's attitude to her friendship with Charlie, but she would now. If her father was annoyed, well, she'd deal with that problem when she met it. She would go and ask Basil as soon as she had a moment. Not to where Basil and Eleri lived on Trellis Street. She would go to the Griffithses house on the edge of town.

She admitted to herself that asking Basil by finding him at the Griffithses instead of at home was pure nosiness. She wanted to know what was happening between Barry and Caroline. She felt a bit guilty at her inquisitiveness, but she was only human and if Barry had messed things up between himself and Caroline, she was curious to know how.

* * *

Frank was angry with Ernie, this time because he'd convinced himself it was Ernie's fault he had got mixed up with Percy Flemming. If his stupid cousin hadn't started meeting Helen on the sly and used the van for his courting, it wouldn't have happened, he reasoned. His anxiety was growing hour by hour as he waited for Percy's appearance. To ease his stress and justify his restless mood, he picked a fight with his cousin a week after Caroline had returned home.

* * *

Voices were raised in anger when Rhiannon approached the house where, as usual, the windows and door were wide open. She recognised the voices; Frank and Ernie. 'Who else?' she muttered. Frank stormed out before she could call out a greeting and forced her to stagger against the stone pillar that had once supported a gate.

'Sorry, Rhiannon, I wasn't looking where I was going,' he said, catching her by the shoulders and steadying her. 'That Ernie is

172

winding me up something wicked.'

'You can put me down now,' she laughed, as his hands were still on her shoulders.

'Sorry, I — ' He glanced through the doorway and asked, 'Fancy coming for a walk do you? If I don't get some of this anger out of my system I might do something stupid like kill our Ernie.'

'Not planning to beat *me* up, are you?' she asked in mock alarm.

'No, nothing like a good walk and good company to let the steam out.'

It was such a surprise being invited to walk with Frank, who was someone who normally seemed unaware of her existence, that she agreed. 'So long as I'm back in time to see Basil and Eleri,' she said, explaining about the bike.

Frank's long legs made her hurry to keep up until she stopped and told him to slow down. 'I'd have to be in a real bad temper to keep up with you,' she laughed.

'Sorry.' He grinned and offered his hand, which she took as they walked on more slowly and Rhiannon waited for him to tell her what had made him so angry.

'Ernie and I were going out tonight. And we'd planned a fishing trip on Sunday morning. He's just told me I won't be coming. Left me high and dry he has and all because that Helen Gunner wants him to take her somewhere.'

'Seems reasonable to me, that he wants to go out with a girl,' she said. 'But unreasonable to break a previous arrangement to do it.'

'Ernie and I have always been pals,' he told her. 'I suppose you'll think me childish if I tell you I'm angry with him for finding himself a girl who he thinks more about than me?'

'I can understand the anger, but it has to be short term, or you'll lose his friendship altogether,' she said as she began to understand his distress. 'Meeting someone and realising they're going to be special is like that. You want to forget everything else in your life, old friends included, just to spend time with your new-found love.'

'It was like that with you and Barry, wasn't it? Before he married our Caroline.'

'It was, but I'm over that now. I'm sorry it isn't going too well for them.'

'You've heard?'

'I've heard.'

'What went wrong, d'you think?'

'Living in the flat where she had intended to live with Barry's brother can't have helped.'

'Why?'

'Oh Frank! Can't you see that living where she had dreamed of making a home with Joseph would be painful?'

Frank didn't see at all but he nodded and grinned at her. 'Mam always says you have to spell everything out for me because I'm thick,' he said sheepishly.

'I think she's right!'

'You think I'm thick?'

'No,' she sighed, 'just a man!'

Frank didn't understand that either but thought it best to say nothing. 'Barry believes that Caroline sees him as big and clumsy, comparing him to Joseph unfavourably all the time,' he said. 'I heard him once, telling our Dad. That sounds daft to me but that's what he said. Yes, it seems as though our Caroline's home for good. Best if our Ernie does marry and move out. More room for the rest of us!'

'They're living in that flat with a ghost,' Rhiannon said sadly, 'both feeling guilty about cheating on Joseph, who they both loved.'

'Why don't they tell each other?' Frank said, frowning. 'Mam and dad talk to each other all the time. It's hopeless if they can't talk to each other.'

Rhiannon agreed. 'Hopeless and sad. What

about you, Frank? Aren't you hoping to marry one day?'

'Who'd have a thicko like me?' he said glumly. Then he smiled, turning her to face him. 'You wouldn't fancy going on a date would you, Rhiannon?'

'I'm off men at the moment,' she said with a laugh. 'But I'll keep you in mind!'

'You and that Jimmy Herbert, is it?'

'No, not any more.'

'No one you fancy then?'

'No one.' She spoke firmly but thoughts of Charlie made her feel guilty of an untruth.

As they returned to the cottage to discuss the bicycle, still hand in hand, she was still thinking not of Barry, who was weak, or Jimmy who was amiable and kind, but of Charlie Bevan and his powerful determination to make a success of life and give his son a chance. There was something very attractive about a determined man.

7

While Frank and Rhiannon had been out, the living room of the Griffithses cottage had filled up. Helen was there with Ernie, who was nursing a reddening bruise on the point of his chin. Rhiannon's brother, Viv, and Joan Weston had called in. Jack was there with Victoria who was laughing at something Hywel was telling her and blushing prettily. Basil and Eleri were just preparing to leave.

Rhiannon looked at the sea of smiling faces and felt a pang of loneliness. All couples except herself, and Frank; and although she had enjoyed the walk through the fields with him, she knew there would be nothing more than perhaps extra friendliness between them.

'Rhiannon!' Caroline waved a greeting from the doorway of the kitchen and she mentally amended her list. Caroline was on her own too. Barry had failed them both.

'I've called to see Basil,' she called across, before making her way through the throng to where Basil was packing his work-bag with extra food supplied by his mother.

'I didn't do it! It wasn't me!' Basil joked

and she smiled as she approached him and asked if he knew of a bicycle for sale, suitable for Gwyn Bevan.

'I'll keep an eye,' he promised as he gathered together his family plus the paraphernalia of pushchair, spare clothes and the rest. 'I think I know where there's one that will do.'

'I thought you would. Thanks.' She smiled, then she stooped to talk to seven-month-old Ronnie and tell him he was wonderful.

'Don't go, Rhiannon,' Caroline called as she began to follow Basil and Eleri out. 'Stay and have a chat.'

A glass of home-made cordial was pushed into her hand and a place found between the bodies sitting and lolling and arguing and teasing. Caroline sat beside her and they talked of general things, but, as the evening wore on and the talk became desultory, Caroline asked whether Rhiannon had seen Barry.

'He comes and goes to the flat and I think he's gradually bringing more of his photography equipment back in,' she was told. 'At least, more stuff seems to be coming in than goes out.'

This was confirmation to Caroline that Barry was glad to be rid of her but she smiled and said nothing.

Rhiannon was aware of Frank watching her and every time she looked up and caught his eye he grinned and looked away. She turned to Caroline and whispered, 'I think your Frank has his eye on me.'

'Not surprising, you're a lovely girl,' Caroline said without any falseness. 'I love Frank dearly, but I don't think he'd make an interesting boyfriend, do you?' she added with a smile.

They chuckled and Frank continued to smile. When Rhiannon finally stood to leave he stood also.

'Better walk you home, Rhiannon, it's dark out there.'

'It's all right, Viv and Joan will come some of the way with me.'

'They've gone,' Caroline said. 'Best you do go with Frank. It is late, Rhiannon.'

They were shrugging themselves into their coats and walking away from the house when they saw Rhiannon's father approaching. He was arm in arm with Nia; the owner of Temptations and her father's mistress.

'Where are you off to, Rhiannon, love?' Lewis asked, looking suspiciously at Frank, who stood aside, hands in pockets, shoulders drooped, cap slanted over one eye, self-consciously waiting for them to pass him.

'I'm off home. Frank was going to walk me to the road.'

'No need!' Lewis glared at Frank and although the night was dark, the glare didn't need to be seen for them all to know it was there.

'I — we — we didn't want her walking through the fields on her own, Mr Lewis,' Frank said, still hanging his head like an accused man. 'Mam said I should see her safe, like.'

'I'll do that.' Lewis was still sharp as he told Nia to go on in and he would be about fifteen minutes. Hardly allowing his daughter time to thank Frank for his offer, Lewis hurried her away. 'Stay away from Frank Griffiths. He's trouble that one. And his brother Ernie. Never been a time when they weren't.'

She glanced back, certain Frank would have heard. 'Dad, he was only being kind, making sure I was safely home.'

'Don't come here again unless you have Viv or Jimmy with you. Right?'

'I'm not seeing Jimmy any more.'

'More fool you. Good lad he is, better for you than wandering around at night with the likes of Frank Griffiths.'

Irritation seethed inside her. Banned from talking to Frank and forbidden to talk to

Charlie, although, she thought defiantly, she couldn't have promised to obey *that* demand.

Just ahead of them, lights from the streets gave a glow. 'There's the road, you can go back to Nia now,' she said, choking on anger and humiliation. 'And Dad, I like the Griffithses. Caroline is a friend, and Basil is a good husband to Eleri. Don't tell me not to see them.'

'Of course I won't, love,' he said, his tone softening as he realised from her voice that she was upset. 'I just don't want you mixed up with Frank or Ernie. In and out of court they are and no sign of them changing. Be careful, eh?'

She walked down the road, a little girl who had been scolded by a much-loved father. Why was life such a mess? First Barry, then Jimmy and neither of them the man she wanted to spend her life with, even if she had been close to becoming Mrs Barry Martin. Now that *would* have been a mistake. His indifference to her, all the times he had promised to meet her and had forgotten, were being repeated with Caroline. He was not a caring man and certainly incapable of adoring anyone. To be adored was her dream. She shuddered at how close she had come to disaster.

Now, without having a thought of taking

the friendship with Frank any further, she was being warned off him. Naturally she resented that parental judgement and felt a rebellious determination to be extra nice to Frank in future. How could he be dangerous? What harm could he bring her? Frank's father had been similar to his sons as a young man and everyone could see how happy Hywel and Janet were. Perhaps someone like Frank, so unconventional, so like Hywel, who had made Janet's life a good one, would be a good choice for her?

As she turned the corner where Temptations stood silent and dark, Frank was waiting in the doorway.

'Sorry if I got you a row,' he said, walking with her towards her door. 'I raced through old Booker's farmyard to get here before you and your father. Set the dogs off proper I did.'

'I'm sorry, Frank. Dad was rude.'

'Only looking after you. I don't blame him. If I had a daughter as lovely as you, I wouldn't want her mixed up with someone like me,' he grinned, his teeth shining, strong and regular in the glow of the lamp. 'So long, then. See you soon.'

'Bye, Frank. And thanks.'

As she put her key into the lock a voice called 'Goodnight, Rhiannon.'

'Charlie? I've asked Basil about a bike for your Gwyn. He might have one by the weekend.'

'Kind of you to bother, specially after the trouble my Gwyn's been to you in the past.' He strolled across the road to join her.

'Taking sweets from the shop you mean?'

'That, and the earring.'

'Earring?' she frowned.

'Your father had told him off for something and when he found an earring on the pavement, and saw your father's car door open, he threw it in the back seat and hoped your mam would give him a bout of what-the-hell and demand an explanation.'

Rhiannon was smiling as she went inside. Perhaps one of the times Dora had thrown Lewis out, he really had been innocent! The smile exploded into laughter.

★ ★ ★

A letter arrived for Janet from someone who had seen the enquiry in the village of Cwrt y Celyn. It was brief but said his mother had recently died and among her possessions were letters from a Marion Jolly, one being a thankyou for a wedding present sent by his mother and father. 'It seemed they must have been good friends, as the correspondence covered several years,' the letter went on. 'And, as the letters bear three different addresses, you might like to see them.'

Janet showed the letter to Hywel before replying, then arranged to visit the man on the following Sunday, the last in May. She and Caroline would go, leaving Joseph, who was now almost two years old, with Eleri and Basil.

Setting off in the old van on Sunday afternoon, Hywel called after them, 'Behave, the pair of you, you look like kids off on a Sunday School outing instead of two respectably married women!' Turning to Frank he said, 'Go with them, I don't like them going off meeting strangers. Better if they've got you keeping an eye on them.'

Loping across the fields, skirting the farm of Mr Booker, Frank flagged them down on the corner and climbed in beside them. After exaggerated complaints about his mother's road-worthiness, he changed places to drive.

'I'm not sure what a chauvinist pig is, Frank,' Janet complained, 'but I think you're one!'

The man, a Mr Walfree, invited them into the terraced cottage that had been his mother's home. Janet saw at once that although the furniture was there, the place was gradually being emptied. He offered them tea and gave them the contents of a cardboard box to examine while he made it. The box contained an assortment of packets, and the letters they wanted were in an old fashioned chocolate box priced at sixpence. There were almost twenty of them.

'I have no idea why my mother kept them,' the man explained. 'There were no others. The rest of the box is filled with postcards sent from holidays and a few birthday cards she had obviously liked.'

The letters gave a surprisingly full picture of her sister Marion's life. They described how she had found work as a kitchen hand and graduated until she was appointed cook in a canteen, then in a cafe. There were three letters announcing the arrival of a child, sons called Fred and Harold and a daughter called Elenor.

'The boys would be forty and forty-two now,' Janet whispered, her mind filled with images of these children, her nephews and niece, whom she had never known. 'And the girl, Elenor, would be — ' she counted on her fingers, 'twenty-four. She had her late, didn't she?' She frowned, and counted again. 'That's never right. She'd have been in her fifties!'

Another letter referred to Elenor as 'our

precious gift', and delving further into the box, another reference disclosed that Elenor had been adopted.

'Just like us and our Ernie,' Janet gasped.

Once the man had been convinced that the letters were indeed from Janet's sister, he gave them to her. 'I hope they help you find her,' he smiled. 'There were so many and obviously treasured, that I couldn't dispose of them without trying to restore them to the right family.'

While they were talking to Mr Walfree, Frank was wandering around the lanes promising to return in an hour. When they went out almost two hours later he was sitting in the van, a flat cap tilted over his eyes, fast asleep.

'You have three cousins, Frank,' his mother announced as they climbed back into the cab.

'If you find them, make sure you check whether they've got money before introducing yourself,' was his sober reply.

When they reached home, Hywel's response was just as cool.

'What d'you want to look for more family for, Janet? Damn it all, haven't we got enough trouble with the one we've got?'

* * *

186

Ernie knew Frank was up to something and surmised that he wasn't being told because of Frank's unresolved resentment towards Helen Gunner. He'd discussed his concern with Mam and Dad and they had promised to talk to Frank, tell him he was being unreasonable, and explain that Ernie having a steady girl wouldn't change anything. Although in his heart Ernie knew it already had. He didn't want to spend time with Frank when he could be with Helen, and because of that, he was excluded from confidences about Frank's activities in a way he never had been before.

All efforts failed to produce any change in Frank's attitude towards him, and the separation widened and disappointment changed to anger. So, when he was offered some produce to sell, he accepted the deal without attempting to include Frank. He needed money if he and Helen were to consider marriage. Why should he share the profits with a surly brother who was in fact only a cousin? A fact regularly pointed out by Frank during these past weeks.

The promise was for a van load of bars of soap and boxes of washing powder. The price was such that he could sell it around the poorer areas of town for less than half the shop prices. He would make a quick few pounds and perhaps earn enough to buy Helen an engagement ring. With a light heart he set off to meet his contact.

★ ★ ★

Viv and Jack enjoyed fishing. They usually went to the river Teifi in West Wales and spent the day in search of supper. It was rarely that they caught enough to share with friends, but on a day in early June, they stayed near home. They were sitting on the grassy wasteland alongside the old dock no longer used, opposite where Victoria's father had drowned several months before. Their keep-net was full and they were drooling over the prospect of a good supper.

It was early in the morning, still not seven o'clock, and they were both having to face going back home to get changed ready for work; Jack to his class of school children and Viv to Jack's grandfather's wallpaper and paint shop. The sun was showing itself mistily and a haze rose from the moist earth as it warmed. As they sat there watching the still water and their presently unmoving floats, the mist began to lift to reveal the freshness of the day. The water showed a surface covered by an oily skin, sluggish movement occasionally allowing the light to catch a ripple and reveal brief glimpses of rainbow colours.

The sounds from the busy docks some distance away were muted, voices calling softly, as if the men about their early morning tasks were whispering, and the touch of metal against metal as ships were loaded or unloaded had been softened by cotton wool in deference to the splendour of the dawning new day.

'I could go to sleep, Jack,' Viv said lazily.

'So could I.' Jack looked at his watch and groaned. 'Only half an hour more and we'll have to leave.'

They lay back on the grass, screened by blackberry and blackthorn bushes and stunted trees which were still struggling to clothe themselves in fresh new leaves, and closed their eyes. The sun, strengthened by the dissipating mist, shone on their faces and they relaxed into sleep.

★ ★ ★

Gwyn finished delivering his morning papers and went to where his father had left his breakfast ready for him. It was eight-thirty when he realised that Polly wasn't with him waiting for her share of the cereal and cold toast. In a panic he ran out of the house and round to the garage where his father worked.

'Dad! I can't find Polly! She was with me when I delivered the last paper, but when I got home she wasn't there.'

Arranging to work late to make up the time, Charlie left the car he was working on and went to join the search for the puppy.

Rhiannon was coerced into helping, and Gertie Jones came out in slippers and a dressing gown to call and whistle, but when it was time to open the shop and for Gwyn to be at school they still hadn't found her. Rhiannon promised to look out and keep her safe if she found her and with that Gwyn had to be content.

★ ★ ★

At the dockside, Viv and Jack dreamed on until the puppy saw them lying down and in what she presumed was a position in which to play games. She leapt on Viv's stomach and bounced off onto Jack. In a tangle of lines and fishing bags and wriggling puppy they awoke and let go of their rods, wondering for a second or two where they were, and why.

The pup gambolled around them, getting herself more and more tightly entangled in

190

the lines as the reels spun lazily out.

Viv stood up, tried to walk, tripped over the line and fell backwards. He struggled to sit up, then sat trying to free his feet from the line while Jack hastily reached over to take in the keep-net in which the fish still survived. In despair, they wrapped the sabotaged lines around the rods in the hope that they might be able to sort out the bird's-nest later.

'Young Gwyn's puppy isn't it?' Viv said irritably. 'What's she doing here?' He looked around, hoping to see either Gwyn or his father on whom he could vent his anger, but the puppy appeared to be on her own.

'God 'elp! Look at the time!' Jack gasped. 'Lucky she woke us, we might have been there till dinner-time!' He bent over the keep-net to decide which of their catches they would keep and which would be thrown back. He decided to take two good-sized ones each, and it was as he was bending forward to release the others that the puppy sensed her favourite game. She jumped on Jack's back and they both went into the water with a loud splash.

The puppy reached the edge first and Viv lay full length and hauled her out then he looked at Jack, treading water a few yards out, outrage on his face as he spluttered and swore. The sudden transformation of the once peaceful scene was so ludicrous he felt a bubble of laughter rising.

'Don't stand there you fool. Help me out!' Jack shouted and this made Viv laugh louder. The more angry Jack became, the more his laughter increased until he was bent double, giving in to it completely.

He couldn't talk for laughing, and his arms were too weak to help. He just watched as Jack trod water, coughing and spluttering, and finally made his way towards the edge until his feet touched, then crawled out up the stone-built slope, water pouring out of his clothes in a torrent. Viv couldn't see properly for the tears that filled his eyes. His loud laughter continued unabated, even when Jack stood, dripping wet, offended and angry, but without hope of sympathy, before him.

'D'you think they'll believe me when I tell them you dived in after the fish?' Viv asked eventually, as the bedraggled pair stood with the pup, restrained on a length of line, cheerfully waiting for the next stage of her adventure. 'Damn me, what I wouldn't have given for a camera!'

'What fish?' Jack asked sulkily. 'They all went back into the dock!' Which remark brought a renewal of laughter from Viv and more scowls from Jack.

Gladys and Arfon Weston considered themselves one of the important families of Pendragon Island. The fact that not everyone agreed did not make any difference. Gladys felt her position as example-to-the-rest very strongly. Which was why she had to make sure the weddings of her grandson, Jack and of her grandaughter, Joan showed others how it should be done.

As usual, when something was likely to cause great local interest, and particularly now when so many waited to see the Weston family fall on their faces, Gladys gave a 'royal command' for all the family to attend a meeting. The first one she asked was always Jack, these days. He was the least likely to attend and if she arranged a time he was sure of being free, the rest of the family had to fit around it. On an early June morning, with birdsong rousing her gently from sleep, she woke, prepared herself for the day and realised, as she waited impatiently for her servant, Mair to arrive, that it was not yet seven o'clock.

Making herself a cup of tea and a piece of toast on which she spread the last of the butter ration, she decided to go out and try to catch Jack before he went to school. Arfon was already out. Going up early to visit the shop which was now run by Viv Lewis and his granddaughter, Joan, was a regular part of his day.

She knew he only glanced through the books and examined the stock, looking for faults and rarely finding any. He missed the involvement and was full of regret at the way his sons-in-law had let him down and almost cost him the business.

Gladys had to admit that, although she had hated the idea of Viv Lewis taking over, he, with her dear Joan's help, of course, had saved the business from liquidation. She had secretly hoped that one day the family would run it once more and Viv would be sent on his way. Now, with her lovely granddaughter determined to marry the man, she had to accept that he was there for good.

She set off to walk to Trellis Street in the quiet of the morning, the sounds clear on the summer air, with few background noises to mask them. Someone dragging boxes out of a shop to start a display. An errand boy whistling the Eddie Calvert hit, *Oh Mein Papa*. A woman scrubbing her front step. A rattling sound as ashes were dropped into a bin followed by the echoing clang as the lid was slammed back in place. Gladys felt an excitement at being up and about as the town was waking and identifying the various sounds, and her smile widened.

Then the smile was wiped off like chalk from a blackboard as, around the corner strolled two men, dressed in peculiar fashion, one holding a string against which a lively young dog pulled. They were obviously drunks returning from a night of debauchery. They were laughing and staggering slightly and she looked around for some escape from them as they approached. At that moment, Henry Thomas, the postman, stepped out of a short cut, a gap where a house had once stood, and he greeted the two disreputables cheerily. Perhaps she would walk with him until she passed them.

'Hi, Grandmother,' one of the 'drunks' called and she stared with horror as she recognised Jack and Viv.

She listened to the story as she and Jack went to number forty-four and she smiled grimly at her daughter, Sian. 'At least after this embarrassment he won't refuse to attend the family conference!'

'What is the conference about, Mother?' Sian asked. 'I don't have much time to spare during the day. I'm a working woman these days and Rose Tree keeps Dora and me very busy you know.'

'It's a serious family matter, Sian, dear.

The weddings. Your Jack's mainly. Jack is being extremely difficult.'

'As ever,' Sian said with a sigh.

★ ★ ★

The large house in which Arfon and Gladys lived was not in a fashionable area of Pendragon Island. It was the house in which they had begun their married life and neither saw reason to change. Now, with family fortunes greatly reduced, they had only one person to help run it. Mair Gregory had once been sacked, when Victoria had returned, but now Victoria was engaged to marry Jack, Mair had been called back. Not as a maid to deal with Gladys's whims and fancies this time, but to do as much of the cleaning as Gladys could persuade her to do for the money she paid her.

For the family conference, Mair was ordered to work during the evening to serve the food and add to Gladys's self-illusory belief that the Weston family was still superior to most.

When the whole family was gathered Gladys took out a notepad and began to run her fingers down a list.

'Jack first, as he and Victoria are the slowest at getting things organised. Now,

196

have you chosen your dress, dear?' she asked the shy girl whom she had so recently ordered about, for three pounds ten shillings a week.

'No, I haven't seen anything suitable,' Victoria replied, looking at Jack for support.

'Come into Gwennie Woodlas's shop and I'll choose something,' Megan said in a bored voice.

'Don't you mean help Victoria choose?' Jack said sharply.

'Of course she does,' Joan retorted. 'Stop nit-picking, Jack or we'll be here all night.'

There was an obstruction at every suggestion to every item on Gladys's list. No, they hadn't thought about flowers, they weren't sure whether they wanted a choir, and no they would prefer not to have a peal of bells. In despair, Gladys snapped the notepad shut and turned with a forced smile to her granddaughter.

'Joan, dear, shall we start with you? Now, you've chosen your dress haven't you? And we are going into town on Saturday to select headdresses and a veil.'

'Here's what we've managed so far, Grandmother.' Joan handed her a piece of paper. 'These are the hymns Viv and I would like and we've already discussed them with the organist. The choir is singing *Ave Maria* while we sign the register, and colours have been discussed and the flowers are ordered.' She smiled sweetly at Gladys and glanced, with a hint of triumph, at Victoria.

Jack stood up and offered Victoria his hand. 'Well, that's quite a lot achieved then, isn't it Grandmother? Now, if you'll excuse us, Victoria and I have some plans of our own to prepare. You coming, Viv?'

'Plans?' Gladys looked alarmed at the prospect of things being taken out of her hands.

'Colour schemes and all that, for the house we'll live in.' He looked lovingly at Victoria as he added, 'Victoria is dealing with it, so our future home is in very good hands.'

'Joan is the one to help with colour schemes, dear.' Gladys said.

'Not this time. Victoria is having the first and the last word. I'm just the slave who does the work, aren't I love?'

When Jack and Victoria had gone, Gladys tapped her notepad again. 'Now, Joan dear, I've consulted several caterers and — '

'No, Grandmother,' Joan said. 'You and Mummy have already been told. Viv and I haven't changed our minds. We want a buffet. And,' she added with a warning gleam in her eyes, 'Viv and I have decided that his mother and my aunt will prepare it.'

'But they can't, dear. Seriously, how can the mother-of-the-bride be responsible for something so vital when she's there as a most important guest?'

'Don't worry, Mother,' Sian said. 'Dora and I have it all worked out. Most of the cooking will be done on the day before. After all,' she added with a hint of rancour, 'you've taken over all the wedding arrangements, so I'll have plenty of time.'

It was a quiet Gladys who put aside her lists and poured tea a while later. Quiet, but simmering with frustration. She blamed Victoria for Jack's stubbornness, although, she admitted, he had never been easy to persuade. But this time it was Victoria who, as the daughter of a drunk and a poverty-stricken washer-woman, was dragging her grandson down to an unacceptable level. She would have to have strong words with Victoria's mother.

Megan and Joan discussed Victoria's certain lack of taste.

'Can you imagine what she'll choose?' Joan said.

'Can you imagine what she'll look like if she tries to carry off one of Gwennie's model dresses?' Megan added.

'You will let me know what happens?' Joan smiled.

'Girls,' Sally said. 'I don't want to hear another unkind word. You should be helping Victoria, not standing by, waiting for her to ruin her special day.'

Neither girls showed regret at their unkind remarks.

'Sorry, but you must admit, it's rather odd, her marrying our cousin, Mummy. We still think of her as Grandmother's maid sometimes, forgetting she's marrying Jack.'

'Then don't forget!' Sian snapped. 'We must all help her through a day which is sure to be an ordeal. But especially you two!'

★ ★ ★

For the Griffithses, the goat milk idea was not a success. Janet had not remembered the basic rules and, having neglected to 'strip out' the goats to ensure the last milk had been taken, the goats dried up in a very short time. Until they were mated and produced a kid, they would simply be unproductive eating machines.

'Not one of your father's best ideas,' Janet told the boys.

Ermintrude still treated Frank like her best friend and he spent some time with the affectionate creature, talking to it and telling it how hurt he was by Ernie's deliberate rejection of him the moment a pretty girl winked her eye.

He was sitting in the pen, out of sight of the house one morning, when he heard Ernie come in. The van trundled along the rough path and stopped outside one of the outbuildings that Hywel intended to repair one day, but on which the corrugated iron roof still lurched drunkenly on weakened walls.

He watched as Ernie unloaded boxes and stacked them in the shed. When the unloading was done and the van driven away, he went to see what was there. Soap and soap powder. So much for Ernie's avowal that he wasn't dealing without him. For the first time in days he felt easier about his involvement with Percy Flemming. He'd make a lot of money and was glad Ernie wouldn't share it.

The first hint of trouble was in The Railwayman's later that evening. Someone at the bar was complaining that a warehouse had been broken into. When he began to describe what had been stolen, Frank left his pint and hurried home. There was no time to find Ernie. He'd be out of sight somewhere kissing and canoodling with that Helen Gunner.

Working at a speed he rarely found, he

took the boxes and dropped them all over the edge of the quarry beyond Pigog Wood. Then he swept up and burned the litter, and went to bed.

When the policemen came and insisted on searching the place, he woke up and stood beside Janet, Hywel, Caroline and Ernie, his hair across his face hiding the wink he gave them, and waited until the police had given up and gone away.

Then he poked Ernie in the chest with a bony finger.

'You owe me one, mate!'

8

Helen Gunner was becoming a regular visitor at the Griffithses, settling in and becoming an approved member of the family circle. Gradually, Frank accepted that she was going to remain so. Helen and Ernie were casual towards each other when they were with the family, there was none of the embarrassment Barry had caused by kissing Caroline, and making love to her with his eyes, in the time leading up to when they had decided to make their marriage real. No need to cough before entering a room where they were sitting. And for that Frank was grateful. He grudgingly admitted to his mother that, 'She isn't half bad.'

On the Sunday following the visit from the police, Helen invited Frank along when she and Ernie were going to tea with her parents.

'Mam and Dad would like to meet you,' she said, smiling as she lied. She had lost count of the hours spent persuading them to lower their defences and talk to a Griffiths. 'I've told them about you, but it isn't the same as meeting you themselves.'

He got out of it by insisting the goats and chickens needed cleaning out and set to with a vengeance when Hywel agreed with him.

'I think you're afraid you and Ernie will lose touch with each other because of me,' she said, following him to where Ermintrude was bleating her delight at seeing Frank.

'He can do what he likes. It doesn't worry me. I've got my own life. Just tell him to make sure he doesn't bring stolen stuff to the house again, that's all.'

'That was stupid, he knows that. But you and I know he is a bit thick,' she teased, 'and I doubt if I can change that. I'll have to think for him, like you've done over the years. Thank you for getting rid of it before the police came searching.'

'Needs a keeper he does.'

'And what about you, Frank? You're planning something, aren't you?'

'What d'you mean? I share my deals with Ernie and we both check to make sure it's safe. I'm not stupid enough to bring dodgy stuff home.'

'Not planning something to get your own back on him?' She tilted her head and looked at him thoughtfully.

'That's what Ernie says is it?'

'That's what he thinks. Be careful, Frank. Because when I've persuaded Ernie to propose, he'll want you to be his best man. You can't do that if you're in prison, can you?'

'You don't have to worry.'

'But I do, Frank. About all of you. I know you do these little 'deals' as much for the devilment as profit, but if you step over the line of mild trickery into the world of the real villains, your life will never be the same again.'

'If you know what Ernie's like, why bother with him?'

She tilted her head again in that fascinating way and laughed. 'Even the Griffithses have to grow up some time, Frank.'

'Oh, I see, marry the bloke and then change him so his best friends won't know him.'

'I confess I have something like that in mind. I'll tell you in confidence, Frank, Ernie wants to marry me but I won't agree until he gives up this stupid way of earning a living. I don't intend to survive by grubbing along on the bottom in the sludge. I want to swim in the clean, fresh stream. No, your Ernie'll have to get a job before I say yes.'

'You think he'll ask you?'

'He'll ask,' she said with a confident smile.

'Good luck,' he said doubtfully.

Rhiannon answered a knock at the door and saw a smiling Gwyn there with his father.

'Hello, Charlie. Don't tell me. You've lost the pup again!'

'No, it's about my bike,' Gwyn replied. 'Basil Griffiths, in Trellis Street, he reckons he's got one.'

'We wondered if you'll come with us to look at it,' Charlie said.

She gathered a jacket and slipped on some tidier shoes and they set off with Gwyn chattering non-stop about where he was going when he had transport. Rhiannon shared a smile with Charlie and felt a wave of pleasurable excitement.

Basil was sitting behind a heavily loaded dinner plate and helping to coax Ronnie to eat a spoonful of mashed vegetables that he was spitting out as fast as his father was pushing it in. Basil was laughing as Ronnie wrinkled his little face in outrage.

'Doesn't think much of your cooking, Eleri, love,' he said as the visitors sat down.

'So long as he's had a little,' Eleri said, coming in from the kitchen with cups of tea.

Basil pushed his plate aside. 'Keep this hot for a few minutes will you, love? I'll show them the bike before I eat.'

'We can come back another time.' Charlie began to rise. But Basil shook his head.

'You can wait but I don't think your Gwyn can, eh, son?'

The bicycle had been in a bit of a crash and the paint was badly scraped, the handlebars had been slightly buckled and staightened, but Charlie and Basil examined it minutely and decided that it was safe, and in need of cosmetic treatment only. Delving in a shed, Basil found several tins of paint and promised to help clean the vehicle so it would be ready for the weekend. Then he pulled from the back of the shed his own bicycle and said,

'Borrow this for a week or so, Charlie, so you can go with him and make sure he's behaving sensible on the roads.'

'Can I take it home now?' an anxious Gwyn asked.

'Go on then, but don't ride it 'til we've greased it and checked the brakes, right?'

When Rhiannon and Charlie walked back with an excited Gwyn 'scooting' on the pedal beside them she wondered at the kindness of people.

Charlie had announced that he was determined never to break the law again and he had been taken at his word and offered help.

'Aren't people kind,' she said. 'Basil only charged two pounds ten shillings for the bike and I don't think he made a profit.'

'And Mr Windsor giving me, an ex-jailbird, a job in his garage. Yes, I'm lucky to live around here where people care.' He looked at her and smiled ruefully. 'Most of it's thanks to you,' he said. 'Knowing you trust me and treat me like a friend has made a difference. People wouldn't have accepted me so readily and I certainly wouldn't have been offered the job in the garage if you hadn't told Mr Windsor I was a reformed character. Thank you.'

'Oh, I didn't think you knew I'd spoken to him?'

'He told me what you said and I promised him I'd never let you down, Rhiannon, and I meant it.' He leaned towards her and placed a gentle kiss on her cheek before turning away, and hurrying across the road to help his son push his bike inside.

★ ★ ★

Afternoon tea with the Gunners was not one of Ernie's most enjoyable experiences. As Frank was 'unavoidably' detained, he went into the living room alone, to see Mr and Mrs Gunner standing side by side

208

behind a lavishly set table, as if intending to ward him off with forks and knives. He had been warned in advance to insist on washing his hands before sitting down but failed her mother's first test of a gentleman by going into the kitchen and not the bathroom to do so.

The conversation was nothing more than a series of questions which, Ernie surmised, were more tests. From the look on Gloria's face, he failed.

Walking along the road afterwards, with an amused Helen escorting him as far as the corner, watched by her mother from the gate, he said,

'I'm getting very fond of you, Helen Gunner, and I want you to be a part of my future plans, but only if we can exclude your Mam from the whole thing. How d'you fancy Australia? Or the Arctic? Or the middle of the Sahara?'

Defying her mother, who still watched from the gate, Helen kissed him and started to walk back home. 'Not unless you promise to marry me first, Ernie Griffiths,' she teased.

★ ★ ★

When Caroline had first moved back to her parents' house, Barry called every day to play with Joseph, and sometimes to take Caroline to work. Whenever possible, he had tried to talk to her about moving back to the flat. But although Joseph greeted him with delight, Caroline firmly avoided being alone with him. She only allowed him to take her to work when her mother or one of the others needed a lift as well. It had reached the stage when he dreaded meeting her. Although he practised speeches when they were apart, when he saw her he no longer knew what to say.

He wasn't deliberately avoiding her, he told himself, although it would have been easy to do so as she worked every weekday in the wool shop. Calling during the day to see Joseph, who was happy in the care of Janet and Hywel, he only had to avoid Wednesday afternoons to be sure of missing her. Unless she took a day off for some reason.

Thinking of this possibility, he tensed himself every time he went to the cottage, afraid that he would open the door and see her there. Yet every time he felt a sinking disappointment when she did not appear. He felt so ashamed at his failure and at the same time disappointed in her for letting him down and making him look such a fool.

He only had to imagine pleading with her to come home, and then would come the second part of his imaginings and he was watching the sadness cloud her lovely dark eyes as he stepped towards her. Walking away was misery but to stay would be impossible.

It wouldn't work. It couldn't work. Why had they ever thought it would? Stepping into dead men's shoes was impossible, specially when the dead man was a brother, loved by them both.

Yet, unpleasant though it might be, he needed to talk to her. There was the money for one thing. They had decided to use her wages for the week to week expenses and allow his earnings to be ploughed back into the business. But business was slack, although there was a spate of weddings booked for June. He didn't have enough money to pay the bills and find food.

He walked across the fields one evening and resentment simmered. He was building a business for her and for Joseph, wasn't he? So why couldn't she be patient and wait until it was up and running? Time he spent away from the house was one of the things she had hated, but it was only until the business grew. Then he could pick and choose his appointments and find more time for her. Things would be all right if only she would show more patience.

His shoulders drooped. It would never be all right. He was lying to himself and what was more pathetic than that? She didn't want him. His absences, the long hours he worked, she hadn't missed him, or wished he was there, they had been no more than an excuse on which to hang her regrets.

Almost within sight of the cottage, he stopped at the edge of a field and leaned against a stile. Life seemed so empty. If it wasn't for Joseph he might be tempted to emigrate and start somewhere new. Surely as a photographer he could find work wherever he lived?

'Watcha, Barry,' a voice called and he turned to see Basil walking along the hedgerow towards him. 'On your way to see our Caroline are you?'

'I suppose so, although I doubt if she wants to see me,' he replied morosely.

'Why? Aren't you going to make arrangements about her coming back home? She must have had enough of our Mam and Dad's house by now?'

'I don't think she wants to come back. Ever,' Barry said. 'Our starting a home together was a terrible mistake.'

'Come on, boy, I thought you and she were made for each other?'

'It's my brother she loved and I was a fool

to think I could take his place.'

'You were stupid to take her to the place where she and Joseph were going to live, I'll agree with that.'

'You mean that might be the trouble?'

'It couldn't have helped could it, daft 'aporth!'

'I never thought,' Barry frowned.

'You'd better do some thinking straight-away then, hadn't you?'

'Perhaps the flat was a part of the trouble, but not all. Caroline resented my going out evening after evening on appointments. But what could I do? I have to work.'

'You have to keep her, I can see that.'

'I didn't actually keep her, Basil.'

'What d'you mean?'

'It's the business. I'm putting everything I earn back into the business.'

'Apart from house-keeping you mean?'

'We used Caroline's wages so I could put any money I earned into improving the premises and getting better equipment.'

'Wouldn't it have been better to build your home first, then start your fanciful plans?' There was an edge to Basil's voice that startled Barry.

'I was doing it for them!' Barry defended. 'It was all for them. I had this plan — '

'I see. So that's why your wife has left

you and gone back home to Mam and Dad? Some plan! I'd never had a regular job in my life until I married Eleri. Now I take great pride in handing her my wage packet every Friday. I take out all the small change and give her the rest.'

'It's different for you. You're satisfied with a boring job like nightwatchman. I couldn't accept anything like that.'

'Satisfied? I hate it! But I'll do it for my family forever if necessary. Too bloody high and mighty for the ordinary you are, Barry Martin. If I lost this job I'd go right out and get another! I'd do anything. Anything at all, to bring Eleri and Ronnie a wage every Friday. That's responsibility, Barry. Heard of that, have you?'

Barry stared after the tall, spindly figure of Basil as he hurried away from him, his feet sounding like a scythe as he swished angrily through the thickening June grasses. He had never, ever heard the man lose his temper before. And about nothing. Basil was too thick to understand about ambition, he decided. How could someone who worked at an uninspired activity like nightwatchman, realise what ambition was? Irritation and a touch of superiority kept him angry as he turned and walked back to Sophie Street. He was too upset to visit the Griffithses tonight.

★ ★ ★

Victoria went with her mother and the two youngest Joneses to the imposing premises of Gwennie Woodlas's gown shop. She was dressed neatly in a skirt and blouse and carried a shopping bag. She was dreading the visit, although having her mother and the two little brothers with her helped her to feel less conspicuous. They walked past twice without entering as they could see through the glass door that customers were being served.

'I'm not going in until the place is empty,' she whispered to her mother and was rewarded with a nod of agreement.

'She locks the door if she has someone important to attend to,' her mother told her. 'Perhaps, as you are marrying Jack Weston she might do that for you.'

'His name isn't Weston, Mam. No matter what Gladys does, she can't change the fact that he is Jack Heath. The Weston is an affectation insisted on by Gladys on a promise of an allowance. Jack has always thought it silly.'

'You can do what you like when you have money,' her mother chuckled. 'Will I have a daughter with a hyphenated name, then?'

'No you won't! And, if we don't get in

215

there soon you won't have one with a bride's dress either!'

To her dismay, it was Megan Weston who came forward to serve her, Gwennie being busy with books in the small office beyond the showroom.

'Victoria, dear,' Megan smiled. 'Come to see if we can make a presentable bride out of you, have you?' She smiled sweetly and added *sotto voce*, 'Take my advice and don't chose anything too splendid, you need confidence and stunning looks to get away with most of these. Better really for you to go to one of the stores. But I'll get out a few to show you, as you're here, shall I?'

Victoria swallowed the insults and stepped towards the rack of bridal dresses under the dust sheet.

'Don't touch, I'll take some out for you,' Megan said at once. Victoria stepped back as if stung.

'I need to look,' she said rebelliously.

'They're so expensive and the fabric so easily soiled,' Megan said.

Victoria wiped her small hands on her skirt and stood there, tears enlarging her eyes.

Her mother took her arm and began to pull her towards the door. Gwennie had obviously heard something of the exchange as she came forward, pushed Megan aside and smiled her heavily-made-up smile.

'Go and make tea for our customers, Megan. And turn the notice on the door to closed, if you please.' There was a grittiness about the voice as she guided Victoria and her mother to the plush chairs in the corner. 'Now, Victoria, dear, what did you have in mind? I want to make you the most beautiful bride the town has ever seen.'

'I thought of cream, not white,' Victoria began. A stifled giggle was heard from the office and Gwennie stalked across and closed the door.

'Will you try a few of each, dear? You might change your mind when you see how a lovely skin like yours glows against pure white.' Dresses were lifted from the rails one by one and hung around the showroom, each one confusing Victoria more. How could she choose? They were all lovely and, besides, she had no idea of the cost and without some guidelines she was afraid she would select one and then not be able to afford it. Oh, how she wished the dreaded wedding was over and she and Jack were settled in their home.

The trying on was frightening at first, Megan's words running through her head and making her afraid of damaging the pristine garments. But as the second and then a third slipped over her slim shoulders it began to be fun. Gwennie flattered and advised and assured her she needn't worry about the price tags, they were tucked well out of sight and not for her to concern herself with.

The one she eventually chose was white satin. It was ankle length with a full skirt and tight waist. There was a panel of embroidery on the bodice and the neckline crossed low down and rose to the shoulders in sparkling folds. With her shy expression, and the diamanté catching the light and giving her an aura, she had an air of mysterious beauty.

'It's the one,' Gwennie whispered.

The others agreed. Her mother sobbed and blinked her eyes. Her young brother stared and said, 'Blimey,' in great awe.

As Victoria stepped forward to be helped out of it, Gwennie stopped her with an imperious hand. 'Megan?' she called and Megan stepped out of the office with a tray of tea in her hands. 'I want you to look at this beautiful child and tell me, have you ever seen a more radiant bride? Because I don't think I have.'

When Victoria and her family had gone, Gwennie turned angrily to her assistant and said, 'If you look half as stunning on your wedding day as that lovely, shy child — who came to us for help and not insults — will on hers, I for one will be surprised. And I will not tolerate you using my showroom for your pettiness towards a girl because she has the temerity to be marrying your cousin. Now, leave. I don't want you in my shop another minute.'

★ ★ ★

Megan walked home slowly, utterly ashamed. How could she have been so unkind? The days when she and Joan shocked everyone and got away with it because they were free and extremely wealthy and able to do exactly what they wished, were gone. She hadn't even enjoyed it. Certainly not as much as she and Joan would once have done. Joan had always been the one to suggest their most outrageous behaviour. But not now. Joan was marrying Viv Lewis and was wrapped up in Grandfather's business and plans for her future.

She had always been the quieter one, the less devilish of the two Weston Girls. What had got into her? Was she so embittered that she had to use her position to humiliate poor little Victoria, for idle fun? She had imagined recounting the interlude to Joan and sharing the joke, but now she was the one who was humiliated. She had been sacked. Megan Fowler-Weston, one of the famous Weston Girls had been ignominiously sacked!

When she reached home she was relieved to find her mother out. Since taking in boarders to help recover from the financial disasters that had beset the Weston family, Sally was kept very busy, shopping and cooking and making sure the house was as clean as she could make it. For Megan it was a relief to be on her own. She went up to her room and sat at her dressing table staring at her reflection in the mirror. What a pain to have let herself down so badly. Now she would have to find another job and it wouldn't be as enjoyable as working for Gwennie and her 'Gowns For The Discerning Woman'.

She was so intent on the scrutiny of her features, and her thoughts on a search for employment, and how she was going to explain to her mother why she no longer worked for Gwennie, that she didn't notice the envelope for some time. The letter, placed there by her mother, had a London postmark and, frowning, she slit it open.

It was from Terrence Jenkins and for a moment she pushed it aside unwilling to read what he had to say.

Terrence was related to the family who

lived in Montague Court. They were once wealthy landowners but now ran the family home as a restaurant and hotel.

He was the only man with whom she had ever fallen in love. She stared at his writing on the envelope and remembered how he had excited her. If he hadn't 'forced her', they might still be together. She and Joan might have been planning that double wedding they had dreamed of as children. But he had forced her and frightened her half to death by fears of having a baby: and by fear of how much she had wanted and enjoyed it, she admitted with a slight blush.

The Jenkinses had been one of Grandmother Weston's failures, she mused. On learning that they were in reduced circumstances, similar to herself, or so she fondly thought, she had tried to befriend them and had invited them to her Christmas Party at which she had hoped to find husbands for her two granddaughters. Of the Jenkinses, only Terrence had made an appearance and instead of adding a bit of 'class' to the proceedings, he had caused a fight. In spite of her melancholy, she chuckled at the memory.

Terrence's ex-fiancée's brother had turned up and attacked him as punishment for jilting the girl at the altar. Jack and Viv and some of the others had joined in and it was Grandmother's deepest regret that the fight hadn't been started by the Griffithses so she could say, 'told you so', but by her most prestigious guest, Terrence, one of the Jenkinses of Montague Court.

Slowly, she unfolded the letter and began to read. It wasn't very long.

'Dear, Darling Megan,

Please forgive my writing to you after you begged me not to. I can't tell you how many times I have filled pages then thrown them away.

Please will you write back and tell me how you are? And, if you miss me as much as I miss you?

I would give anything for just the briefest of moments with you.

If I visit my family at Montague Court, will you consider allowing me to buy you tea?

Please, dear Megan, put me out of my misery and write,
Yours forever,
Terry.'

Megan tore it into pieces and dropped it into the litter bin with a picture of love-birds on the side.

Frank was dreading hearing from Percy Flemming. Why had he listened to the man? What had he been thinking of, getting involved in something so dangerous? Poaching a few salmon or some pheasants was one thing, but knocking out a watchman? Someone like Basil? That was something very different.

It was towards the end of June when he saw him. He had just finished sawing up a van-load of wood ready to sell the following day around the houses, and was walking across the fields towards The Railwayman's and a pint with his friends. Someone hailed him from just inside the wood.

He wanted to walk on, pretend he hadn't heard, hope that Percy would give up on him and find someone else to do the job. How was he supposed to knock out a watchman? A clout from a spade on the back of the head? With sleeping tablets? Where would he find a spade? Just standing there nice and handy in the watchman's hut? Or walk along with one across his shoulder in broad daylight so everyone would see him? And tablets? How could he get hold of knockout pills? Could he casually tell the doctor he wanted to put someone to sleep a bit earlier than they'd intended? It was madness.

'Frank!' Percy called running to catch up with him. 'Long-legged lot, the Griffithses. Didn't you hear me calling?'

'Oh, hello Percy. Coming for a pint?'

'We don't want to be seen together now do we, boy?' Percy said disapprovingly. 'Meet me at the edge of Pigog Wood tomorrow night at ten.'

'I don't think I'm up to this, Percy,' he said.

'Too late, boy. You're in and in you stay.'

Frank walked on towards the town and wondered idly whether he could leave town for a while. It seemed the only way. But he only had enough money to take him to Cardiff, and from the look of Percy's face that wouldn't be far enough.

★ ★ ★

Rhiannon was worried about the continuing absence of Caroline from the flat. If only she and Barry could be persuaded to talk to someone. Someone who could help them sort out the problem before it was too late. They were both so unhappy; neither appeared relieved at the separation, there had to be a way of putting things right between them.

Barry was filling the flat with a surplus

of things as if to disguise the fact that it had been intended to be his home. Chairs were pushed out of the way and cameras and flash lights and all the paraphernalia of a professional photographer filled every space. She opened the door one day to call up and ask if she could come up and make some tea, and found the sides of the stairs filled with boxes.

'Barry? What are you doing? This isn't safe you know. What if there was a fire? You could be blocked in.'

'It's only until I get my new premises,' he called down. 'Stay there and I'll make your tea and hand it to you.'

The doorbell tinkled and a voice said, 'Make one for me as well, will you Barry?'

'Nia? Is something wrong?' Rhiannon asked.

'Wrong? Why should there be? I was passing and I called to see you, that's all,' Nia smiled.

As customers called in, she helped serve and when their tea was handed to them across the barricade of boxes, she sat beside Rhiannon and asked her in a whisper,

'What's going on?'

'He's trying to forget that he was hoping to live there with Caroline. That's what!' Rhiannon whispered back. 'He's cramming

225

the place till he can hardly move. Any old thing, just to hide the fact it could have been a home. He has the double bed propped against the wardrobe and he sleeps on the couch. He's so stiff he can hardly move some mornings and serve him right too. What's happened to those two?'

'Caroline walked out, that's all he'll tell me. My son absolutely refuses to discuss it, dear.'

'I don't know what's happened either,' Rhiannon said. 'I can make a few guesses though.'

'I think they both lost their nerve and each believes the other regrets the attempt to stay married.'

'I think it's ghosts,' Rhiannon said firmly. 'Living here has unlocked the past for them both, but especially for Caroline. It's brought it all back; the happiness she and Joseph shared and the tragedy of his death. Sorry if it upsets you, saying this, but don't you think they were wrong to set up home in the very place Caroline intended to live with your Joseph?'

'I thought so at the time. I still think so, but I daren't mention it.'

'Pity, it might have helped. They used to meet here before they told anyone they loved each other, didn't they? Secret meetings that must give every room a special memory.'

'Exactly. How could Barry expect her to live with him in a place resounding with such memories?'

At the top of the stairs, Barry was listening. He hadn't given a moment's thought to Caroline's request for them to live somewhere else. What nonsense to think the flat was the cause of their problem! Caroline wasn't a fanciful kind of girl and she understood that it wasn't sensible to pay a high rent when his mother allowed them to live here practically rent-free. But at least it was something to discuss, when everything he said of late was a conversation stopper.

As soon as his mother had gone he went around to the Griffithses in high hopes and asked Caroline if she would start again in a different place.

'Everything else would be the same, would it?' she asked in her quiet, calm voice. 'Nothing else would change?'

'I'll still work hard at building the business and I'm afraid you'll still have to spend a lot of evenings on your own, but it's for our future, yours and mine and little Joseph's.'

'No, Barry. I'm sorry, but I'm staying here with Mam.'

★ ★ ★

227

The wedding dress was delivered to Goldings Street and Victoria carried it upstairs to the small bedroom she shared with her mother. The wardrobe was old and smelled slightly of damp so she hung it on the picture rail and sat on the bed to admire it.

Her mother followed her up and sat beside her. 'Go on, try it on again,' she coaxed. 'The boys won't be home for ages yet and the youngsters are both asleep.'

Together they removed the tissue that protected its shoulders and, with her face aglow, Victoria stood and allowed her mother to slip the dress over her head. It felt crisp and cool and gave her a feeling of excitement the like of which she had never known. Jack would see her in this as she walked down the aisle to become his wife.

Entering the church filled with people would be terrifying, but once she could see Jack, the faces would fade to a misty haze and she would be aware of no one but him. Her face glowed with happiness as she imagined it all.

Stepping onto a stool to protect its delicate lace train, she admired herself in the yellow mirror on the old wardrobe.

'Jack will be so proud,' her mother whispered. 'And so will I. The Westons will never have had such a lovely bride.'

The Westons. For a moment Victoria had forgotten them. That sea of faces in the church became sharply focused and she saw Jack's family looking at her with their false smiles. They would all be there, watching, criticising and waiting for her to do something embarrassing. Turning away from her reflection she gave a deep sigh.

'It's a beautiful dress, Mam, but I still wish Jack and I were marrying in a register office. Don't you?'

'No, dear. Not now I've seen you wearing this dress. I want the whole town to see how lovely you are.'

She guessed the reason for her daughter's show of nerves and, after hanging up the dress and covering it with tissue paper, she hugged her daughter for a long, long time.

★ ★ ★

Frank met Percy as arranged and, this time, he was given more of the plan. He tried to talk himself out of listening. He wanted to get out while he still could. Once he knew the finer details he would be unable to escape, he would be a danger to the other members of the team.

'Don't tell me, Percy. I've changed my mind, I don't want to know. Find someone

229

else will you? I won't say a word about it. You can be sure of that.'

'The stockroom will be full, and at the same time there'll be money to pay the workers. It'll be there for two nights only, so we have to be ready,' Percy said, ignoring Frank's plea.

'We'll be caught.'

'The goods will be taken straight to London and sold on before anyone realises they're missing. You can safely leave that side of things to me, boy.'

'What about the watchman? He'll know if he's been knocked out or coaxed away from his post won't he? And what about me? Won't he recognise me if I sit and have a cup of tea with him all cosy like, and put a few tablets in to close his eyes for a few hours? *No* Percy. I'm out of it.'

'Too late for that. We can't risk anything at this late stage, boy.' He smiled in the darkness and added, 'You haven't asked yet where it's to be.'

'I don't want to know. Count me out before you tell me.'

'It's Waterman and Francis.'

'What? Then you know I can't do it! That's where our Basil works!'

'And that is exactly why you must, boy.'

9

Charlie spent a couple of hours every evening helping Gwyn to ride his new bicycle. Once he had cleaned himself up after his day in Windsor's Garage, he prepared a meal and then gave the boy his attention. After three sessions, Gwyn was able to ride a wobbly course up and down the stretch of road from the corner near Temptations to the next corner and back again but he wouldn't let him go out on his own.

'I want to be sure he's safe,' Charlie told Rhiannon when she had overheard his son's pleading. 'At the weekend I'll go out with him and then perhaps — ' He grinned at Gwyn.

'Perhaps, is it, Dad? That usually means yes,' he confided to Rhiannon.

'If you fancy coming with us,' Charlie invited. 'We won't be going far, just to the beach and back.' He stepped closer and added, 'Gwyn doesn't realise it yet, but he'll be fit to drop after a couple of hours concentrated riding.'

'I'd like to, Charlie, but I'm not sure.'

'Glad to have you with us if you can.' He smiled.

231

She turned to go, giving Gwyn an encouraging wave as he stopped to allow a van, slowly cruising along the street, to pass him. Charlie said,

'That's funny, I'm sure that's the van I worked on when I first started at Windsor's.'

'So?' Rhiannon queried.

'So why is it a different colour and why do I think the number is different?'

'Come on, Charlie, you have to be mistaken. You can't remember all the numbers of vans you've worked on!'

'Plenty of cars and a few motor-bikes, but only two vans and I remember that one because it was the first one Mr Windsor trusted me with. I recognise the damage to the mudguards and the pattern of rust under the passenger door. It was green and now it's a badly-painted grey. It's changed. And that's for definite.'

'If you're sure, shouldn't you tell the police?'

'Ha! I can just imagine them listening to me, an ex-burglar. Listen with bated breath they will!'

'Then you aren't sure,' she challenged.

'Oh, I'm certain. The colour's changed and that numberplate isn't the one it had when I worked on it. In fact I can soon check. The number will be in Mr Windsor's book.'

'Why would someone want to change the number?'

'I don't know,' Charlie shrugged, 'but it can't be innocent fun, can it?'

'Tell the police.'

'Come with me?'

★ ★ ★

The sergeant was very off-hand, but told them the matter would be investigated and when they emerged from his solemn presence, they both burst out laughing. 'Fat lot of good that's done!' Charlie sighed. 'Probably thinks I'm inventing an alibi.'

★ ★ ★

Helen Gunner lived not far from Gladys and Arfon Weston, although her family had never been included in the circle of people whom Gladys considered acceptable. Her father worked as a painter and decorator and had contracts to keep the schools and libraries of the town in good order. Comfortably placed but without pretentions, the Gunners lived simply in a modest terraced house, and had two holidays a year, one in Butlins holiday camp and one at Bournemouth in a boarding house.

233

Helen's father, Wilfred Gunner, knew Viv Lewis as he sometimes bought his supplies at Weston's Wallpaper and Paint Stores. 'Decent chap,' he told his wife, 'and he's a friend of the Griffithses.'

'Pity for him,' Gloria said through pursed lips.

Gloria Gunner was acquainted with Caroline Martin, whom she described as 'the least worst' of the Griffithses. Being a dressmaker, she used the wool shop where Caroline worked for all her sewing needs.

Mrs Gunner continued to be unhappy about her daughter's involvement with Ernie Griffiths, as, besides belonging to that notorious family, he didn't have a trade. Having a list of court appearances against his name, even though they were mostly for poaching and trespass, didn't auger well for his prospects in getting one either. She tried every way she could to discourage her daughter from seeing him, but Helen was adamant.

'I'll look at no one else, Mam. It's Ernie Griffiths or a nunnery!'

'Now you're being ridiculous.'

'So are you, inviting him here and trying to trip him up with all your tests.'

'What is the girl talking about?' Gloria looked at her husband and shrugged. Wilfred grinned and said nothing.

After a few more visits in which Wilfred opened up to the young man and tried to make him feel more comfortable in the neat and orderly house, Gloria relented. 'He's untrained but malleable enough for our Helen to do something with,' she confided in her husband.

'You talk about him as if he's a gorilla,' Wilfred protested.

'Is he the kind of young man you want our daughter to marry? Is he?'

'We could lose her,' Wilfred warned. 'Best we make him welcome.'

Gloria reluctantly agreed, still clinging to the hope that Ernie Griffiths was a novelty, a fascination with which Helen would soon tire.

★ ★ ★

Helen worked in a large grocer's shop and was presently involved in making an impressive display of the new fats they would be selling once rationing finally ended. Pyramids of one pound and half-pound boxes of Spry and Trex, which promised pastry that melted in the mouth, made a window display that attracted a lot of attention. Whole fifty-six pound cheddar cheeses were exhibited with

Caerphilly and Gouda decorated with Danish Blue and the cheerful red Edam and many more. Fruit was added to the eye-catching display, making passersby stop, look, and pop in to ask when these exciting items could be bought.

All this was to remind shoppers that from the third of July they could forget weekly allowances and buy in quantities only limited by their pocket. Bacon and ham had been off-ration since May, but the display in the main window showed models of pigs routing in clean sweet-smelling straw, and artificial sides of bacon amid the rest, all decorated with flags and bunting to mark the end of all food rationing.

It was reported that people were planning to gather together and burn their ration books, the fire a symbol of the end of frugality, and a celebration of a new beginning, the prosperity that was to come.

★ ★ ★

'I'm going to eat butter until it comes out of my ears.'

'Cheese on toast with more cheese than toast.'

'Imagine making proper pastry instead of making do with a miserable scrape of fat.'

'Strawberries smothered in cream!'

Everyone had something they had only dreamed of for the past fourteen years.

Stepping outside to check on her display, Helen almost knocked over Janet Griffiths who was standing there studying the new products, many of them never seen before. Clutching her hand was Joseph. After discussing the window's contents briefly, Janet said, 'Half-day today, isn't it, Helen? Fancy coming over for a cup of tea?'

'Love to. Thanks,' Helen said as she tripped back inside. That was a step forward, being invited to visit Ernie's mother *by* Ernie's mother. She was even more than usually light-hearted as she cleared away the rubbish left from her work on the window, and went to ask the manager to examine and judge her efforts.

* * *

When she arrived at the Griffiths's house, Caroline was there. She smiled and appeared friendly enough, but Helen found it difficult to involve her in conversation. She wondered if her subdued mood was because she didn't approve of her interest in her brother, but being an optimistic young woman, put that idea aside and decided Caroline was feeling low because of the estrangement with her husband, Barry Martin. She wasn't clear about what was going on, as Ernie seemed unwilling to discuss his sister's affairs.

While Janet was in the kitchen preparing tea, she tried to persuade the quiet young woman to open up, but Caroline seemed lost in her own thoughts. All Helen had gleaned from Ernie, was that she no longer lived with her husband. Caroline's withdrawn state made it impossible to bring the conversation around to that personal and painful matter, so while she waited for Janet's return, she talked to the little boy.

She wasn't easy with children. They stared so. But she had to make an effort. She was thankful when Janet had made the tea, set the table and returned to sit with them.

'Have you made any more progress in the search for your sister, Mrs Griffiths?' she asked. 'Wouldn't it be exciting if you found her after all these years? Inlaws outlaws, nephews and nieces and heaven knows who else besides!'

Janet brought out the box in which she kept all the information they had so far learned, and gave her the letters to read.

'A policeman she married, was it? Couldn't you find something out from the police then?'

'He left soon after Marion left the farm.'

'What about an advertisement in a few newspapers, then? That might rouse a few memories. Our brains only need a bit of a jog sometimes for all sorts of forgotten things to spill out.'

She chattered on and Janet marvelled at the ideas she came up with, the most interesting being the newspaper idea. She made a note to remind herself to do something about it the following day. 'Now why didn't I think of that?' she sighed.

'You can be too close to the problem to see it easily,' Helen chirped knowingly. ' 'Can't see the wood for the trees' sounds daft but makes sense really, doesn't it?'

Janet glanced at Caroline and they shared a smile. When Helen had gone, she turned to her daughter and mused,

'I wonder if Ernie knows how that bright, lively girl will change his life? At the moment he's so dazed by love he can't see the wood for the trees either!'

'You can be blinded by love,' Caroline said sadly. 'I didn't see clearly when Barry said he loved me, did I?'

'Perhaps it's now that your sight is distorted, love,' Janet replied as she gathered up the plates and took them into the kitchen.

When Caroline and her mother went the

following week to visit one of the addresses on the letters from Marion, Janet invited Helen to go with them. They took the van and a picnic and went through the pretty villages of Glamorgan Vale. They found the address they were searching for after being confused by false instructions several times, but to their disappointment the house they were seeking had been demolished. Janet shrugged off her disappointment saying,

'What was it about my sister? First Spring Cottage left to fall down and now this one pulled down. A vandal was she?'

Janet was aware that Caroline was even quieter than usual. She was always one to sit back and let others talk, but accompanied by the lively chatterbox that was Helen Gunner, she seemed to have sunk deeper and deeper into her shell. She began to wish she hadn't invited the girl. Perhaps, if she and Caroline had come alone Caroline might have been persuaded to talk about what was troubling her. She was well aware that Caroline had once tried to kill herself, just after the death of her fiancé, Joseph Martin, when she had discovered she was to have his child. Although reassured by all who knew of it, there was always the fear in her heart that her beloved daughter might reach those depths again.

When Helen took the little boy to look for a sweet shop, Janet said firmly to her daughter, 'Caroline, love, you and I are going for a walk this evening when Joseph is in bed, and we are going to talk. Right?'

'No Mam. I'm not ready to talk yet.'

'Pity, because I am!'

Helen returned with a chattering Joseph who offered to share his sweets. Sensitive to the mood of Janet and her daughter, Helen offered to go off again, but Caroline quickly thanked her and shook her head.

After a brief stroll, they studied the houses in the main road of the village and at its centre, they saw the almost obliterated words over a door which said Post Office and General Stores. The shop window had been changed and the house was showing signs of neglect. An elderly man opened the door to their knock and said at once that he wasn't buying at the door. Assured they weren't trying to sell him anything, he listened to their questions about a Mrs Marion Jolly who had lived in a house no longer standing.

'Condemned it was. It was a wreck before Mrs Jolly moved in, her and her three children.'

'You remember her?' Janet could hardly contain her excitement.

'I remember her! And that husband of hers.'

'Her husband?' Janet coaxed.

'Ran off with my wife, didn't he?'

'Oh, I'm sorry.' She was so embarrassed she wanted to turn away but the thought of being close to reaching Marion made her ask, 'You don't know what happened to Mrs Jolly, do you? Marion Jolly? She's my sister and I'd like to get in touch.'

'Marion Jolly you say? Didn't call herself that. Harriet she was then. Perhaps you've made a mistake?'

Disappointment showered her like a sudden downpour. She had been feeling optimistic, sure they were getting close.

'Don't give up, she probably used a second name to hide her shame,' Helen suggested in her bright, cheerful manner.

'It wasn't her fault if her husband ran off,' Caroline said.

'Of course not. But the shame is felt just the same,' Helen replied.

'You're right there,' Janet said. 'Come on, we'll go and knock somewhere else. If she lived here someone else might remember her.'

'Ask who is the oldest inhabitant,' Helen suggested.

'Picnic first,' Caroline said firmly.

'Picnic first,' echoed Joseph.

The day was warm and they found a sheltered spot where they could escape the sun and sit to eat their picnic and where Joseph could play under the trees. Janet's sharp eyes noticed that Caroline ate little, passing her food to her son or throwing it into the bushes for birds or field mice to find. She couldn't ignore this situation any longer. If Caroline had been happier without Barry she might have let things drift, but Caroline was sinking deeper into depression and that couldn't be allowed to continue.

They didn't get any further with their quest that day, but Janet had high hopes of the newspaper advertisements which she had placed in six London papers and two local ones. One of the local papers had sent someone to interview her and the young reporter explained that since the war, many families had lost touch and the paper's policy was to publicise the names and what information was available, and try to reunite them.

'D'you think she went away during the war?' Janet had asked the young man.

'A lot of people moved about. Evacuees came here from the big cities, servicemen and women married and settled in places where they had been posted. Houses were bombed and families moved out to other areas. Plenty of reasons for losing touch.'

She thought it better not to tell him that it was not a war time mix-up, but sixty years since she had seen her sister.

She gave him the old photograph she had found in Spring Cottage and showed him the letters and names she had discovered. It gave her a strange feeling on being handed the local paper a few days later to see her own face staring back at her.

'What d'you think of that, then?' Hywel asked as he held it in front of her.

'When did I get to look so old?' she replied sadly.

* * *

Gladys Weston was not the kind of woman to give up easily. Joan and Viv Lewis might think they had got their own way over their wedding but she was determined to win some of the arguments. The idea of a buffet was acceptable. She had heard of several high-class weddings where a buffet had been chosen instead of a proper sit-down meal. But it had to be a proper one, no niggardly little sandwiches and a few sausage rolls made by Dora Lewis. And the venue.

Gomer Hall, for heaven's sake! That would have to be changed.

Putting on her fur coat and her best leather shoes and gloves, and the hat which had cost three times what she had told Arfon, she went to call on the Jenkinses of Montague Court.

An hour later she returned home by taxi, having booked the function room and arranged for them to add a few specialities to the selection of food.

She told her granddaughter what she had done that evening when Joan called to show her the invitations she had chosen.

'Sorry, my dear but you'll have to change them, I have a surprise for you — I have booked Montague Court.'

Joan kissed her, told her she was kind and generous, then rang and cancelled it.

* * *

Hywel decided to sell the goats. It was when he was working for Farmer Booker, clearing out a barn, that he met a man who said he might be interested in buying them from him. The man, a surly individual, had come to look at some old machinery Booker was selling. Hearing about Hywel's goats he made an offer, subject to them being in good condition. He offered less than Hywel had paid but Hywel knew that some lessons had to be paid for and learning that goat-keeping was not for him was a lesson well-learned.

He arranged for the man to come and look at them on the following evening and Janet stood in the kitchen and watched as the tall, heavily built man strode across the yard and looked into the pen. She couldn't see much of his face as a heavy beard hid most of it, but she saw that his colour was high, his eyes were dull and his nose was pitted and had an unhealthy purplish look.

She beckoned to her husband and, when he came over, she whispered,

'I don't like him. I don't think he'd treat them kindly. Let's wait for someone else to take them.'

'You're right. He looks a cruel bugger. And one who's been in a few fights too.' He went up to where the man was looking over the fence at the goats and said, 'Sorry mate, my wife has changed her mind. We're keeping them.'

The man walked away after grumbling to Hywel about wasting his time and with a sigh of relief, Janet heard his lorry start up and drive away. She shuddered.

'He reminded me of my father,' she explained.

'You don't need to explain, love,' Hywel said. 'I wasn't happy about him myself.'

★ ★ ★

Frank was still uneasy about the commitment he had made to involve himself in the robbery at the warehouse. But learning that Basil had Fridays and Saturdays off, he felt that at least he wouldn't be expected to confront his brother and give him something to make him sleep. Although the worry remained. Even if he convinced the police of his innocence, he knew Basil would know he was guilty. And what trouble was he bringing to him? Basil could be suspected of complicity and could easily lose his job.

When Percy met him as he was walking home from The Railwayman's and told him it was on for Saturday night he was almost relieved. At least action was better on the nerves than waiting.

He was given a flask and a small paper packet, and told to fill the flask with whisky to which he must add the powder. A second fold of paper containing the powder was also handed over.

'If the watchman refuses to drink the whisky you'll have to put this in his beer or tea, what ever drink he has, right?'

'You mean I have to go in there and deliberately give him knockout drops? What about my alibi? He'll see me won't he?'

'You tell the police you were there. You went to see your brother, forgetting it's his night off. But whatever you say, remember to stay as close to the truth as you can.'

'What if he doesn't invite me in?'

'That's what I'm paying you fifty quid for, boy. So you make sure he does. Right?'

★ ★ ★

It seemed far from satisfactory but Frank knew he had to go through with it. By Saturday, he was so tense he was ill. Every muscle ached. His joints felt about to snap apart and the pain in his head was one intense, explosive agony. At five o'clock he sat in his parents' kitchen and stared at the food his mother had offered and couldn't swallow a single forkful.

'Sickening for something, are you?' Hywel asked, his fork poised to take a sausage from Frank's abandoned plate. 'Don't tell me you're love-sick an' all! What a household this is! Ernie mooning about, dreaming of Helen, Caroline in despair because she can't believe Barry loves her, and now you? Who is it?'

'Leave it, Dad.' Frank said. 'I'm not in the mood for talking, or for food.'

'Then you won't want this,' Hywel smiled as he speared the last of Frank's sausages.

At half-past eight, when Frank was pretending to sleep in a chair close to the fire, Basil and Eleri walked in with their baby. Frank was swamped with guilt at the thought of what he was going to do to Basil's deputy in a few hours' time.

'Hello, Eleri, Basil. Glad you don't have to work tonight?' he asked.

'I do,' Basil groaned as he dropped his shoulder bag onto the table. 'Old George, my replacement, is ill and he can't work. So, no sleep for me tonight.'

Frank's stomach curled in fear. He couldn't do it now. How could he? Percy wouldn't expect it. His mind tumbled in a confusion of mixed images; himself arrested, Basil arrested, Eleri crying and accusing him. And Percy, standing threateningly telling him he had to go through with it or else.

But try as he may there wasn't a way to get in touch with Percy to tell him the whole thing was off. Perhaps if he simply didn't go? He thought of walking through Booker's yard with a couple of pheasants and getting himself arrested. That would be enough of an excuse. Or getting drunk and behaving violently and achieving the same result. But there wasn't time. He had to be there, and with an unconscious watchman laid out, in just over three hours' time.

'What's the matter?' Eleri asked, alarmed at the paleness of Frank's face.

'I think I'm going to be sick,' he said, and rushed from the room.

'He hasn't been well all day,' Janet said. 'Best he goes to bed I think.'

Ernie had gone straight to Helen's from work. He had found a few day's casual employment, sawing floorboards to the required lengths at the woodyard. At ten o'clock, Eleri and Ronnie were still there but Basil had gone to start his night-shift.

'What's the matter with him?' Eleri whispered, pointing a thumb at Frank.

'Sick,' Hywel said. 'Don't talk to him or he'll have to make a run for it again.'

'Some sympathy wouldn't come amiss,' Janet said, then she looked at Eleri. 'Are you feeling unwell too, love?'

'I don't feel all that grand,' Eleri admitted.

It was coincidental Eleri being ill at the same time as Frank as there were different reasons for the sickness, but Janet presumed they must have both eaten something that disagreed.

'Hywel will walk you home, love,' she said.

'Or would you like to ride in the van?'

'Best I walk, I think,' Eleri said. 'But I think I'll sit a while longer.'

'You could stay here tonight,' Janet said, 'but Basil will be worried if you aren't there when he gets home at seven o'clock tomorrow morning.'

When eleven o'clock came Hywel was beginning to doze, Janet was making cocoa, and Frank had an idea.

'You make up a bed for Eleri and Ronnie, Mam. I'll go and tell Basil that Eleri isn't well,' Frank said, seeing the perfect excuse for calling at the factory.

'D'you feel well enough?' Janet asked and Frank nodded.

'He wouldn't like it if we let her walk home at this time of night and her not feeling well.'

'I would be glad, Mam,' Eleri said.

'So would I,' Hywel admitted. 'I don't fancy walking to Trellis Street and back.'

Frank set off, remembering to take the flask he had prepared and the extra packet of powder given to him by Percy. It might work. Fifty pounds just for giving his brother a few extra hours' sleep. Thank's to Eleri's upset stomach, it might just work! He shook off the feeling of panic as he hurried through the dark night, across the fields, down a rutted lane, through the wood, his eyes accustomed to being out at night and effortlessly finding the paths.

When he rattled the gates and rang the emergency bell, he saw Basil come out, a torch in his hand.

'It's only me,' Frank called. 'I've got a flask, can I come in?'

'You know I'm not allowed to open the gates except in dire emergency,' Basil said, then added, 'Hang on while I fetch the keys.' He ambled across and as he opened the gates asked,

'What's up then? Don't tell me Mam's locked you out?'

'No, I've come to tell you Eleri and Ronnie are staying at our place tonight.'

'Not ill, is she?' Basil asked anxiously.

'A bit tired that's all. Mam thought she could stay rather than disturb little Ronnie to go home. Fast asleep he is and snoring like a good 'un. We didn't want you to have a fright, going home and finding the house empty. Fancy a drink?'

They went into the cabin where Basil spent five nights of the week, and settled down near the open window. The night was dark but there was a warm breeze. Basil had always enjoyed the night hours. Since he was a small child he had relished the silence and peacefulness of the darkness. He felt privileged to share the secret world that revealed itself once human activity ceased.

He was aware of small sounds that most would not hear. Animals rarely seen during the day were well-known to him. Even here, in his locked-away room behind fences that were supposed to keep the rest of the world at bay, he knew what was going on beyond the arc of light from his window.

He told Frank about the fox that called at midnight for a share of his food and he went outside and bent down close to the wire fence to show his brother where he fed the trusting creature.

Frank watched as Basil sat back on his heels, his long legs bent, his knees up around his ears, his head leaning against the wire. It was several minutes before he realised Basil was fast asleep.

Taking the keys and unlocking the padlock and the heavy locks on the metal gates was easy and he collected the flask and its lid and went home, leaving the keys in the padlock, which he threw into the undergrowth at the side of the lane. When he was well away from the factory he threw the flask away too, after washing it in a stream.

He went home but he couldn't sleep. The sick feeling had returned and he thought of his brother lying on the cold ground and knew he had to phone the police. He had done his part, had kept his promise and how would Percy ever know it was he and not a passer-by who had telephoned the police?

Slipping out of the house without being seen or heard was accomplished with the ease of practice. Trying to disguise his voice, he told the constable, not that there was a robbery taking place, only that there was an unconscious man there.

He walked a little way through the fields, trying to calm his nerves and holding back from running to the factory to make sure Basil was all right. He heard voices raised in argument, a man and a woman, and he went closer to investigate. As he broke through the trees where a pair of cottages stood, the outside lights revealed the two people. He saw one run off, shouting back abuse at the girl, who stood close to the garden wall, her arms around her shoulders as if for warmth.

He recognised her as Mair Gregory who worked for Gladys and Arfon Weston and, not wanting to frighten her, Frank called out and gave his name as he drew closer.

'You all right, Mair?' he asked.

'Yes, but I don't fancy walking home in the dark, and at this time of night,' she said.

'Not much of a man leaving you out here, even if you have had a quarrel,' Frank said, giving her his jacket.

★ ★ ★

Ernie was very late getting home that night. He had gone to Helen's for supper and had stayed playing cards with her and her parents and a neighbour who had called in, until one o'clock.

Walking home, a bit tipsy from the flagons Helen's father had opened and shared, he met Farmer Booker, walking his fields with a broken shotgun across his arm. They stopped, farmer and poacher talking in a subdued whisper and remarking on how still the night was and how warm.

'After poachers, Mr Booker?' Ernie asked.

'Not really. There's an injured cow in one of the fields and I went to see how she was. She's cut herself badly on some barbed wire, silly old girl. She's been stitched but we've left her there, with some hay bales around her. She'll be able to walk back to the barn tomorrow.' He patted the weapon and added, 'I usually carry this. You never know when there'll be an opportunity to give someone a fright.'

'Poaching's for kids,' Ernie said, pulling off

a length of grass and chewing thoughtfully. 'There comes a time when you want to settle down.'

'You? Don't tell me you're thinking of marrying that Gunner girl?'

'You know her?'

'She deserves the best. She'll expect you to get a proper job, and keep it, mind.'

'And that's what I intend to do. The trouble is, I can't think what.'

They talked for an hour, standing in the tall grasses at the edge of the hay field, and when they parted Ernie felt as if he had grown up and come of age.

He went into the bedroom he shared with Frank quietly, but a glance at the other bed showed him Frank wasn't there.

He came in a few minutes later, puffing slightly.

'I've been outside to be sick,' he explained. 'Been feeling bad all evening. Me and Eleri.' He lay on his bed wide awake, all his senses alert and poised as if for flight. He listened intently, his heart pounding, waiting for the dawn, or for the loud imperious knock of the police, whichever came first.

10

The robbery was still underway when two policemen arrived at the factory at twelve-thirty, but most of the goods had already been transferred to the van hidden behind the hedge of the field beyond the wire perimeter. They drove through the open gates and, once out of the car, began to search for the unconscious man. But they were at once drawn to sounds from inside the building and quickly realised that a robbery was in progress. Surprised by the change in their expectations they failed to catch any of the thieves, who ran off in different directions.

They first tried to stop two men who were running, heavily laden, from the open doors. Another appeared, hesitated, then ran towards the wire where a section had been cut away to enable them to pass the stolen items through to another member of the gang. One of the first two darted around the police car and pelted along the lane and was soon swallowed up in the darkness. The other ran in a darting zig-zag manner, and after throwing a carton at the policemen, pushed his way between them, knocking one of them off their feet.

The one who had been loading the van was the driver and, unseen, he made his way to the van.

Whistles blew and the stabbing light of torches broke the darkness, then one of the policemen found the switch and the outside lights flooded the area but failed to do anything useful, just lost the hunters their night sight.

There was the rumbling sound of the van starting up and one of the police made for the gates in the hope of stopping it. But before they could get out of the yard and through the hedge, one of them saw Basil staggering towards them, his elongated shadow before him making him look like a giant. They both turned to face this new threat.

'Easy,' Basil said hoarsely. 'I'm on your side. I'm going home to see my wife.' Then he sat down again and rolled over on his side and slept.

The two representatives of the law gave up all thoughts of following the vehicle they had heard driving away, and went inside Basil's office to telephone for assistance and an ambulance.

★ ★ ★

The van made its way through the quieter streets of the town taking a short cut by driving across the waste ground that had been Philips Street and down Brown Street. In his haste to reach the contact point before the police were alerted, the driver took the corner by Temptations too wide and the van hit the side of Charlie Bevan's house. The driver did a hasty bit of reversing before recovering and driving off.

The squeal of metal scraping against stone woke Charlie and Gwyn and the dog and Charlie went down to see what had happened. Opening the door he saw Rhiannon and Dora standing at their door wondering what had caused the noise.

'Anyone hurt?' Dora called across, and Charlie came out, with Gwyn a small shadow beside him, and looked at the crushed wall near his front door. Behind them the dog was barking and Gwyn went inside to let her out.

'The house isn't damaged and no one is hurt. Damn me, for a minute there I thought that Hitler was back! Just some crazy driver, that's all. Are you two all right?'

Dora and Rhiannon walked over and Rhiannon reassured Gwyn that the house wasn't falling down, that his father would be able to fix it and his bike was too far away from the door to have even suffered a scattering of dust.

'I want a cup of tea,' Dora announced and inviting Charlie and Gwyn across, she went inside.

The dog came too and it was almost three o'clock before they went to their beds.

'The police haven't appeared, so I don't suppose it's anything more than a driver with too much to drink or in too much of a hurry,' Charlie said. 'Sleep well, and don't worry,' he said to his son. 'He won't be back to finish the demolition of our house, Gwyn.'

★ ★ ★

Basil dozed on his way to the hospital, waking occasionally and asking for Eleri, explaining in a mumbling way that she was 'in the family way' and was unwell. 'Our Frank came to tell me, see,' he explained, sounding like a drunk. 'Where's our Frank then? Here a minute ago, he was.'

'Oh, he was was he?' the constable smiled. 'Now that's interesting.'

Still drowsy, Basil laboriously explained again that his brother had called to tell him Eleri was unwell.

'Don't worry about Frank, he'll be well looked after.'

'Worried about my wife,' Basil slurred slowly.

When Basil woke again, he was in a hospital bed. A constable sat beside him with his notebook open, and a pencil poised and ready in his hand. Basil was alert enough now to realise that Frank needed a good explanation for being there immediately before a robbery, so he suffered instant amnesia and feigned sleep, which soon became real.

The inspector who took charge of the robbery, Inspector Leonard, ordered one of his men to go first to interview Ernie.

'Dab-hands they are at inventing alibis, them Griffithses. This could be down to Frank, and if so, Ernie will be Frank's alibi for sure, so get Ernie's story first. And make sure they don't have a chance to talk to each other!'

★ ★ ★

It was still very early when there was a knock at the Griffithses door. Janet had finished her first cup of tea and was about to start getting breakfast when the two uniformed men asked for Ernie. Ernie and Frank were sitting with their father, looking half asleep, listening to the news on the radio. Caroline was boiling an egg for Joseph to eat with bread soldiers.

Eleri and Ronnie were still fast asleep.

Janet was alarmed when Ernie was asked to go to the police station to answer some questions. Frank rose in his seat and sank down again slowly. If this was about the robbery, they couldn't have anything on Ernie, but it might be a trick to make him talk. He reminded himself to be careful and remember he knew nothing about what happened at the factory a few hours before. He took a thick slice of bread, pressed it onto the long handled fork and held it in front of the glowing fire. Act casual, he told himself. Act casual.

Janet's fears grew when she was told that Basil was in hospital, and, as the policemen gradually told them what had happened, she turned to look at Hywel in alarm. Ernie's head jerked around to stare at Frank. A movement not missed by the policemen.

'I'll go and wake Eleri,' Janet said, hurrying from the room.

One of the policemen arranged for her to be taken to the hospital where Basil was sleeping off his 'brush with death', as he was calling his strange memory loss. 'What happened must have been so frightening and dangerous I've shut it out of my consciousness,' he told everyone who asked. 'Just like in an adventure story.'

'But you haven't forgotten your wife?'

'No chance. Look at her, isn't she lovely?' he smiled as Eleri entered the ward and ran to his bedside. 'All I've forgotten is how I came to be sleeping against the wire.'

* * *

When the police gestured for Ernie to follow them to the car he was sick with anxiety. What if he said a wrong word and Frank was arrested?

Ernie could not believe Frank was involved in such a daring robbery. He just wasn't in the know at that level of thieving. But perhaps he'd better make sure he had his story straight just in case. He had to talk to Frank and find out what he was going to say about the previous evening. Dammit, why hadn't they been together? If only he hadn't been to see Helen there would be no problem about an alibi.

How could they get away from the police long enough to exchange a few words? He tried to tell the police he had to see to the goats and the rest of the menagerie, but they shook their heads. He was given no opportunity to speak to Frank in private. Not for a second.

Over the past weeks he had sensed Frank

was doing a deal with someone, and from his attitude guessed it was something about which he was not happy. He regretted not asking him about it. This stupid argument, due to him seeing a lot of Helen Gunner, could land them in real trouble. But surely Frank couldn't have been involved in this? He wouldn't have agreed to anything like breaking into a warehouse, and certainly not one where their brother, Basil worked. So why had the police come here? Had someone set them up? Again he had doubts. They were small-time and certainly hadn't trodden on any of the big boys' toes.

'That sort of caper's well out of our league,' he told the police when he was interviewed at the station. 'A few pheasants, well, yes, we'd hold up our hands to that, haven't we often done so in the past? But robbery on this scale, you must be mad to think that has the ring of the Griffithses. We wouldn't know where to go to set up something like that, and where would we sell a lot of tools if we did? Pontypridd market? Don't talk daft, man!'

'And you insist that Frank was ill and had been all evening.'

'Never left the house. He didn't even go to The Railwayman's that's how bad he felt.'

'Funny that. Basil said he went to the

factory to tell him Eleri was ill.'

'Well, damn it all!' Ernie gave them a beatific smile of wonderment. 'I must have fallen asleep and missed that. Now there's a thing!'

'This was before you were home, while you were at the Gunner's, playing cards,' he said to remind Ernie they had checked.

'There you are, then.' Ernie smiled again, apparently content that the matter had been satisfactorily cleared up. The policeman sighed and wrote something on his notepad.

★ ★ ★

Basil was allowed home later that day, although he was warned that he would be called upon to answer further questions. That evening his boss called to see him and, after asking if he was fully recovered, told him he was sacked.

★ ★ ★

Frank sat and waited for Ernie to come home, unable to move from the house. His thoughts were jangled and full of dread. Eleri came to tell them Basil was home and apparently unharmed and that he had

265

lost his job, accused of neglect.

'He insisted someone had put something into his food or drink and attracted him to the fence. Falling as he had beside the wire, they would have found it easy to reach in and take the keys from him,' she said, her voice thickening as she was near to tears. 'But Inspector Leonard wasn't convinced. He insists Basil set up the whole thing, that he was an accomplice,' she sobbed. 'Poor Basil. He's so upset. He feels he's let me down.'

'Did the police say anything about me?' Frank asked as Janet soothed the distraught girl.

'Only that they would want to talk to you later today. Did you know there's a policeman standing at the corner of the lane? And there's another outside the back gate,' she replied. 'I think Ernie's in the clear, so I expect they're making sure *you* don't wander off before they've talked to you.'

Eleri didn't stay. Having assured his family that Basil was relatively unharmed, she went home to comfort him. She decided not to mention to him that his brothers were being questioned, although he would probably guess.

'I wish our Ernie was back,' Janet sighed. 'Perhaps he'll be able to tell us what's going on.'

'Why are they worrying us?' Frank asked. 'As if we'd rob a place where our Basil works.'

'It's because it is the place where our Basil works I suppose,' Hywel said. 'But why aren't they looking for that van? Better if they stopped pestering us and concentrated on that, and the men in it. That can't have vanished into thin air!' Hywel's anxiety made him sound irritable.

It was eight o'clock that evening when a police car arrived and took Frank in for questioning. A few minutes later another brought Ernie back.

'They're making sure you don't have an opportunity to exchange stories,' Hywel said seriously. 'They must be certain that you two know something about it.'

'I'm tired of the interest shown by the police whenever something happens around here,' Janet said with a rare surge of anger. 'It's time we Griffithses stopped being the first thought when anything goes missing, or Booker loses a few rabbits, or a bit of off-ration meat is confiscated. Always the Griffithses. It's time you all grew up!'

She ran upstairs and stared out of the window, willing Frank to return quickly and safely. Frank wouldn't have done anything as stupid as this. The police were way out this time. Her boys had always been pranksters. Forever looking for a bit of a dare, a lark spiced with danger that might make them a few shillings. But when were the Griffithses ever more than foolish young men?

★ ★ ★

'One of the Griffithses is in trouble again, or so I've heard,' Nia said as she poured coffee for Lewis that evening.

'Which one?'

'Frank, I think.'

'I knew it. There's never a moment when one of them isn't involved with the police. Rhiannon was talking to that Frank the other day and I warned her to keep away. I don't know what Dora's thinking of allowing her to mix with people like Frank Griffiths and that Charlie Bevan. Very cosy those two were last Wednesday afternoon, until I made her get in the car and be driven home.'

'Oh, Lewis, love! You didn't embarrass her in front of Charlie, did you?'

'I did. She ought to have more sense.'

'D'you know, Lewis, whenever I think of our Joseph and his death at such a young age, it isn't the things I allowed him to do that I regret, it was all the times I said no.'

'The Griffithses are different.'

'Are they? Joseph wanted to marry one of them, remember. And Barry did marry her.'

'And a fine mess that is. Caroline is a lovely girl, the best of the bunch for sure, but look what she's done to your Barry. Married him and refused to be a wife.' He was silent for a moment, aware that he had been insensitive, talking about the Griffithses, forgetting for a moment that Joseph had been in love with Caroline. 'I wonder what Mrs Gunner thinks of having a Griffiths as a son-in-law?' he said later.

'Not happy. But if she's sensible she'll go along with it or Helen might just choose to give allegiance to the Griffithses.'

'She probably will anyway. I have to admit that there's an attraction there. They seem to have more fun and happiness than most.'

'They aren't happier than we are, love,' she said softly, reaching out for his hand. 'Even if our happiness destroyed Dora's.' She frowned, then added, 'I wish we could have gone on loving each other without her knowing. While our affair was a secret no one was hurt. I hope we don't have to pay for our happiness in some way.'

★ ★ ★

Frank was away for three hours. He returned, looking pale and exhausted and complaining of being hungry, just after eleven and Janet set-to to prepare him some supper while he washed and changed and settled down to tell them what had been said.

'I told them everything that happened,' Frank began. 'I told them about Eleri being ill and me going to the warehouse to tell Frank she was staying the night with us. I went in and stayed a few minutes then I left and came home across the fields. I didn't see a van and I didn't meet a soul. That's all I know about it.' He didn't mention meeting Mair Gregory and walking her home, as she might have noted the time and that would confuse things. He had seen her later than he told the police he had returned home.

'And there's me telling them you were in bed sick as a poisoned pup and never moving from the house,' Ernie said sadly.

★ ★ ★

Frank's thoughts went over and over what had happened and his subsequent story. Was there anything he had forgotten? Then he remembered the flask. He should have been more careful about disposing of it. He had washed it out as thoroughly as he could but

270

the police were clever and they might be able to find traces of the powder Percy had given him. And fingerprints, he thought in alarm. He had to go and find it and dispose of it more permanently.

Dodging the policeman who was still watching the cottage was easy. Through the goat's enclosure and through the hedge while Mam gave the constable a cup of tea, then through the woods to the lane.

The lane went straight to the factory in one direction but he travelled along it in the opposite direction intending to leave it and double back. But a voice called him as he was passing the farmworker's cottages and he stopped and walked back. It was Mair Gregory walking her dog.

'There's been a robbery where your Basil works, I hear. That was the time you were out and near the very spot, wasn't it?' she said as he approached her.

'Me? Oh, yes, I went to give our Basil a message. Much earlier though. Lucky it wasn't any later, eh? I might have been caught up in that burglary. Could have had my head bashed in!'

'You must have gone the long way round if you were there before the robbery,' she said, tilting her head on one side. 'Midnight they say it happened. I saw you about that

271

time, didn't I? Wrote it in my diary I did, the time I told my boyfriend to get lost.'

'Mistaken you are. I was home and fast asleep when thieves raided the place. My brother works there! D'you think I'd be involved in something like that?'

'Who said you were involved, Frank? I didn't. Getting hot and bothered about something, aren't you?' She smiled and asked, 'Guilty conscience is it?'

'I do feel guilty, me being there before the incident and not knowing or able to help him.'

'But you did help, you rang the police didn't you?' she said in a hoarse whisper. 'Saw you while we were in the trees getting all steamed up and into our quarrel. Gary and me, we saw you. We could tell them when we saw you, exactly, to the minute.'

'Are you going to tell the police? They would be very interested in times and places.' He tried to sound casual but he was quaking.

'Take me out this evening and I'll think about it,' she said.

'Take you out?'

'That's right. So I can make Gary a bit jealous. You do me a favour and I'll do one for you. You don't want the police pressing for more details of what you were up to, do you, Frank?'

'I've done nothing wrong,' he mumbled.

'For sure. But meet me so we can discuss it, is it, Frank? Seven at The Railwayman's.'

'The Railwayman's? Your Gary often calls in there, doesn't he?

'Too often. That was what the quarrel was about.'

Frank made sure she didn't follow him before doing a U-turn and finding the place where he had hidden the flask. He found it easily and this time stuffed it well down into a sack of rubbish then threw it into the quarry nine miles from where he had first hidden it. Having to walk home was daunting but he set to and plodded across the fields heading for home and food and sleep.

At the gate he saw the police guard had been changed and there were now two men standing beside the back gate. He stopped, filled with alarm, and in a fluster of panic turned away from supper and sleep and went once more into the fields.

He went first to where Mair Gregory lived, and explained that he was under suspicion for something he hadn't done and pleaded for her help. With a slightly doubtful expression, she packed a bag with food and drink, and gave him a blanket. He left to find a place to hide for a few days. Once they found the van, and a few fresh clues they'd have enough to keep them busy and perhaps they'd leave him alone.

He felt sick. Why had he been so stupid? How could he have been so upset at Ernie finding himself a girl that he had allowed himself to get into this mess? Mam was right. It was time they all grew up. It seemed that he was the last one to do so!

* * *

Mair's date with Frank didn't happen, but Mair stood rather self-consciously in the Railwayman's and when Gary turned up told him she had a date with Frank. A talk of talk, a bit of flattery and Mair agreed to give him one more chance. She'd say nothing about Frank's midnight ramblings. Of course she wouldn't. Her mother might want to know what she was doing in the trees with Gary in the middle of the night.

* * *

When it was clear that Frank had run off, they all began to worry. Ernie was unwilling to go out, instead Helen came to the cottage and sat with them, as they waited for news. She played with Joseph, making pictures for him to colour until it was time for him to go to bed. She went up the stairs with Caroline and the little boy and Caroline told her she was trying to imagine where her brother would go to hide from the police. 'I wish he had spoken to me before running off,' she told Helen. 'I'd have pointed out the idiocy of such a move.'

'Your brothers must know a dozen places where they could shelter,' Helen said. 'They've spent their lives in the fields and woods. Know it like the back yard, don't they?'

'But all the places they know would be known by others. It won't take long for the police to find him.'

'Can't you think of somewhere further afield? Ten, fifteen miles wouldn't be too much for someone like Frank or Ernie or Basil. With their long legs they can eat up the miles.'

Caroline frowned and shook her head. 'I've never been involved in their ramblings, being a girl,' she replied sadly.

Barry arrived, having heard about Basil's troubles and he was told everything that had happened.

Typically, Janet's main worry was whether Frank had enough to eat and whether he was sleeping somewhere safe. Hywel didn't voice his suspicions but wondered grimly whether his stupid son *had* been involved in the robbery in some way. Why else would he have made a run for it? Neither parent considered his continued absence meant anything else but that he had gone into hiding. But where? The 'why', they didn't want to consider.

* * *

Charlie Bevan was not taken in for questioning, but the police made repeated visits, obviously curious about the scrape marks on his house and the possibility that the van that made them was involved in the robbery.

'Bashed the wall as they stopped to drop you off, did they?' he was asked.

Rhiannon went over there late one night when she saw him standing in the doorway, reminiscent of how poor Maggie Wilpin, Gwyn's great-grandmother, used to do.

'Don't let it get you down, Charlie,' she said. 'You must have expected this. With a record like yours you'll be pestered for a long time before the police are convinced you're going straight. Let it wash over you. Accept it as part of the punishment and don't let it get you down.'

'You're right,' he said and touched her arm with a hesitant affection. 'You're cold,' he said and took off his coat and put it around her. His arm stayed across her shoulders and she moved slightly towards him, a tacit acceptance of the move.

'Gertie Thomas told me that Maggie used to sit here for hours at night, unable to sleep, and waiting for me to come home,' he said softly.

'We all tried to persuade her to go inside and keep warm but she hated the night. I think she was afraid she'd die before you came home and Gwyn would be left with no one to care for him.'

'If she'd been sitting there when that lorry passed — ' He shuddered.

'Mam used to take her food sometimes.'

'I've caused a lot of trouble, haven't I?'

She moved a little closer. 'No more though. All that's finished now and your future looks good.'

'Does it?' he asked quietly. 'With you in it I'd ask for nothing more.'

She turned her head to look at him and his head came down slowly, and they kissed.

'If the frustrations and stupidities of these past years were leading me to this, Rhiannon, it will all have been worth it,' he whispered.

★ ★ ★

Ernie walked Helen home late that night and when he returned, Caroline and Barry were talking to Janet and Hywel.

'I think I know where Frank might be,' Caroline said, her dark eyes shining.

'I want to go and see, now this minute, but she insists on going herself,' Hywel said.

'I'll take you in our van,' Barry said and to Janet's sharp ears, he emphasized the penultimate word. Not *his* van but *their* van. For the first time since Caroline had left the flat, Janet felt the stirrings of hope.

Leaving word that Caroline would not be in work the following day was easy. Barry dropped a note through the door of the wool shop as he drove back to Sophie Street. They had decided to set off with a laden picnic basket, during the afternoon. That would make the reason for the drive more believable. Janet added a few words to the policeman watching the comings and goings at the gate, that the young couple had been having difficulties which they were trying to resolve.

Although it was July, the weather had refused to co-operate and there was a cloying mist over the trees that blocked out the sun and made the day humid and dull. They drove around in silence, each wanting to talk but afraid of saying something that would be misunderstood. Joseph asked questions about everything that caught his eye but they didn't answer him as fully as they would normally have done. The ride seemed long as they made their way to the village of Cwrt y Celyn, where Janet had sought news of her sister.

Taking the picnic basket and the toys, and offering a hand to Joseph, Barry walked up the overgrown muddy lane and tried to make fun of the difficult walk, for the sake of the little boy who had been so excited at the prospect of a day out with his mother and the man he had learned to call daddy. When they came out at the other end, they went to the ruinous Spring Cottage and dropped their baggage on the floor of what had once been a kitchen.

'Frank?' Caroline called. 'Frank? It's me, Caroline, and Barry and Joseph. We've come to see you.' No response so Barry joined in.

'Come on, Frank. We have a picnic to share.'

There was a rustling sound, a disturbance of straw, followed by footsteps across the partly collapsed ceiling above them, and a face peered down through a gap.

'How did you know I was here?' Frank asked.

'Caroline remembered how you had

wandered about, exploring when you drove them here to look for the missing aunt,' Barry explained as Frank moved cautiously down the staircase.

'Did you help in the robbery, Frank?' Caroline asked.

'Would I? With our Basil there?'

'Basil wasn't supposed to work that night, was he? Only George was ill and he had to change his nights.'

'Come on, Caroline, you know Frank wouldn't be that stupid,' Barry said uneasily. 'How can you ask?'

'Then come back with us,' Caroline pleaded. 'It has to be sorted and you're only prolonging it by running away like a frightened chicken.'

Frank bent his knees, crouched down, flapping his elbows and moved around doing an imitation of a frightened chicken to amuse his nephew, but Caroline was not deterred.

'Frank? Will you come with us? You can tell the police you needed time to think and if you go to them, rather than wait for them to find you, they'll have to believe it was nothing more than nerves after what has happened.'

'Caroline's right, Frank. Don't make everything worse by staying away any longer. After all, your brother was attacked, even if the weapon was only some knockout drops. To be accused of that, well, you're bound to be upset.'

'You have every right to be scared,' Caroline added.

Caroline and Barry were sitting as far apart as they were able to in the tumbled down kitchen. Both drawn and unhappy, yet so obviously aware of each other. Frank wasn't a highly intelligent man, but seeing them so afraid to touch each other, so obviously unwilling to make a move to put right their estrangement, he used their plight to take the pressure off himself, to allow himself time to ponder on what they suggested.

'At least I'm afraid of real live people. You two silly buggers are afraid of a ghost!' he snapped.

'What are you talking about?' Barry demanded. 'What ghost?'

'Your Joseph, that's what ghost!'

'We're here to talk about your problems,' Caroline said, and Barry stood up and walked about in an agitated way not looking at Caroline.

'That flat is filled with memories of Joseph and you two were stupid enough to try and make your home there.'

'You don't know what you're talking about, Frank,' Barry began, but Frank interrupted.

'And that flat is only part of the trouble, mind. Trying to make your marriage work is madness while you're both feeling guilty of cheating on Joseph.'

'Leave it, Frank,' Barry warned.

'No, I won't leave it. You both believe you're betraying Joseph, don't you? There in the flat where he was going to live with Caroline? Well, let me tell you both, the Joseph I remember would laugh at that bit o'nonsense and wish you both the best of luck!'

Frank had heard all this from Rhiannon and his parents, but had managed somehow to make it sound as though the ideas were his own. Caroline and Barry stared at each other in amazement.

'Frank! I would never have marked you up as a thinking man,' Barry said.

'I'm not stupid,' Frank retaliated.

'No, you're not,' Barry said thoughtfully.

'Can we get back to you, please,' Caroline said in a shaky voice. 'Then there's this food to eat.' She beckoned to her son and said, 'Come on, Joseph, help me set out the food on this cloth then we can have tea.'

They ate, Frank talking about anything that came into his mind to break up the horrendous silences as Barry and Caroline avoided each other's eye, and Caroline served food without coming close enough to Barry to risk their hands touching.

Frank felt ashamed of interfering and wondered if he had made things worse between them.

'All right,' he said as the food was wrapped and packed away and they prepared to leave. 'I'll come with you, right? You've talked me into it.'

'If they hadn't, we would,' a stern voice said, and four policemen appeared around the broken corner of the building.

'You never told them you were coming on a picnic, did you?' Frank said raising his eyes in disbelief. 'They'd be daft not to work out that you were meeting me and bringing supplies!'

Frank was marched back to a car waiting at the end of the lane and Caroline and Barry followed.

'They were probably listening to everything that was said,' Barry remarked. 'Thank goodness he didn't confess.'

'You don't think he *was* involved, do you?' She was trembling at the thought of the lengthy sentence that robbery on that scale carried.

Barry saw her distress and tentatively put an arm around her shoulders and drew her to walk closer to him. 'It'll be all right,

Caroline,' he said. 'Everything's going to be all right now.'

★ ★ ★

When they reached home, Basil and Eleri were there with baby Ronnie, and Caroline told them about the police following them and finding Frank.

They discussed the possibilities and Hywel went with Janet to the police station to find out what was happening.

'There's some good news,' Basil said. 'I've got another job.'

'Well done,' Caroline smiled. 'What will it be this time? Not another nightwatchman?'

'No, there's a new factory starting, making plastic brushes and combs and the like. They're importing the raw materials from America, would you believe.'

'That sounds very technical, Basil,' Barry said.

'They give you training and I don't think it'll tax my brain too much. And it's not nights, it's days, eight till five-thirty, so I'll be with Eleri every evening. Worked out for the best, it has.'

'You love being out of doors, Basil,' Barry said. 'Can you face working inside day after day?'

'For Eleri? Yes, of course I can! I'll do anything I have to, to make her happy.'

'It does sound good,' Barry said and for the rest of the evening he was deep in thought.

To everyone's relief, Frank was released. He came home with Hywel and Janet a few hours after he had been taken into custody.

'We don't know what happened, but we think one or two of the men have been caught,' Hywel told them.

'And they believe it was one of them who persuaded Basil to open the gate.'

Frank was delirious with relief, although he did have a moment of sadness when he realised he would never see those fifty beautiful pounds.

A few days later, when he saw Percy Flemming walking purposefully towards him, he began to quake. His legs went to jelly as the man drew nearer. Now would come the accusations, the reminder of his failure, the threats and warnings, but, without looking at him and hardly pausing as they passed, Percy handed him a roll of ten shilling and one pound notes.

Basil was unharmed, he and Ernie were friends again, he seemed to be in the clear, and he had his fifty pounds!

11

The excitement at the end of rationing on July 3rd 1954, which had built up during the preceding weeks, faded quickly. By the following week, people were ordering their requirements of the previously restricted foods with panache. Sandwiches were spread with butter and margarine was banned from many pantries by people who swore never to touch it again. Joints of meat and rich pies rapidly became the norm and if any ration books escaped the ash-bin they were thrown into the back of a drawer as novelties to show the children when they were grown up and could laugh at it all.

As the grocery shop closed its doors behind its final customer of the day, Helen Gunner looked at advertisements and drooled over pictures of wedding cakes made with butter, and elaborately iced, making the shortages of the war years and those that followed melt away from memory. She wondered if she would be ordering one of her own before 1954 ended. Ernie Griffiths showed no sign of becoming bored with her, in fact there was hardly an evening that they didn't meet.

She collected the simple ingredients she had bought and, dragging her gaze from the magnificence of the wedding cakes, set off home to make a butter-based sponge with real cream filling for tea the following day, which was a Sunday. Ernie was coming to tea and — that important development in the ritual of courtship — he was bringing his parents with him. Everything depended on whether her parents got on with Mr and Mrs Griffiths. Dad was all right, he wouldn't make trouble while they were there, although he would certainly kick up a fuss when they'd gone.

No, it was Mam. As long as she didn't start showing off to Mr and Mrs Griffiths about how much better the Gunners were than most of the inhabitants of Pendragon Island, all would be well, and Ernie might pop the question. From what she'd heard of the Westons, her Mam came second only to Old Gladys.

★ ★ ★

Helen's mother, Gloria, had begun life as Gwen Dunn and when she reached the age of fourteen she had decided that she deserved a more interesting name. So, against all her mother's pleadings she had renamed

287

herself Gloria and it was as Gloria she had been known ever since. Mrs Wilfred Gunner wasn't really to her taste either but she didn't know how to change it into something like De Gunnair, or she would have persuaded Wilfred to do so.

When her daughter Helen was born she had visions of the girl living out her dreams for her and becoming someone famous and important, but Helen had ignored her mother's attempts to launch her into the world of the prestigious, and left school at fourteen to start work in a grocery store. The only compensation for Gloria was that it was the largest one in the area and her daughter was quickly promoted to shop display and window dresser, besides running the provisions side of the business.

And now, when her daughter had reached the age when she might reasonably be expected to marry someone of note, Gloria had once more seen her hopes deflated. Helen had brought home one of the Griffithses. It was more than a loving mother could stand.

★ ★ ★

Helen knew there would be trouble when the two sets of parents met and had warned

Ernie not to be worried by her mother's behaviour. Ernie and she had been able to laugh at Gloria's condescending attitude once they were free from the house. But this was different. She could hardly warn Ernie's parents to ignore her mother's little digs!

The event was worse than Helen had expected. She and Ernie shared looks of embarrassment as Gloria altered her voice, quirked her little finger and performed in what she considered to be a well-bred, mannerly way. She talked with a clipped politeness and condescendingly helped them understand the correct way to hold their knives by reminding her daughter. 'Remember, dear, not like a pen,' and that was embarrassing enough. But her father joined in too.

Wilfred had been primed. That much was obvious to his anxious daughter. He didn't hide the fact that he was unhappy about his daughter marrying into the Griffiths family, although he got on exceptionally well with Ernie.

He was normally such a quiet, inoffensive man, but goaded on by looks from Gloria, he insisting on discussing why Frank had been arrested, and brought up more than once the suspicious fact of Basil working for the place that had been robbed, although Janet

289

and Hywel, with voices getting louder with each telling, explained that their sons were not, and never had been, under arrest for the crime.

'Frank was only helping with enquiries as he had been at the scene previous to the robbery,' Janet said with the light of battle in her eyes.

'And our Basil was knocked out before he even knew a robbery was taking place!' Hywel said. 'How many more times have I got to tell you? You must be *twp* if you don't understand what I'm saying. Innocent they are, the pair of them and I'll fight anyone who thinks different!'

Hywel was boiling with rage but the imploring glances from both Janet and Helen persuaded him to hold back from attack. 'Like a bad-tempered bull-dog on a frayed lead,' was how Janet described it later. So he managed to keep his temper reasonably intact, ignoring Gloria's attempts to remind them again via a reminder to her daughter, of the 'mannerly' way of using a fork. 'Index finger above the prongs, dear.'

He swallowed anger with each mouthful, as the constant gibes came fast and furious. According to Gloria, the Griffithses were honoured to be invited, not everyone was as understanding about a family known to the police. Janet saw her husband's face getting redder and redder and knew the end was near. It happened as Gloria began to serve pudding, which Gloria insisted was called dessert. He threw a dish of blancmange over Wilfred and told Gloria she was lucky he was 'mannerly' enough to hold onto the dish.

Gloria left the room and was followed by Wilfred and, as the door closed behind them, the unrepentant Hywel burst into laughter and was joined by Janet and Ernie and Helen. Life with the Griffithses was not going to be easy, Helen thought, and neither would it be dull.

'I was only trying to help,' Gloria's voice wailed through the door, and Helen began to rise.

'I'd better go and see that they're all right,' she said.

Hywel held her back and pointed to the table's centre-piece.

'What about a piece of your cake, Helen?' he whispered. 'Better than lumpy blancmange. Now, quick, before they come back and chuck us out.'

Ernie stayed back when his parents left and in the private darkness of the porch, while Wilfed and Gloria called for their daughter to, 'Come in now, this minute', Ernie proposed and Helen accepted.

'Best we wait a while before telling our mams and dads,' a happy Ernie suggested. 'At least till the blancmange is dry.'

★ ★ ★

Another couple who were seeing each other very often as the summer wore on, was Rhiannon Lewis and Charlie Bevan. Although they hadn't walked out together, Rhiannon's father had seen to that. He had forbidden his daughter to talk to Charlie, insisting that he was a jailbird and a convicted thief. No amount of argument would convince Lewis that Charlie would or could change. Until Dora stepped in.

'Don't you know that forbidden fruit is always the most coveted?' she said, when she overheard him warning Charlie off one evening. 'Besides, what's it to do with you, Lewis Lewis? You walked out of this house to live in sin with Nia Martin, so what we do is not your concern any more.'

But Rhiannon still looked up and down the street in case he was near before running across and knocking on Charlie's door. On the day she heard that someone had been arrested for the robbery of the warehouse, she went across to let Charlie know.

'They won't be bothering you again,' she said.

'Till next time,' he said sadly. 'I don't blame them, mind, once a thief always a thief. That's what most people believe.'

'I don't. I know you're trying to make a success of your life.'

'Thanks, Rhiannon. You don't know what a help that is, to know you trust me, to know you care.'

The word 'care' seemed intimate and suggested a closeness that didn't really exist and it made her blush. She started to walk away but he held her arm and said,

'I'd be so proud if you really cared about me, like I care for you.'

'Of course I care. You're a good man and I know you'll do well.'

'That sounds real boring. 'A good man'. I want you to think of me as something more than that. I like you a lot, Rhiannon, and I enjoy the time I spend with you. D'you think you could come out with me some time? For a walk perhaps? Or to the Gomer Hall dance?'

'I don't think Dad would be pleased,' she said, hesitantly.

'Good, I wasn't thinking of asking your Dad.'

She smiled and said, 'All right, I'll go

for a walk with you and Gwyn on Sunday morning. Later, perhaps we can try the dance class. I haven't been since I stopped going with Jimmy Herbert.'

One Sunday afternoon they took a very excited Polly to the crowded beach. Families were making the most of a sunny weekend and had come in their droves to enjoy a day out on the sands. The puppy smashed his way through sandcastles and picnics and headed for the waves, gambolling through them to the consternation of some and the amusement of others. Most people presumed they were a family and for Rhiannon, her outings with Charlie and Gwyn and the pup were beginning to feel like it too.

They began to go out most evenings. After a week or two, when most people had seen them together and stopped criticising her choice of companion, they began going to the dance class where they met Viv and Joan, Jack and Victoria and many others. Dora willingly looked after Gwyn, for whom it was a luxury to have someone care enough to stop him wandering the streets as he had done before his father was released from prison.

Charlie, with his easy-going manner, and with Rhiannon beside him, soon became an accepted member of the crowd. Then they began to join the crowd on Sundays for cycle rides, their walks and the rides including Gwyn. Their friendship rapidly flowered into something Dora suspected was love.

★ ★ ★

Lewis Lewis was angry; and hurt because his daughter refused to obey him any more, and he complained to Nia Martin one Sunday morning as they worked in their large garden.

'She's your little girl no longer, Lewis, love,' Nia smiled as she pruned back a straggling forsythia bush. 'She's grown up and doesn't need your advice any more.'

'If I'd been at home she wouldn't even be talking to that Charlie Bevan. I wouldn't have allowed it even if she is grown up. But I suppose by living here with you I've lost the right to say my piece.'

'Any regrets?' Nia asked.

'None.' He smiled at her affectionately. 'This is the happiest part of my life and I wouldn't change a thing.'

'I know you still miss being a part of the family and occasionally feel the loss, don't be afraid to say it.'

'All right, I do find it strange to think that Viv is getting married in a few weeks and I don't have a part in the build-up like I did when Lewis-boy was marrying Eleri. But I couldn't be happier, you must know that.'

'I know it.' She kissed him on the cheek and handed him an armful of branches. 'Shall we have a bonfire this evening?'

'For heaven's sake stop cutting then, or we'll set the road alight!'

'I do love an excuse to stay outside.' She looked up at the oldest tree in the garden, an ancient ash. 'We'll have to do something about this tree soon. Several branches look dead and next winter will see an end to it I think.'

'Don't try and do it yourself, Nia. We'll make that a job for me, and Barry when he comes. Right?'

'If you say so, although I can use a saw, you know.'

'You can, but please don't.'

'Come on, let's get the bonfire built.'

★ ★ ★

Dora was very busy. She didn't spend a lot of time worrying about her daughter, trusting Rhiannon's good sense and hoping she wouldn't be let down by the appealingly gentle Charlie. Apart from the usual warnings, about 'giving in', she allowed her to live her life without too much interference.

Beside the cafe which she ran with Sian Heath-Weston, she and Sian were using every spare moment deciding on the buffet menu for Joan and Viv's August wedding. Sian had made the cake, thankful that with rationing finally abandoned, she could follow a pre-war recipe and not struggle with replacements for the best ingredients. It was already covered with almond marzipan and awaited the final coats of icing before she somewhat nervously began the decoration.

Dora had practised a few of the most intricate designs on plates and dishes and Sian had done the same. Between them they felt moderately confident of achieving something of which Gladys would approve.

Gomer Hall, where the dances were held, was not a glamorous place, 'functional rather than ornate', was how Sian described it, but it had an adequate kitchen and there were enough trestle tables and chairs to easily accommodate the number of guests. Most families had a special tablecloth, stored in blue tissue and brought out only for special occasions. Begging and pleading didn't suit Dora's personality but as it was for her son's wedding she swallowed her pride and did so, asking everyone she knew to lend her one, and had managed to acquire fifteen white, starched cloths that would be the foundation of the table decoration.

Although rationing was no longer in force, there were many things still not easily available and cake decorations was one item they found difficulty obtaining. More scrounging, this time on the part of Sian, produced a pre-war bride and groom for the top of the cake, and Dora developed her newly found skills in making roses from icing, coloured a garish pink with cochineal.

Once the cake was ready to be iced, Sian came to seven Sophie Street and they told everyone to stay away until the job was finished. Shutting themselves in the kitchen, they began. Trying out each stage of the work before applying it to the cake, they worked in almost complete silence, following the plan they had drawn and each one concentrating on her section of the pattern. Getting the right consistency for the various designs was the hardest. Firm enough to loop without dropping in some sections, and soft enough to make the tiny flowers in another, they often felt despair approaching, but each was encouraged by the other until they recovered from the disappointments, scraped the area clear and began again.

When it was finished, they hugged each other and laughed in relief. It was finished, their first wedding cake and it was perfect.

White cake, pink roses, and leaves and stems that were white with a tinge of pink.

'It isn't moving from this spot until the wedding,' Dora announced. 'If that mother of yours wants to see it she can come here, right?'

'Right!' Sian laughed. 'And we'll warn her not to breathe, shall we?'

They arranged for Gladys and Arfon to come that evening to admire their handiwork and they arrived at seven-thirty, with Sally and Ryan and Joan and Viv.

'What the 'ell are *vol-au-vents*?' Viv demanded when he looked at the list of food Dora was planning to produce.

'Stop behaving like a lout and pretending to be as ignorant as the hoi polloi, and tell your mother how thrilled we are with what she is doing for us,' Joan demanded.

'Thank you, Joan,' Dora smiled, 'time someone reminded him about his manners. Now if you promise not to touch, come and look at the cake.'

Standing beside Sian now, and listening to the ooh's and ahh's, Dora couldn't help wondering at the remarkable changes that had taken place in the Lewis household in the past months. Entertaining people like the Westons in her small kitchen would have been unheard of a year ago. And now she was soon to be related to them. Her son was marrying the daughter of Sally and Ryan Fowler-Weston, and she was running her own business, in partnership with Sally's twin sister, Sian. And most remarkable of all, their formidable mother Gladys, was actually congratulating her on her skill.

'Now the cake is done, we ought to concentrate on Jack and Victoria. Their wedding isn't much more than a month away and so far as we know, nothing has been arranged,' Sian said.

'Victoria and Jack insist that everything is in the hands of Victoria's mother,' Dora explained. 'They'll ask for help if they want it.'

Gladys sniffed. 'I do what I can, dears, but Jack has always been stubborn. In fact all my children are strong-minded. I booked Montague Court for Joan and Viv and they went straightaway and cancelled it. I thought that was bad enough, but Jack and Victoria are worse! I can't even persuade Victoria to agree a guest list. And as for Jack, Sian dear. You and I both know he has always been stubborn, but surely a wedding has to follow some conventions?'

'Planning it all themselves aren't they?' Sally said. 'You mustn't mind if they do. Victoria is shy and I don't think Jack wants her to be unhappy on her wedding day.'

'Sally's right,' Sian said. 'Jack has made it clear that they want a small ceremony, and as few people there as possible.'

'Even Jack has to accept that the family is involved.' Gladys's voice was loud and disapproving and Dora quickly changed the subject.

'If you've all finished breathing over our cake you can sit down and Sian and I will fetch you some tea.'

'I think she means bring us some tea, dears,' Gladys said in a audible whisper.

'Any more of that and she can fetch it herself!' Dora hissed towards Sian, her blue eyes blazing.

* * *

Barry put his business, including the showroom and workshop, in the hands of an estate agent and told him he wanted a quick sale. Using every moment he could spare between appointments and clearing the flat, he finished decorating the place and making it look as attractive as possible. As a going concern it had to look tempting, if he wanted to get rid of it before Viv and Joan's wedding.

At the flat above Temptations, he sorted

out the mountain of equipment he had gathered for the photography business he no longer intended to run. Most of it would be included in the sale of the business but there were a few special items he would dispose of separately. A large advertisement in the trade magazine would hopefully see the lot cleared, then he could concentrate on the new stage of his life, a stage that would include Caroline and Joseph as a close part of it.

Caroline had no idea of what he planned. Barry didn't want to tell anyone, even his mother, before everything was settled. He had taken Basil's and Frank's words to heart and faced up to sharing his life instead of doing what he wanted and leaving Caroline on the periphery of his dreams and plans. Going to the new plastics factory he got himself a job which would start a week after Joan and Viv's wedding, which was arranged for August 14th.

* * *

With only a couple of weeks before Joan and Viv's wedding, Gladys and Sian, Joan and Megan were at the Lewis's house liaising with Dora over last-minute changes and discussing what they would each be wearing.

It was Saturday evening, and Rhiannon came in after closing the shop, with Charlie beside her.

'Mam, I've just seen Mrs Jones, Victoria's mother. She said Victoria has disappeared.'

'What on earth is the child talking about?' Gladys demanded to the others.

'That's what she said. And she went around to Jack's place and Jack's father told her that Jack has gone away for a few days.'

'Are you saying that both Jack and Victoria have disappeared?' Sian frowned.

'Together?' echoed Gladys, in the tone used by Lady Bracknell when she said 'A handbag?'

'Apparently. He didn't say where he was going, just that he and Victoria needed a break.'

Dora couldn't help feeling a bit gleeful at the consternation the couple's departure had caused. She felt quite lighthearted when, on the following Monday, several members of the family, including Viv and Joan, received postcards with the local postmark of Pendragon Island, telling them the young couple were going on holiday. There was so much consternation about them travelling together before they were married, that for a while no one thought about anything else.

'They'll be back for the wedding,' Gladys assured them repeatedly. 'Jack is Vivian's best man.'

But when the eve of the wedding arrived the only news anyone had of the couple's whereabouts was another card, posted in Eastbourne, telling them all that they regretted they wouldn't be back to see Joan and Viv married.

Gladys went from the Lewises to her daughter's house and back again hoping for news, bending the taxi driver's ear about the selfishness of the younger generation.

When they were once again gathered in Dora's house where she and Sian were making their last-minute preparations for the wedding on the following day, the only news was another card, this time from London. Ignored by Sian and Dora, who were frantically checking food lists for their largest and most important occasion, Gladys made herself a cup of tea and demanded to know what they were going to do about Jack.

'Jack's too old for us to send out a search party, Mother,' Sian said rather more sharply than usual. 'Now could you go in the other room while I take these pastries out of the oven? I don't want to risk dropping them on the floor.'

'What are they thinking of?' Gladys wailed

from the doorway. 'It's that girl's idea, all this. I know it. That's what you get when you marry beneath you!'

'Oh, Mother,' Sally sighed, wiping her arm across her hot forehead, 'Forget Jack and think about Joan. Tomorrow she is getting married to Viv, who is hardworking, clever and who loves her. Let's concentrate on that, shall we?'

'And there's another one, that Vivian Lewis.' Gladys seemed to have forgotten she was standing only a few feet from Viv's mother. 'Refusing to hold their reception in Montague Court, indeed. As if what he wants should matter a toss! Why can't you see what a disaster it all is?'

'Mother! I'm worried about my son, I'll be relieved when he and Victoria come home and explain, but, as Sally pointed out, Dora and I have a wedding to deal with tomorrow, and what can I do about Jack and Victoria anyway? Except wait and hope that they return without coming to any harm?'

'Harm? You think they're in danger?'

'No, Mother,' Sian interrupted, 'but you might be! Please move back a bit, I want to put these hot baking trays outside.'

'You shouldn't be doing this for your niece's wedding, Sian. And what about the arrangements already made for *Jack's*

305

wedding?' Gladys went on. 'Do I confirm them? It's only a couple of weeks away.'

'Put everything on hold,' Sally said, and Sian agreed.

'Tell everyone we'll let them know when we know ourselves.'

'That should give the gossips something to chew over,' Dora chuckled. 'You Westons are having quite a time of it, aren't you?'

'If people knew their place none of this would have happened!'

Dora's blue eyes took on a warning sparkle and she took a deep breath to respond, but instead she shared a smile with Sian and let the matter drop. Wherever Jack was, and whatever trouble he was making, the wedding of her son, to Gladys's granddaughter, was starting in about fifteen hours and that had to be everyone's priority.

* * *

The morning of the wedding day began with moist, thin cloud which burned away as the sun rose and strengthened. Gladys looked out of her bedroom window and wondered how it would all turn out. She had to admit that even if Viv wasn't a son of one of the better families in Pendragon Island, he was honest and he certainly had a good understanding of business. She went downstairs in her dressing gown to make her morning cup of tea, a routine she still hated not having done for her, and made up her mind that she would enjoy the day and think positively about her darling Joan's future.

At least they hadn't invited Rhiannon's awful new boyfriend, a convicted thief. He wouldn't go to the church, would he? She shuddered delicately at the thought. What were the Lewises thinking about, allowing their daughter to mix with such people? A convict was what he was, and there was no wrapping that up in delicate words to make it acceptable. The Lewises were about to be related to the Westons, surely they ought to show a bit of social conscience?

When she walked into the church, the first person she saw was Rhiannon. She sighed with relief to see that the seat beside her was empty. At least she'd had the decency to leave that Charlie Bevan out of it. Gladys studied Rhiannon and admitted to herself the girl was looking very pretty. She wore a flouncy blue silk dress with a low neck, frilled with paler blue ruffles, and a hat that seemed to frame her thick red-brown hair and make it look more luxuriant. The Lewises were quite handsome, if in a common way, so at least Joan's children would be beautiful.

She turned away to smile regally at the other guests as they arrived and were seen to their places by the ushers. Turning back to Rhiannon she covered her mouth to stifle a gasp. Charlie was there and with him his son, Gwyn. Gwyn sat beside Rhiannon but Charlie walked towards the front pew and stood there beside an elegantly dressed and startlingly handsome Viv. Surely they couldn't — they wouldn't — She turned to clutch Arfon's arm and whispered, 'Arfon, dear. Tell me, please tell me I'm mistaken. They haven't asked that Charlie person to be best man, have they?'

'Afraid so, my dear. Grin and bear it. This is Joan and Viv's day and the choice has to be theirs.'

Gladys thought she would never live down the shame, but at that moment, the organist stopped what he was playing and began the wedding march. She turned to see her granddaughter walk through the doors, a vision of loveliness, on her father's arm, and her twin sister behind her organising a recalcitrant train, and she forgot all her worries and lost herself in utter enjoyment.

★ ★ ★

Jack was working in a bar, serving drinks with skills learned in The Railwayman's over the past weeks. Sitting in the back room, having prepared lunch for the owners of the public house and their family, plus food for a few guests, Victoria sat at a small table on which stood a casserole and dishes of vegetables. She looked up expectantly as the door opened a few moments later and Jack smiled at her, kissed her and sat down opposite to share the meal.

'Are you sorry we've missed Joan and Viv's wedding?' she asked as she served him.

'Not a bit. This is much more fun,' Jack smiled. He looked at his watch. 'The wedding's all over now, except the party tonight and I'm a little bit sorry to miss that, aren't you?'

'It would have been fun, with all of your friends there.'

'*Our* friends,' he corrected gently. 'Everything I have is yours and that includes my best friends.'

'Oh Jack, this is scary, but it's fun too. Imagine everyone's faces if they knew where we were. They'd never believe we were here, in Scotland, waiting to be married in Gretna Green.'

★ ★ ★

Jack had perfected his skill as barman during their time in Scotland, and Victoria had learned to cook for a crowd and had enjoyed experimenting with new recipes. In their spare time they had walked around the lovely border countryside and taken photographs and treated the weeks of waiting as a honeymoon but without the loving. That would have to wait, Jack had decided. When they were back in Wales and settled in their own home, then he could introduce her to the magical joy of sharing their lives completely.

He looked at Victoria as she rose to take their dishes over to the large sink below the window. Her hair was escaping from its pins and her face was flushed from cooking. How lucky he was to have found her and faced the criticism and teasing. There would never be a moment in the years ahead when he would forget how lucky he was.

'Come here, Victoria my love,' he whispered. 'I have an overwhelming desire to kiss you.'

Victoria had relaxed and opened out in the absence of Gladys and Arfon and the rest of Jack's family. Warm and loving, and finding the natural social skills that had previously been hidden by shyness, she had easily made friends among the softly spoken Scots in the friendly border town.

Attending to the bedrooms when guests were staying was nothing new and cooking meals — sometimes at short notice — no longer held terrors for her.

'Nothing could be more terrifying than working for your grandmother, Jack,' she admitted, making him laugh at one of her rare and mild complaints.

Wild flowers, opening a little later than at home, delighted her. And the wild animals with which the fields abounded seemed less afraid and would allow them to step quite close.

'Better not tell Basil, Frank and Ernie,' she warned.

★ ★ ★

Frank was working in the house Jack and Victoria had bought to begin their married life. While time dragged a little for them in Scotland, impatient as they were to spread their news, Frank was thinking how quickly the next couple of weeks would pass. He had to finish papering the main bedroom that day to keep to his schedule and it was going hard. He was counting the days to the time Victoria and Jack were due to return and there didn't seem enough hours in the day or days in the week for him to complete the surprise Jack had arranged for his bride.

He had promised to finish redecorating the whole house and make sure all the furniture was back in place and the curtains re-hung, and time was too short. He was even missing the party to celebrate Viv Lewis's wedding. If ever a man suffered, he moaned to himself.

If only he had persuaded Ernie to forget Helen for a few nights and help, the task wouldn't have been so daunting. But he and Ernie were not the friends they once were. He wondered whether Basil might take pity on him and give a hand. To help the job along he promised himself a pint after hanging three more lengths and cheated by choosing short ones.

★ ★ ★

Gladys put on a brave expression, but the wedding was a disappointment. Apart from Joan making such a stunningly beautiful bride of course. But the day wasn't over and there were other shocks awaiting her that day. The first being the arrival of Terrence Jenkins, a cousin of the Jenkinses of Montague Court, on the arm of her other granddaughter, Megan.

The last she had heard of him was a

whispered hint from Sally that he had not been very gentlemanly towards Megan. That was after two thugs had invaded her Christmas party and picked a fight with him. Such embarrassment her family had suffered. She frowned at Megan and beckoned her over.

'Why is Terrence here, dear? I thought after his dreadful, loutish behaviour at Christmas he wouldn't show his face.'

'I invited him, Grandmother.'

'But why?'

'Oh, we had a few misunderstandings and I thought if we cleared them up we might be friends again.'

'I suppose we might give him another chance,' Gladys frowned. She couldn't face another confrontation at the moment. And, she reminded herself, he is a Jenkins of Montague Court. 'Invite him to tea tomorrow,' she added.

Terrence had written several times to Megan and receiving no reply hadn't deterred him. The letter from Jack, with postcards enclosed which Jack asked him to post in various parts of London and Sussex, was intriguing, and using the excuse of visiting his family, he had arrived at Megan's door in time to be invited to attend the wedding of Viv and Joan.

He hadn't been able to forget Megan, and even though he had probably ruined things by his lack of patience, rushing her into taking their friendship too far too soon, he thought it worth another try.

Megan had greeted him coolly when he had knocked on her door, but there had been an expression in her dark eyes that had given him hope, and when he asked her to go with him to have tea at Montague Court with his cousins, Margaret and Edward, she had accepted. That had been a few days ago and now they were attending the wedding of Megan's sister and, albeit through gritted teeth, Gladys Weston had invited him to tea on the following day.

★ ★ ★

Megan had always been as outrageous as her wealth and social position had allowed. Although it had usually been her twin, Joan, who set the pace and dared the most audacious dares, Megan had been a slightly more hesitant but nevertheless willing partner. With Joan married and Jack about to do the same she had felt an upsurge of resentment fired by the fear of loneliness, and opening the door to see Terrence there, smiling his special smile, she had seen a way

314

to bring a bit of excitement into her life.

It was more than the chance to upset her family, although that was something she would enjoy. She knew that amongst the boys and men she had encountered, Terrence Jenkins was the only one with whom she could imagine falling in love. There was a strange restlessness about her, a disturbance of her deepest nerve endings when she saw him, and when he touched her it was electric. Perhaps she wouldn't need to be alone for long.

★ ★ ★

Dora watched her daughter dancing with Charlie and saw a love affair in the making. Charlie was far from handsome. Ordinary-looking in fact, she mused. But then, her Lewis had been the best looking young man in the town and look how far that had got her! Here she was celebrating their son's wedding on her own and Lewis was skulking about with Nia Martin on his arm, wanting to be part of it all and at the same time wishing he were miles away.

Amid the celebratory chatter and the dancing and laughter, there was an under-current of concern for the whereabouts of Jack and Victoria. Mrs Jones, Victoria's mother was the only one aware of the secret and she smiled to herself as she watched the family discuss the disappearance in their various ways. Another two weeks and they will all know the truth. Two whole weeks. It was a long time to hold the secret. More than two weeks had already passed since they left, each day dragging itself to a close. Not sharing Frank's workload, she knew that for her, the next two would go so slowly.

* * *

Two weeks after Joan and Viv were married, Victoria and Jack walked down the aisle in the small village of Gretna Green. Their wedding day was as perfect as Jack had promised. A large number of local people who had got to know the young couple turned up to see Victoria arrive at the church in her beautiful dress. And they stayed to cheer and throw flowers as they walked from the church to the Blacksmith's Shop, an ancient site where the traditional anvil weddings had taken place for centuries.

For this second ceremony, several people dressed up in historic garb and one man played the role of the marriage priest, another became 'father of the bride' and sat there looking fierce with a shotgun on his arm, while the happy couple repeated the traditional Scottish oath.

It was all great fun and once it was over they both longed to return home and tell their friends all about it. But both admitted to feeling the sadness of leaving their new friends behind.

'We'll be back,' Jack promised her. 'Next year perhaps, as an old established married couple, we'll be back.'

12

Janet was surprised at the sudden change in Ernie. Since meeting Helen he was anxious to find work and seemed for ever to be asking around begging someone to give him a start. He had tried the woodyard and furniture factory, applied for the post of school caretaker and of assistant gardener at the hospital. He finally found a job, and came running through the yard filled with excitement to tell Janet and Hywel, 'I'm going to be a bus conductor. A public servant.'

'But you can't add to save your life, man!' Hywel said. 'Public servant? Public embarrassment you'll be.'

'No trouble,' Ernie said his eyes bright with excitement. 'Teach me, they will, and I want the job so much I'll be their star pupil, you just watch me.'

'Came in all fuss and feathers and told us he's got a job,' a smiling Janet told Caroline later. 'It's because of that Helen Gunner. All fired up to be respectable he is. I can hardly believe it.'

'To love someone and want to work for

them, that's wonderful. I'm so pleased for him, Mam.' Caroline's gentle smile relaxed into sadness.

'Barry worked for you, love,' Janet admonished, reading her daughter's thoughts. 'Whatever his faults you have to admit he worked for you.'

Caroline shook her head sadly. 'For himself, not me. He wanted to build up a photography business. That was his dream and Joseph and I weren't a part of it.'

It was a Sunday morning and the weather was calm. There was no wind and a weak sun bleached colours and presented a peaceful backdrop to the scene. The essence of the day, that special Sunday quiet, reminded people they didn't have to rush to work, and many took the opportunity to stay a little longer in bed and go through the motions of the early morning rituals slowly and sleepily. Outside, where the Griffiths family often took their breakfast of toast and a cup of tea, was warm and still.

Janet and Caroline had taken the card table outside and were shelling peas and peeling potatoes ready for the midday meal and in the oven the meat was beginning to send forth tantalising smells.

They heard a van but neither looked up. It would be Frank, back for something. He

319

was working at Jack's house and always running out of materials. He had become forgetful in his hurry to get the job done; dashing off very early each morning and having to return to beg or borrow things he had forgotten. Paint brushes that had to be replaced because he'd neglected to wash his own. Sugar soap he'd forgotten to buy, and which he needed to wash walls. Sandpaper for rubbing down. And always rags for wiping up mess.

'What is it this time, Frank? Run out of elbow grease?' Caroline asked, without looking up.

'It isn't Frank, it's me,' Barry said. 'I've come to ask you to come for a walk after lunch. There's something I want to discuss with you.'

Caroline looked startled at seeing him. His visits were becoming less and less frequent. She looked at her mother who nodded imperceptibly before saying,

'In that case, Barry love, you'd better stay and eat with us, unless your Mam is expecting you?'

'No, I don't go to Mam's very often. I shift for myself,' Barry replied.

Guessing that there was something very important on Barry's mind and hoping with fingers crossed so tightly they hurt, that it wasn't divorce, Janet insisted on looking after Joseph.

'You go and have your talk in peace,' she said. 'Hywel and I will entertain Joseph. He can help us make cakes for tea, eh Joseph? Dab-hand he is at mixing cakes.'

★ ★ ★

Barry drove Caroline to where they could park the van and look over the town and the sea beyond, in front of a small patch of woodland. They had left the van in a layby and walked through the fields where they had often walked in the days when they were married but just friends. Barry felt that a place where their relationship had been happy and uncomplicated, was the best place to discuss their future.

'I've sold the business,' he began, and at once Caroline's eyes clouded with alarm. This was it, he was going to tell her goodbye.

'You're going away?' she asked. 'Making a new start?'

'Only if you'll come with me,' he said. 'Caroline, I've gone about things all wrong. I expected you to support me and help in the business but gave nothing in return.'

'It wasn't easy for any of us.'

'Something went wrong right at the start

321

and I avoided it instead of trying to put it right.'

'I was to blame,' Caroline said but Barry shushed her with a gentle hand.

'It was both of us, love. We both started off with such a handicap we couldn't succeed. We both loved Joseph. Your Frank said we're both carrying a sense of betrayal and he was right. You felt you were being unfaithful to Joseph and I felt I was cheating on my brother.'

'I haven't stopped loving Joseph, I don't think I ever will, but that's in the past, only a memory.'

'Can we forget all that and start again? Right from the beginning I mean, courting like we've just met, not rushing into a double bed so we have to have Joseph between us to give us the space we both need. Just slowly and gradually, no plans, just to see where it takes us.'

'You said you've sold the business. What will you do?'

'I've got a job in the plastics factory. I started last Monday. It's a funny sort of job, machines pressing out things like combs and hair brushes and the like, but it's reasonable money and no evening work, so we'll be able to do things together like a family should.'

'You did this for me?'

'For us,' he corrected with a smile.

'You're still living at the flat?' she asked, afraid to hope that this time their rocky path might lead to something better.

'Only until you find us a place where you'd be happy,' he said. 'You and young Joseph. Somewhere far from the memories of Temptations sweet shop, but not too far from your Mam and Dad. And with places to walk and play football and do all the things I neglected to do before. Will you try again, love? D'you think we have enough to make something of our lives together?'

'I don't want to start again by making conditions, Barry, but will you promise me something?'

'Of course.'

'That if doubts creep in, we talk about everything openly and honestly.'

'That's an easy promise to give. If we'd done that to begin with we wouldn't have wasted so much precious time.' He stood up and offered her a hand to rise and they walked slowly back to the van. As he helped her in, Barry touched his lips against her forehead. 'We have to lock away the past.'

'No, neither of us wants to forget Joseph. I think we have to learn to live with our ghost, remember him with love and affection, but make sure the past doesn't ruin our future.'

Back at the Griffiths's cottage, Janet had made a cake in the hope that there was cause for a celebration. 'If not I can always feed it to the goats,' she told Hywel.

★ ★ ★

Jack and Victoria arrived home on Sunday, and the following day Jack had to be at school for the first day of term. They went first to Victoria's mother's house in Goldings Street and the whole family woke and ran down stairs to hug and kiss them both. Jack left Victoria there and went to the house he would now call home, to check that Frank and his new mother-in-law had done all he had asked and that the house was in a fit state to receive his new wife. It was six-thirty when he returned to Goldings Street to collect his bride.

They called at his parents' house at seven, banging on the door and when it opened, standing there with Jack holding out Victoria's hand for their inspection. Sian didn't say a word, she just hugged them both and burst into tears. Islwyn laughed and said, 'What a laugh! Well done, boy, well done.'

Jack wondered whether his father meant well done on finding such a lovely wife or well done for outwitting Grandmother

Gladys! He didn't care. He was home, and every day in the future his wife would be waiting for him when he returned from school, a prospect that filled him with joy.

Mrs Jones had done all they had asked and their pantry was filled and the house looked perfect when they went inside, with Jack romantic enough to insist he carried Victoria over the threshold. Supper was toast, which Jack burnt, and eggs which were forgotten so they stuck to the pan, as Jack kissed her.

His plan to take things slowly faded as she responded to his kisses and, switching off the gas cooker, he led her up the stairs.

★ ★ ★

Janet was so overjoyed to learn that Caroline and Barry were together again, or would be when they found somewhere to live, that the thoughts of finding her sister were temporarily forgotten. So receiving news of her was something of a shock, made more so by the way she came by it.

The long, stiff envelope sitting on the mat the day Jack and Victoria began their married life together, looked ominous. It had the certain look of officialdom and for the Griffithses that usually meant trouble. She took it through the house to where Hywel and Frank and Ernie were eating breakfast in the lazy morning sun and offered it to her husband.

'You two haven't been up to anything, have you?' Hywel asked of the boys, his wiry eyebrows meeting in a knitted frown.

Janet watched as Hywel's thick fingers struggled with the flap and sat as he unfolded the crisp pages and began to read. His face took on a deeper frown, then he smiled and said,

'Bad news and good, love. Your brother, Adrian, died and you inherit something or other. You have to go to the solicitor's office tomorrow morning and arrange an appointment to read the will.' He put the letter down and touched her hands, covering their smallness with his large palms and curling his fingers around them in reassurance. 'Sad to hear of a death, but don't grieve for someone you never knew.'

'I'm not going to grieve, but I wish I'd seen him before he died, just to see if he'd changed. He might have changed, Hywel.'

'No love, he hadn't changed. And I didn't like to tell you but you have seen him.'

'I have?'

'Remember that man who came to look at

the goats when we thought to sell them? The man you disliked so much you wouldn't let him have the goats?'

'That was Adrian?'

'Nasty bit of work he was, you were right to stay away from him.'

'I wonder why he came? He must have known who we were. Why didn't I recognise him? My own brother?'

'You did, love,' Hywel said softly, 'You didn't name him but you saw what he was, said he reminded you of your father, remember? You recognised that cruel streak for sure.'

'Perhaps he knew he was ill and came to say goodbye?'

'Maybe, if you can imagine him being sensitive enough to do such a thing.'

★ ★ ★

Hywel went with her to the solicitor and waiting outside the office door were two women, a small, tired-looking lady who looked about seventy-five and a woman who, Janet guessed, was in her fifties.

'Janet?' the elderly woman queried. Janet had found her sister, Marion.

★ ★ ★

327

Caroline found a flat overlooking the docks in a large house that had been converted into three flats. It had been given the grand name of Valencia Villa, and to Caroline it was perfect. The front rooms looked across the road towards the docks and from the back they looked out on a long garden which would be a perfect playground for Joseph.

When she took Barry to see it, one evening after work, she showed him around as if she were a saleswoman and he a prospective purchaser.

'Three bedrooms if you count the room they call a box room, and a kitchen and a proper bathroom and,' she announced as she opened the final door, 'the biggest living room anyone could want!'

They stood at the bay window and looked out to where ships from every seafaring nation called, bringing food and luxuries in ships with foreign names, and foreign crews, and which, once emptied of their treasures, were loaded with Welsh coal and steel to transport it far and wide. Joseph would never grow bored with watching their comings and goings.

'What d'you think?' Caroline asked, apprehensively. So far Barry had said hardly a word. He seemed to be looking at her more than the rooms she was so proudly presenting.

'Perfect,' he breathed. 'Perfect, like you.'

Caroline turned to him and in an agony of shyness, revealed by the rich colour rising on her face, said, 'This time I'll try really hard to make it work, Barry.'

'We can't fail, my love.' He kissed her and desire hardened his lips and his arms became a vice and she pulled away in something akin to fear and stared up at him, her dark eyes full of reproach.

'I'm sorry, Barry. It's no use. I can't belong to you, not like that.' Tears flooded her eyes and she whispered, 'There have been too many difficulties.'

He walked away, leaving her in the flat. After standing in the silent room for an age, she went out, closing the door on her hopes of a marriage and a home of her own, with a loud click of the key.

* * *

The two newly-wed couples settled happily into their new lives. Joan and Viv Lewis worked together at Weston's Wallpaper and Paint, and dreamed of further expansion. Victoria and Jack Heath — who to Gladys's further dismay had abandoned the addition of the name Weston — were developing a pattern of living that suited them both. Victoria was content to stay at home and keep the house perfect for Jack's return, when she would have a meal ready to put before him which they would share while they discussed the events of their hours of separation.

★ ★ ★

Rhiannon knew something was wrong with Caroline. After hearing of her meeting with Barry and their plans to find a home and begin their tortured married life again, she had expected Caroline to be excited and filled with plans. Instead, she was subdued and when they met refused to discuss her hunt for a place of their own.

'I'm sorry if I'm being nosy,' Rhiannon said when her innocent enquiries met with a blank silence. 'I thought you'd like to talk about your progress. I'm sure I would if it were me.'

'There isn't any progress. Barry and I seem to take a few steps back every time we take one forward. We seem further apart than when we made the foolish decision to marry.'

'Things are bound to be difficult, starting

with a mock marriage, but if you love each other — '

'He says he loves me but I think he's in love with the idea of being married and having a home. After all, roughing it in the discomfort of the small flat over his mother's shop isn't much of an existence, is it? No, it's that hollow miserable life he's living that makes him want to try again. Unable to go home to his mother, who's blissfully happy, settled with Lew — your father,' she amended in embarrassment. 'I think even marriage to me would be better than night after night on his own in that flat with no hope of change. Don't you?'

'That isn't why he wants you to be together! He loved little Joseph before he loved you, I think,' Rhiannon said trying to be completely honest. 'But love for you quickly followed. I could see it happening, remember. In his heart he gradually left me and turned to you. He wants a home and a family, but only with you.'

'I keep seeing Joseph when he comes near,' Caroline whispered. 'Instead of seeing Barry I see Joseph and then he's all wrong. Oh, I know it sounds as if I'm in love with a ghost but it isn't like that. I want to love Barry but I can't help thinking that we both still love Joseph too much.'

'Perhaps Barry knows that, he might even think that every time he touches you, you're wishing it was Joseph.'

'Then how can we ever put things right between us?'

'Determination to make it work is the only way.'

'Wanting to isn't enough,' Caroline sighed.

'I'm dreaming of having a place of my own, too,' Rhiannon told her.

'You and Charlie Bevan?'

Rhiannon nodded. 'Most people accept that he's given up his criminal past, all, that is, except our Dad.'

'It's never easy, is it?' Caroline sighed.

★ ★ ★

Rhiannon and her courtship with Charlie was once more the subject of conversation in Nia and Lewis's house in Chestnut Road. Lewis was trying to think of ways to persuade his daughter to stop seeing the man.

'Leave them, Lewis, love,' Nia pleaded when he complained to her about how often Rhiannon was out with 'that damned ex-jailbird'.

'He's more than an ex-jailbird, my dear. No one is simply how one person sees him. You have one opinion of Charlie, I have another and Rhiannon a different one again. Three impressions and Charlie is all of them. Rhiannon believes he will stay on the path of honesty and why should we think we know better? Let's give him the support she wants us to give. That way she'll relax and look at things more calmly. If we continue to fight her on this she might jump too soon into the biggest mistake of her life.'

Lewis saw the sense of her words and when Nia suggested inviting Rhiannon and Charlie and young Gwyn for tea that weekend, he agreed.

'Whole-heartedly mind, Lewis love,' she warned gently. 'If you're thinking of using the invitation as an excuse for gibes and accusations, best we leave it.'

'All right,' he smiled, kissing her cheek, 'you've convinced me I have to behave.' He kissed her again and added, 'I'll get sweets and a present for young Gwyn. What d'you think he'd like, a jigsaw puzzle?'

'A water bottle or a new bell for his bike might be better,' she suggested. 'He loves that bike, and he goes for quite long rides with Rhiannon and Charlie on Sundays.'

Lewis agreed, told her she was wonderful and decided to buy all three.

★ ★ ★

It was with some trepidation that Charlie, dressed in his smartest suit and a new tie bought for him by Rhiannon, walked up the drive and knocked on the door of Nia's house. Lewis answered the door, and, with what was obviously a forced smile, welcomed them inside. Nia kissed Rhiannon and gave Gwyn a hug and led them out into the garden.

The garden was quite large with shrubs and a few old trees with one or two flower beds, a perfect place for Gwyn to explore. Leaving him to his own devices, the four adults sat in the chairs set out near the rose bed and talked.

Lewis said little. Promising Nia he would say nothing impolite had robbed him of anything to say. But Nia and Rhiannon chatted easily and brought Charlie into the conversation like experts. He eyed the young man warily and had to admit that he seemed genuinely fond and respectful of his daughter.

Charlie continually glanced around checking on what his son was doing. When he hadn't heard or seen him for a few minutes he went to investigate. Lewis followed him as he left the group and wandered towards the largest tree. Looking up, Charlie called,

'Come down, Gwyn. You should ask before

you do anything like climb a tree. This isn't a park, remember.'

Clambering down easily, then hanging onto a branch with one hand, Gwyn swung until his father stepped forward and helped him to the ground.

Nia had followed them and she said,

'I really don't mind you climbing the trees, Gwyn, but that one isn't safe. A few branches have fallen and I think it should come down. I'm so worried that it'll fall while little Joseph is here.'

'Next weekend, I promise,' Lewis said.

'Want a hand?' Charlie offered and with a glance from Nia, Lewis accepted his offer.

'Next Saturday?'

'Right then,' Charlie said happily. 'Saturday afternoon it is.'

Rhiannon went home feeling reassured that, once her father really knew Charlie, he wouldn't raise any objections to their marrying.

* * *

Since that first brief meeting at the solicitor's office, Janet Griffiths and her sister Marion Jolly hadn't met. Marion had made excuses for every suggestion that their families should meet. There was a lack-lustre look

335

in Marion's eyes as if the thought of getting to know her relations was too much of an effort. Now, at the meeting arranged to hear the reading of Adrian's will, while she stared at her sister and tried to encourage her to smile, Janet learned that they were joint inheritors of their father's farm.

It was a shock for Janet. Having had no news of her brother during all the years she had been away, she had presumed he had married and had children of his own to whom the farm would pass. Knowing he had lived his life alone, with only occasional help, saddened her.

'I should have at least made enquiries and tried to help him,' she told her newly-found sister. 'I was so glad to get away, and Hywel and I have been so happy, I've hardly given Adrian a thought.'

Marion, who lived less than fifty miles from Pendragon Island, shrugged away the regret. 'You can't think with today's attitudes and information of what you should have done years ago. Then you were still hurt and angry at the way he treated us, and of his cruelty to anyone near enough to be at the receiving end of his fury. That couldn't be altered. From what I've learnt, he didn't change even slightly from the bully we remembered. So, no regrets as we see him go to his grave.

'Unpleasant and ugly,' she went on in her monotonous voice. 'That was how he was and always had been. Neither you nor I could have changed him, no matter how we tried. We'd have been hurt, and perhaps we'd have hurt our families too. We were right to leave him be.'

Marion spoke without compassion and she seemed to Janet to lack all humour, as her small attempts to raise a smile were ignored.

They had arranged for Adrian to be buried in the churchyard near the farm, and the branch of the family hitherto unknown to Janet, that had begun with Marion, were coming to the cottage for the internment. Marion's sons, Fred and Harold were there with their families and her adopted daughter, Elenor.

On the day of the funeral, all these strangers filed into the small house and nodded in an uninterested way before sitting down; the men with their flat caps on their knees, the women with hands in their laps, folded, palms up.

Such a houseful. People from all over the town of Pendragon Island, many who hardly knew of the existence of Janet's brother, walking across the fields, sure of a welcome. Marion's family were all neatly dressed but showed a distinct and unmistakable lack of money. For Marion and her family, life had obviously been far from kind. Looking at the bunch of her younger generation, Janet was proud of the way her sons and daughter looked.

Ernie had been persuaded by Helen to buy a new suit which he assured everyone would do for hatches, matches and dispatches for at least ten years. Barry and Caroline came in smiling in pretence of being a couple, and were dressed in best clothes, and had even bought Joseph a suit as a mark of respect for the man only three people there had ever known. Basil and Frank looked as though they were employed as official mourners so experienced were they in following funerals for a small fee and setting the solemn tone.

At the cemetery the grave-digger carried his tools to Adrian's grave in preparation for filling it in. He was cursing his assistant, who hadn't dug the plot deep enough. Now he'd have to sort that out before filling in, or there'd be hell to pay. Afternoon burials were a real bind, and he muttered to himself as he made his preparations. There was to be another burial early the following day, so he had to get this one looking tidy so as not to upset tomorrow's mourners. Tomorrow's was a second burial, a widower to be buried with his wife. He checked his plan briefly and began. With the help of his assistant he hauled the coffin to the surface to dig deeper as instructed.

Leaving the coffin covered with a tarpaulin and flowers, he decided that there was time for a pint before tackling the task and he dug his spade into the earth to leave it standing upright and walked off. The spade wavered a while then fell with a spurt of earth, to land between Adrian's plot and the next.

The grave-digger walked across the church-yard and out of the gate, the thought of a beer increasing his speed, and was hit by the car carrying a family bringing flowers to a deceased loved one. He was taken to the accident hospital for treatment, so it was his assistant who later went up to finish what the man had begun.

★ ★ ★

At the Griffiths's cottage, more and more people arrived, muttered their condolences, and their congratulations on the inheritance. They were introduced to Marion and offered food and drink. The sawn-off tree-trunks were brought into use again, as well as boxes and bins to seat them all. Marion and her sons and daughters were bemused by it all.

Lewis came with Nia, and sat beside his estranged wife, Dora, without any obvious signs of anger. In fact, Dora and Lewis talked easily and seemed more like friends than the combatants of a bitter separation.

After the pain of Lewis's betrayal of her with Nia who had once been her friend, Dora had learned to accept the situation, although she still felt the agony of loving someone who had spurned her. She was, if not content, well pleased with the way her life was developing.

Marion and her family remained formal and left early. For the rest, the gathering didn't disperse until about two in the morning. The lively chatter had reached a peak and subsided and all those present were sated with news of people they didn't know, passed on by those whom they rarely met. The occasion had gone through the usual phases of uncomfortable shuffling and over-politeness, with the unfamiliar mix of people hardly known to each other, and the uncertainty of how to behave, and on through the relaxation of becoming friends, until the party spirit was reached and everyone had a good time.

When the last of the mourners left, laughing and joking in the way of many funerals, Ernie and Frank went to stand outside in the cool of the night, too hyped-up to think of sleep. The finality of death had made them both consider their disagreement and reminded them how easy it would be for their separation to continue into the years ahead.

There was a full moon and together they made their way to the cemetery, not with any goal in mind but with the casual wandering that had often taken them to places unplanned. The open grave looked eerie in the moonlight and they went closer, daring each other to lean over and see whether the coffin was visible or if the grave had been filled. To their surprise the grave appeared empty.

'Someone's stolen the old bugger,' Frank muttered.

The grave next to that which they had been told was intended for their uncle, was filled, the earth left loose and rather untidy. Frank reached across to try and see the label on one of the wreaths and his foot sank into the soft earth. He gave a yell and they both decided to leave the churchyard to its ghosts and go home to bed. But they were still puzzled by the fact that the wrong grave appeared to have been filled.

* * *

The following day they were still unsatisfied and they went once again to the cemetery. The funeral at the grave next to Adrian's was of a Mr Gareth Pryce-Yeoman, and would take place at eleven that morning, so Ernie and Frank attended and stood beside the grave with the rest of the mourners. When the service was over they asked the grave digger's assistant where they could find information on the graves and the allotment of them.

Enquiries told them that the grave they had just seen filled with the widower was in fact the wrong one. His predeceased wife was buried in the one alongside. Their uncle had been buried in the grave intended for Mr Pryce-Yeoman.

'Something will have to be done!' Frank gasped. But although they gave the facts to as many people who would listen, it seemed impossible for the wrong to be put right. No one believed them. The two graves, in a row of seven recent internments, appeared to be correct, as set out in the reference books. So far as everyone associated with the church and its cemetery were concerned, the burials had been carried out as planned. The flowers decorated the correct grave, the labels and numbers all tallied. Their uncle was apparently buried in the correct grave and Mr Pryce-Yeoman was sharing his final abode with his wife.

Frank and Ernie were so incensed by this treatment of an uncle they had never known, their damaged friendship was instantly repaired. Even Janet and Hywel were unconvinced that a mistake had been made.

The relations of Pryce-Yeoman were also unconvinced and politely, if a little anxiously, said they were only too glad to trust the efficiency of the service, and advised them to forget it. The complications that such a puzzle entailed were alarming and they insisted that everything was sure to be exactly as it should be. Only Frank and Ernie refused to accept it.

'That grave was empty!' they insisted.

'Drunk you were, mind,' Hywel pointed out. 'I bet you couldn't remember which one it is even now, if we took the flowers away.'

'I would,' Frank insisted and Ernie echoed his assurance, insisting that he'd be blowed if he'd been too drunk to make a mistake like that.

★ ★ ★

The farm was for sale and a buyer had already made moves towards taking it over before the funeral had taken place. In fact the animals were being cared for by him and it seemed that the sale would go through with little delay. The solicitor sent for the two sisters and told them that when the farm was sold and outstanding debts paid, they could expect a sum of around nine hundred pounds each. They looked at each other when the solicitor told them this, each feeling pleasure that was mixed with guilt.

'How can we accept so much money from a brother we disliked and never saw?' Janet said.

'If you don't it will go into the coffers of the government and it's hardly enough to effect the National Debt, is it?' the man smiled. 'These things happen so rarely in life I advise you both to take the money and enjoy it. It could change much of what you dislike in your lives without ruining the things you enjoy.'

'I live in two little rooms, and with Henry and Fred and Elenor so busy with their own lives, I get a bit lonely,' Marion said. 'Perhaps I could buy a house in Pendragon

344

Island and share some time with you?' she said to Janet.

'From what you've told me, you two have a lot to catch up on, so if it's what you both want, I think it a splendid plan.' He wished them both well and promised to help them in the future should the need arise and they went out of his office feeling dazed.

Janet and Hywel's first idea was to share the money between their children.

'After all, we have all we want and they're just starting off,' Janet said. But when they mentioned it to the family there was a loud chorus of protest.

'You and Dad should have some fun with it,' Basil said. The others agreed but Hywel looked around at his family and shook his head.

'Fun we have in plenty with you lot!'

'A holiday then?' The ideas flew for days but as nothing they suggested appealed to Hywel or Janet all thought of the importance of Adrian's money faded.

★ ★ ★

Frank and Ernie finally convinced Basil that their uncle was buried in the wrong grave and as time passed their determination to put the matter right increased.

'We can't have an uncle lying on top of Mrs Pryce-Yeoman for ever and ever, Amen, can we?' Frank shouted one day. 'It isn't decent!'

'Put like that, I have to agree,' Basil said with a grin. 'All right, but what d'you suggest? You've told everyone we can think of and no one believes you.'

'Swop them over ourselves, that's what,' Frank said.

Without allowing too much time to pass, believing that time might persuade Basil they were wrong, Frank and Ernie arranged to go to the cemetery with spades and shovels that night. Being a Saturday, Basil was in the habit of calling at The Railwayman's for a drink with his friends. So he did the same as usual, only he had taken the precaution of snaring a dozen or so rabbits first. As long as they weren't caught in the churchyard actually in the act of desecrating the graves, they would be able to justify their late night walk.

Viv was in The Railwayman's on one of his now rare visits, preferring, as he did, to go out with Joan. He was sitting with Jack as the brothers walked in. Viv and Jack guessed at once that the Griffithses were up to something.

'Tell me or I'll call the cops,' Viv warned

and Jack repeated his threat.

'It would be handy to have a few extra hands,' Ernie said hopefully.

Thinking of all that heavy digging, Frank agreed.

They left the pub at intervals, Jack going home to warn Victoria he would be late and to pick up a spade. Viv running home to tell Joan.

But unlike Victoria, who was content to wait until Jack decided to explain, Joan insisted on being told exactly what was going on.

'I'm going with you,' she said when she had been told. And when Viv argued she threatened to telephone the police.

'That's what I threatened,' he grumbled. 'And now I'm involved in an illegal act.'

'I'll be your lookout, I bet none of you thought of that! I'm coming to make sure the lot of you don't end up in prison!' Joan wore her most determined expression and Viv knew it was useless to argue further as she reached for her coat.

Basil undid the door of the churchyard maintenence shed half-hidden by the prickly remains of last summer's roses, and took out a large rubber sheet which they placed beside the grave to hold the excavated earth. They emptied the two graves without much effort, there having been little time for the earth to become compacted. Joan shut her eyes tightly as the coffins were exchanged. But she listened to the comments and was relieved to hear them agree that Frank and Ernie had been right and the graves had contained the wrong bodies.

They had achieved the job so far with very little noise and it was only when confidence grew and Frank and Ernie began to noisily scrape their tools to reduce the amount of mud sticking to them as they filled the last inches, that the tramp, who had been sleeping behind one of the ancient mounds, woke and looked across to see what had disturbed him. Then, on silent feet he ran to the phonebox and dialled 999 and sat back to watch the fun.

* * *

When they heard the sound of a car approaching, the five gathered their tools and ran, Viv grabbing Joan's arm and hurrying her along, heading for the shelter of a wood. Once there they whispered together and decided that they should cross the fields belonging to Farmer Booker and if possible, rouse him and make sure they were seen. It would give them an alibi of sorts.

Walking close to the farm house and disturbing the dogs was simple enough and when Booker came out with a shotgun in his hands, Basil, Frank and Ernie made sure they were seen and recognised.

When Janet heard that her sons were under arrest for poaching she looked at Hywel and gave a sigh.

'And there's us wondering how to spend Adrian's money!' she sighed. 'We need to keep it for paying our sons' fines!'

13

The Rose Tree Cafe was a popular place for women to meet after their shopping, for a coffee and a chat with friends. By extending the range of food offered, Sian Weston and Dora Lewis had developed a lunchtime trade that attracted more and more men. Businessmen, reps mostly, would call, sure of a reasonably priced, well-cooked meal.

'When the women go home, the men come in,' Sian smiled. 'The business is as sexually divided as parties are, women in one group the men in another.'

'And the men have the best stories!' Dora sighed.

It was eleven in the morning when Jimmy Herbert called in. He looked at the crowded room and, realising the occupants were all women, he hesitated, then began to retreat.

'It's all right, Jimmy,' Dora called, 'come through to the kitchen and I'll find you a cuppa.'

Between serving, Dora chatted to him, guessing he had come to ask about Rhiannon. 'I didn't see you at the Griffithses at the weekend,' she said. 'Didn't you get an invite?'

'Yes, but I thought I'd better stay away. I asked Rhiannon but she was going with Charlie.'

'Don't give up on her, Jimmy,' she advised. 'Charlie has her sympathy. He's a whipped dog, isn't he? Her interest might be short-lived. Once he's on his feet and secure and no longer needing her help, he might lose his appeal.'

Sian's twin sister, Sally, came as Jimmy was leaving. The cafe began to empty and she came into the kitchen where Dora was setting out the lunchtime menu and declared she was exhausted.

'Ryan does nothing to help and it's a full-time job looking after house-guests,' she complained.

'Kick him out,' Dora muttered.

'Mother was very upset about Jack's Gretna Green wedding, Sian,' Sally said. 'What can I do to cheer her up? I do think you should have stopped them running away like that.'

'How could I? I didn't know any more than anyone else.'

'Victoria's mother knew.'

'Well she didn't tell me! Now, if you aren't going to help, can you move out of the way,

Sally? Dora and I have about half an hour before the rush.'

'You couldn't let me have half a dozen pasties could you? I'm stuck for supper for my paying guests and I want to have my hair done.'

As Sian began to collect six pasties, Dora said, 'No, we can't, Sally. Sorry, but I spent two hours last night after a day working here, to make them.'

Sally looked put out and turned to her sister for support.

'Sorry, Sally, Dora's right, time is money.'

'Then don't let me take any more of it!' Sally picked up her coat and rushed out.

'Sorry, Sian. I should have put that more diplomatically.'

'My fault. I didn't think. Your time is as valuable as hers.'

Their next visitor was Lewis. In her forthright way, Dora said, 'If it's lunch you want it'll be half an hour yet.'

'No, I haven't come for lunch, although a cup of tea would be welcome. It's about Rhiannon.'

'She's all right, isn't she?' Dora frowned. 'Nothing's happened?'

'If you call being seen with Charlie Bevan and that son of his all right, then she is!' he snapped.

'Oh, go away, Lewis. So far in the last hour we've had Jimmy flopping about in lovelorn despair, Sally telling us how hard she works and how hard done-by she is, and now you. We're trying to run a cafe, not a problem page!'

Lewis put down the tea Sian had handed him and left.

Dora gave a deep sigh. 'Who next?' she asked, hands on hips. 'Because whoever it is, while we're sorting out their problems I'll set them to wash these pots!'

★ ★ ★

Getting to know Marion and her children was fun for Janet, at first. She quickly realised they were going to prove difficult to integrate, for, try as she might, the new members of her family were reticent, afraid to relax and join in the lively gatherings. There was also a hint of disapproval which she tried to ignore. Elenor, Marion's adopted child, was unmarried and had worked as a live-in housekeeper for several years, content to own little more than most children possessed, in a tiny room with a lavatory and wash-basin close by.

Elenor loved children but, at fifty, had long forgotten her yearnings for one of her own. With her un-tapped motherly skills she indulged her nieces and nephews, the children of her two brothers, Harold and Fred. Not extravagantly, she assured Janet, she considered that was wrong; spoiling children was not character-building. But she gave them a small gift on their birthdays and on occasions a non-frivolous book that would help them with their schoolwork.

Janet thought Elenor was the most boring person she had ever met.

Elenor's life was quiet and orderly with three and a half weeks at the house where she worked, then a long weekend spent sharing her mother's tiny flatlet, catching up on news of the family and walking in the fields near their home.

To have suddenly been introduced to the Griffithses was a shock, and one which she did not seem to enjoy. They broke all the rules of behaviour she had learned over the years of living in other people's houses, rules which insisted she remained at all times unobtrusive and hardworking. The old Victorian family's adage of children being seen but not heard applied with greater force to their servants.

To her, the Griffithses were unmannerly and rowdy, and she frequently took offence at their natural friendliness, and considered their questions an affront.

Marion excused her to Janet and Hywel, explaining that, with so little experience of people, she had been taught by her various employers that people in her position were expected to behave in a manner deemed not to cause offence to others. To this end Elenor had quashed her curiosity and with it any thoughts of betterment.

Janet bravely decided that, dreary though she might be, her 'poor dear niece' was not too old to change.

'Although,' she admitted to Hywel, 'I know I have an uphill battle on my hands if I hope to persuade the poor, dear woman to liven up and come out of the shadows.'

Marion's sons, Harold and Fred, were settled in the first job they had been offered, and seemed content to remain there. Harold was a sweeper-up in a factory and his brother travelled on a bicycle as a jobbing labourer working on a number of farms in the area.

They were abysmally formal and uneasily over-polite. Even when confronted by Frank wearing underpants wandering around looking for trousers that Janet had 'stolen' to wash they said nothing, but backed away looking at each other like cornered mice. Janet and Hywel had invited them to spend an evening with them, but as the talk became more uninhibited and the laughter loud and regular they made their excuses and left. Only Marion seemed prepared to learn to like them and for this, Janet was grateful.

'How sad it would be if, after finding each other we had nothing to say,' she sighed when she and Hywel had seen the family off after another tedious visit.

'Truth is, love, there isn't anything *to* say. You and Marion have led such different lives. Hers is considered a success if she 'keeps herself to herself', pays her bills, and is thought to be a decent and honest woman. They're strangled in respectability and keeping their place. How can you expect them to understand why we live like we do? Best you don't hold out too much hope of becoming friends,' he said gently. But Janet was still convinced that all her sister needed was encouragement to open out and let some fun enter her life. Surely a sister of hers couldn't enjoy being manacled by convention?

As time passed, the invitations still went out, but the new family members, apart from Marion, always declined. Janet waited for an excuse to arise to have a real party. It wouldn't be long, excuses to invite friends around to celebrate something or another weren't that infrequent in the Griffiths' household. That would make Marion and her children relax and enjoy being a part of the family.

Ernie and Helen's engagement was what Janet was waiting for although, having to suffer the inhibitions of her new family as well as the pretentiousness of Helen's mother might be a lot to cope with. Ernie's future mother-in-law, Gloria Gunner, was worse than Gladys Weston. At least Gladys once had money and background to account for it.

Once Ernie had confided in her that their announcement would be soon, on Helen's birthday, the first thing she had to do was convince Gloria and Wilfred that their house was not a suitable venue for the celebration, while hers and Hywel's was the perfect choice.

To her relief Gloria readily agreed.

'Wilfred and I will be getting the back rooms decorated for the young couple, the house will be in too much disarray to think of a party,' she explained.

And when is mine not? Janet asked herself.

Helen's mother had generously told Ernie he and Helen could start their married life with her and Wilfred, using the two back rooms and sharing the kitchen. Gloria wasn't too happy about this arrangement.

She wondered whether Ernie — him being a Griffiths — had been taught the basic rules of cleanliness. But at least she would be able to keep an eye on him and make sure he treated her daughter properly.

The engagement party was planned for the end of November and with no rationing to outwit, Hywel thought the preparations seemed rather tame. But with the house filled to bursting and all the food they could need, Janet was sure it would be a success, and it would show Marion's dull lot how to have fun.

★ ★ ★

Nia was looking out of the window at her garden. Since Lewis had come to live there, she had been left with little to do. He insisted on someone to help with the housework and had taken over much of the maintenance outside. He came with her when she chose new shrubs, ostensibly to help carry them, but she usually ended up with his selection and not her own.

She didn't really mind, she knew Lewis had always enjoyed working on a garden and when he had lived with Dora he had produced large quantities of vegetables and flowers from the plot behind seven Sophie

Street. But besides doing the heavy work, he had taken over the organising of it and on occasions she missed not having an excuse to spend the day outside. She had always found satisfaction in spending a day sorting out, cutting back then having a huge bonfire to get rid of the unwanted vegetation.

Today was a particularly long and lonely one. When he worked locally, Lewis always managed to call in at some time during the day, sometimes even to eat lunch with her. Travelling in the Brecon area as he was today, he wouldn't be back until late this evening and the long hours stretched before her and made her restless.

She looked at the tree he had promised to cut down weeks ago. Charlie had been more than willing to help, he had even offered to do it himself, but Lewis always made some excuse. He didn't want to show in the slightest way that Charlie could become an accepted member of the family. He had to discourage Rhiannon from seeing the man, he told Nia frequently, and not actively encourage him, by accepting his help. So, because of Charlie's offer to help, which Lewis couldn't — or wouldn't — accept, the tree remained in its precarious state.

The large branch on which young Gwyn had swung looked dead and must be weak.

And with winter approaching with its storms she knew it represented a danger as it hovered over the place Joseph liked to play with his toys, several of which were still there, under the tree waiting for him. His tricycle, and the cars and lorries filled with earth, and the beautiful ride-on waggon Barry had made. When weather permitted, she and Lewis often sat, even now with winter on the way, to sip a drink and enjoy the peace of the place.

It was Wednesday, so Caroline might come with Joseph. But they wouldn't be here until at least three o'clock. Plenty of time to take a saw to the branch and make it safe. Lewis would be cross with her but it would be too late to stop her, she mused. And he was never cross with her for long.

★ ★ ★

Caroline left her mother's house, intending to go straight to Chestnut Road, but on the way she changed her mind and went instead to see Rhiannon.

'I'm on my way up to see Barry's mother — why don't you come with us?' she asked when Rhiannon had told her she had nothing planned for her half-day.

'Love to. Let's go the long way round

360

and walk through Pigog Wood first,' she suggested. 'Little Joseph would love to play a game of hide and seek with us among the trees.'

Taking a few cakes and some chocolate in case Joseph got hungry, they set off intending to reach Nia's by four o'clock.

'Just in time for tea,' Caroline said. 'She looks forward to seeing Joseph and always makes a cake on Wednesdays in case we call. I think she's a bit lonely sometimes after being used to working in the shop, so I try not to disappoint her.'

'Does Barry see his mother regularly?'

'Not really. She doesn't say, but I don't think she sees him as often as she would like.'

'Life's never perfect is it?' Rhiannon sighed. 'With plenty of money and my Dad to keep her happy, she still has her disappointments.'

'And I'm the worst of them,' Caroline said sadly. 'My failure to make Barry happy.'

'You and Barry, there's been no change?'

'No change.'

★ ★ ★

Nia soon realised the saw wasn't as easy to handle as it appeared to be when used by

361

Barry. She had watched him making a variety of items from large pieces of furniture to the many smaller things, like toys for Joseph and picture frames for his photographs and, like most experts, he had made it look simple.

Now, balanced on a step ladder and using both hands to push the awkward tool through the branch, she was aching with the effort as the saw continually stuck in the cut. Her hands were blistered, and her head ached and her wrenched shoulder muscles felt as if they were about to split.

She was tempted to abandon the idea, but knowing her visitors might arrive at any time she pressed on, with the intention of boasting of her success. Today she would have earned her tea and cakes.

The weather was humid. The sun had disappeared, the clouds had dropped low and were threatening rain. She was about halfway through the heavy branch when she had to stop and rest and get a cool drink.

She pulled the saw clear of the branch and threw it down before stiffly climbing down the steps. For a moment she stood, stretching her aching muscles and taking deep breaths. Why was the wood so stubborn? It was old and had not shown a leaf for years. Lewis said it was rotten so why didn't it give way to her efforts? She went underneath it and looked up, trying to gauge how much more she would have to cut before it would break free with its own weight. She touched it and wriggled it about and then stretched some more before going into the house to get the drink she so desperately needed.

★ ★ ★

Lewis was on his way home with only a few more calls to make on the way. In a small market town, he stopped and bought flowers for Nia and a couple of story books for Joseph. He enjoyed reading to the little boy and chose them with care. Getting back into the car after collecting his final order of the day, he smiled to himself. It had been a lovely day, more like spring than dull November. Driving through wonderful scenery between Swansea and Brecon, he wished he had brought Nia with him. She would have loved a day out. But she liked to stay home on Wednesdays in case Caroline came with Joseph. He wondered idly whether they were there. He wouldn't be home in time to see them, but perhaps he and Nia would go to the Griffithses after they had eaten and give the books to Joseph.

★ ★ ★

Nia returned to the tree, standing and looking at how much she had managed, smiling, thinking about how impressed Lewis would be when she showed him her handiwork, when there was a creaking sound. She didn't pause to look up but darted away from the danger area. Then she turned to see the huge branch break with an awesome snap and lurch towards her. She turned to move further away, but tripped over the waggon Barry had made, and twisted onto her side. Her head landed heavily on a metal lorry and she was stunned. The branch caught on another, twisted in an elegant dance before falling, falling, like a clumsy arrow. Nia took all its weight on her temple, pressing her down onto the toy lorry. She didn't have time to call out. If she had she would have called 'Lewis'.

★ ★ ★

Rhiannon and Caroline stayed longer than intended in Pigog Wood. Joseph was delighted with the game involving two devoted adults who were relaxed and having fun. They put Joseph in his pushchair and hurried along the road hoping Nia wouldn't be too disappointed at the short time left for their visit. They turned in the drive and Joseph, having been released from the pushchair he hated, ran ahead of them calling, 'Nana, Nanny, it's me!' He disappeared around the corner to where the kitchen door stood open and to their surprise returned, slowly walking backwards around the corner towards them. When he turned his face to them, his thumb in his mouth, his eyes were large with fear. 'Nanny,' he said, taking the thumb out of his mouth and pointing.

'You wait here with Joseph,' Rhiannon said and went to see what had frightened the child. She came back white-faced, her eyes as wide and frightened as Joseph's.

'Oh, Caroline, there's been a dreadful accident!' she said running to hug them both. 'How awful that Joseph was the first to see her.'

★ ★ ★

When Lewis came home, whistling cheerfully, with the books for Joseph and the flowers for Nia and a small brooch he had bought for her at a market in one of the towns he had visited, he was surprised to see a policeman waiting at the gate.

'Hello? Is anything up?' he asked.

'Are you Mr Lewis Lewis, sir?'

'Yes, daft isn't it? What a stupid idea, eh?

When I was at school they called me Lewis Twice.' He chattered on; 'Did the same thing to my son would you believe? Lewis-boy we called him so we didn't get mixed up.' He slammed the car door and tilted his head on one side and frowned. 'How can I help you? Nothing wrong, is there?'

'I'm afraid there's been an accident, Mr Lewis. Mrs Martin, the lady who owns this house. I believe you live here with her?'

'Yes. Yes. Go on, man!'

'I think you'd better come and sit down sir.'

'For God's sake, tell me!'

'I'm afraid the lady had an accident, in the garden it was.'

'That bloody tree! I'll bet it was that tree! Where is she? What hospital?' He turned to open his car door again and the policeman held his arm.

'I'm very sorry, sir, but the lady is dead.'

Lewis stared at the man, unblinking, just staring, waiting for something more to be said to take away the nonsense of the last sentence.

'She can't be,' he said finally. He smiled and stepped forward as a figure appeared around the corner and the smile faded as he recognised not Nia but his daughter,

366

Rhiannon. With her was Caroline, who was carrying Joseph. From the expression on their faces he knew he hadn't been mistaken, the policeman really had told him Nia was dead. He began to wail, a low eerie sound that seemed to emanate from the earth beneath him.

Rhiannon ran to him and together they cried and all Lewis could say was, 'What happened?' over and over again, seeming not to hear the oft-repeated reply. That she was dead, the woman he had loved all his adult life was gone from him, that was the only thought that filled his mind.

His head was filled with a strange buzzing sound and it was a long time before he realised it came from himself. His eyes were glazed, seeing a future that didn't include Nia. He stumbled towards the back door and then he looked at his daughter.

'D'you know, Rhiannon, on her headstone it won't say Nia Lewis. Not even Nia Martin. She'll be Nia Davies after some man she was married to briefly, when your mother found out about us and she fled to London. She should have been Nia Lewis and now it's too late.'

Like a child he allowed himself to be led inside and sat in a chair, and to be hugged by his daughter and his frightened grandson.

Caroline stood like a statue, wondering how to comfort Barry.

★ ★ ★

Barry didn't finish work until six o'clock. When he saw the foreman approaching him more than an hour before that, walking hesitantly along the benches at which the packers worked, he smiled a greeting.

'You look fed-up. The machines playing up again?'

'You'd better come to my office, boy,' he was told.

Caroline was there and her face told him something serious had happened. The foreman left them together while Caroline told him the awful news and they walked out together, arms around each other before driving up to Chestnut Road in the van.

★ ★ ★

Later that night, when all who needed to be told had been informed and the seemingly endless line of people trekking in and out had finally stopped, and Lewis had been put to bed with sleeping tablets supplied by the doctor, Caroline and Barry were left alone.

'Please don't go home tonight,' Barry said. 'I don't want to leave here and I don't want to spend the night alone.'

'Lewis is here,' she said.

'I want you.'

He looked so confused, so unhappy and so young. She stepped towards him and held him in her arms. Holding back tears he took deep breaths, and gradually calmed down. Neither of them moved for a long, long time.

Caroline put her fingers to his cheeks and turned his face to meet hers. The kiss was like the culmination of years of need. Ice to fire. A need greater than hunger, greater than thirst. An all-consuming need that his enfolding arms and his lips and the scent of him and the warmth of him, melted away.

★ ★ ★

Lewis was a man in pain. He wandered around, dealing with the arrangements with Barry, and seemed only half aware of what he was doing. He continued to live at Chestnut Road but went every evening to sit in Dora's living room, hardly saying a word, but attending to the chores like adding coal to the fire or making cups of tea as if his mind had tripped back to the time before the break-up of his marriage.

On the night before the funeral, he began to talk and Dora thought he would never stop. He talked about Nia, about their life together, and how they had always loved each other. As an afterthought, as if suddenly aware of who he was with, he told Dora that he had loved her too, but Dora only gave Rhiannon a grim smile and said nothing.

He talked until he fell asleep but instead of allowing him to stay where he was, on the couch near the still glowing fire, Dora woke him.

'Lewis, tomorrow's the funeral. You have to be at the house and go with it from there. Barry needs you, and you need to be there.'

'I don't know what I'll do,' he said as he shrugged himself into his coat. 'The house is for Barry and Caroline, I've always known that. I don't know where I'll go.'

'There's always The Firs.' Dora's eyes gleamed with malice as she remembered the discomfort of the shabby rooms in that place, where Lewis had spent some time after walking out of their home. 'It isn't as if you don't know the place, is it?'

Dora stood at the door as the car drove away. She still loved him, she always would, but he wouldn't come back. She had more pride now, and would never make a fool of herself over a man again. Not any more.

★ ★ ★

The funeral was a large one. Nia had been in business in the town for many years, taking over Temptations from her mother, and she had been well-liked. Lewis walked with Barry, and the Griffithses were with them, offering support.

Lewis stood between Viv and Basil and kept looking around as if waiting for Nia to come and tell him he'd had a nightmare, unable to accept what had happened. He stared at the coffin in which his happiness lay. 'I've lost Joseph, and now Nia, why am I being punished so?' he murmured.

'You lost our Lewis-boy too,' Viv reminded him. But the words of reproach seemed not to penetrate the haze of misery and despair.

Dora was standing near and she said, 'You had years of happiness, some never manage any.' Her voice was tender. She ached to comfort him but didn't know how. Even a hand reaching out to touch his arm had been quickly withdrawn. Best to wait. Then,

371

gradually aware of her concern and angry with herself for feeling it, her expression hardened and she walked away.

'He's not coming back,' she told her daughter, wagging a warning finger. He had loved Nia too much for that to be possible. He wasn't going to come back and treat her as a bolt-hole in his misery. Never again would she accept second best.

★ ★ ★

Farmer Booker saw the mournful Basil and Frank and Ernie at the graveside and murmured,

'Not planning any more shennanigans here are you?'

'What the 'ell d'you mean?' Frank asked.

'That bit of poaching you were supposed to have done the night the graves were disturbed. The rabbits in that bag were as stiff as a load of firewood.'

Frank and Ernie, Viv and Jack took him on one side and explained to him what they had been doing. Booker's laughter startled the mourners and frightened a few sparrows away from the newly-turned soil of the graves.

'Well, what could we do?' Frank demanded in a hoarse whisper. 'Old sod he might have been, but we couldn't have an uncle lying on top of Mrs Pryce-Yeoman for ever could we? It wouldn't have been proper!' The laughter came again, louder, and Booker had to walk away from the crowd to enjoy it.

'I'll drop the charges,' he said between helpless hoots of laughter. 'You've given me the best laugh this ages.'

Full of consternation at Booker's generosity, the three Griffiths boys went to see him later that day and, somewhat bemused, he agreed *not* to withdraw charges of trespass and poaching. They needed the trespass charge. It was an alibi, of sorts, for being innocent of the more serious charge of desecrating the graves.

★ ★ ★

Barry and Caroline quickly confirmed that the house in Chestnut Road was theirs.

'What shall we do about Lewis?' Caroline asked after the visit to the solicitors. 'This is his home. We can't just tell him to go, can we?'

'Let him stay for a while. Until he finds somewhere else. There's plenty of room until our Joseph has a brother or a sister,' he said, touching her rosy cheek with his lips.

'We have to find this Mr Davies, the man she married in London. He ought to know, and there's the painting and the other things she left him in her will.'

Lewis had the man's name and address and, on the advice of the solicitor, they wrote to him.

The reply came very quickly. He offered his condolences and said how sorry he was that they had never met. He would be very happy to receive the small gifts and the Paul Nash painting, which he had bought for Nia as a wedding present. Without delay, Barry parcelled them up and posted them off.

★ ★ ★

The party to celebrate the engagement of Ernie and Helen was attended by half the town's young people. Or so Hywel thought as they trooped in; a never-ending stream. The T.V. was pushed into the shed and Farmer Booker surprised them all by turning up with a gift for the young couple and playing them a few tunes on a piano accordion. By eight o'clock the party was off to a good start.

Caroline and Barry were there, sober and looking pale, although Janet was relieved to see a different light in Caroline's eyes when she and Barry exchanged glances. When she had a chance, she asked how things were, and Caroline hugged her and said, 'It's going to be all right, Mam. Barry and I are all right.'

Grieving for Nia hadn't been allowed to stop them celebrating the engagement of Caroline's brother. As Barry reminded them, they were his only family now and he was going to treasure them.

As Lewis wouldn't be there, Dora walked across the fields with Rhiannon, Charlie and Gwyn, and Viv and Joan, who made excuses for her twin Megan, explaining that Megan had a previous engagement.

★ ★ ★

Megan was discontented. She missed the company of her sister and on the occasions when they did meet Joan was no fun any more. Marriage had sobered her. Once, The Weston Girls, as they had always been known, had a reputation for doing the unlikely and even the unacceptable and outrageous. Now things had changed and Megan hated it. She, who had mainly followed her sister's lead, was looking for excitement.

Knowing that her family did not want her to involve herself with Terrence Jenkins, with whom she had once had a brief affair, she invited him to go with her to the Griffithses party. An hour after Joan had made her

375

excuses, she walked in. The expression on Joan's face alone, made it worth the bother.

On Joan's insistence, Viv told Megan they would walk her home, but Megan clung to Terry's arm and shook her head.

'Terrence will look after me, won't you?' She smiled up at Terrence, a handsome if rather haughty-looking individual, and stretched up to touch her lips against his chin, which was as far as she could reach. 'You don't have to worry about me while I'm with him,' she assured everyone.

Terrence was far from comfortable in the shabby and over-filled house. He thought of other places where they could have spent their time and constantly glanced at the clock and wished it was time to leave. He was afraid to suggest escaping too soon, he was anxious to please Megan even to the extent of staying in this awful room with these awful people she amused herself by calling her friends.

Marion and her family arrived at nine o'clock and left again at half-past. They hardly spoke, in fact Fred stood clutching his cap, wringing it out, obviously embarrassed in company. Janet waved them off and thought it unlikely she would see them again. It had been exciting, searching for them. 'But sometimes it's better to leave the past locked away,' she whispered to Hywel.

'You had as much chance of teaching that lot to enjoy themselves as teaching a goldfish to ride a bike!' was Hywel's reply.

During the evening Megan stayed close to Terrence and made sure she was seen kissing him, behaving in a way that embarrassed those present. She looked at the others with thinly veiled contempt. All these couples doing the conventional thing. Surely life could hold something more?

When it was time to leave, she walked to Terrence's car, clinging to his arm with the concentration of a drunk.

'Megan, love, does this mean you've forgiven me?' Terrence asked. 'I promise you I haven't seen a girl since we parted. I want to marry you.'

'Oh no, Terrence, don't let's be boring. The town has had a surfeit of weddings and engagements, for heaven's sake! Let's run off to London and have some fun.'

'Run away and get married like Jack, you mean?'

'*No*! No, just have some fun before life squeezes us into our allotted rut.'

★ ★ ★

The Gunners were determined to disapprove, and were helped in that aim by Ernie's announcement that he had lost his job. His days as a bus conductor had ended ignominiously after starting a fight with a passenger who dared to tell him his bus was late.

Gloria told him he could forget his hopes of marrying Helen until he found a job and kept it. Helen smiled and cancelled out the threat with a wink. For the rest of the evening, Gloria tried to show everyone how upset she was, but the laughter got to her and the teasing which included herself and Wilfred softened her resolve and she enjoyed the evening in spite of her determination not to.

Charlie and a sleepy Gwyn walked across the fields with Rhiannon and Dora and Viv and Joan. On the doorstep of seven Sophie Street, sitting huddled against the cold night air, was Lewis.

'Wrong house, Lewis,' Dora said sharply. 'Memory going is it? You live at Chestnut Road now, or The Firs if Barry's thrown you out.'

'I just wanted to hear how the party went, Dora. That's all.'

'It was the usual lively evening, with the Griffithses on top form and poor Helen on a knife-edge, trying to be her mother's polite little girl and at the same time hold her own with the Griffiths boys. They'll be all right, Helen and Ernie.'

'I suppose they're my family now, aren't they? Nia's son married to Caroline, their little Joseph my grandson.'

'We're your family,' Viv said, with an arm around his mother. 'You turned away from us, we didn't leave you.'

Viv stood with an arm around his wife and his mother, Charlie stood with Rhiannon and his son. Lewis stood up and nodded to them all before walking slowly to the car. Before getting in he listened to the sound of them, laughing and chattering as they closed the door on him, then he drove away.

* * *

When the guests had gone and the debris of the evening was scattered around them, Janet and Hywel summed it up.

'Well, so much for our new relations, love,' Hywel sighed. 'Stayed less than an hour, showed their embarrassment at our uncouth ways and walked off with their pathetic noses in the air. How dare they think themselves superior to us?'

Janet chuckled. 'Who doesn't? Did you see

the way Terrence glared at us all? And the way Helen's mother looked at the food? A soul-sister to old Gladys Weston she is for sure, or tries to be! She actually shuddered when I brought in that plateful of brawn sandwiches and a seven-pound sweet jar filled with pickled onions!'

'She was more likely upset at the way everyone tucked in! They all ate as though they'd been starved for a week. Small-minded lot, our new relations, you'll never change them. Some people never change.'

'You're right, love.' Janet laughed and pointed to the mantelpiece on which stood a long envelope. 'Nothing changes. Our Basil and our Frank and our Ernie are in court again next week, for trespassing and poaching.'

THE END

Other titles in the
Ulverscroft Large Print Series:

THE GREENWAY
Jane Adams
When Cassie and her twelve-year-old cousin Suzie had taken a short cut through an ancient Norfolk pathway, Suzie had simply vanished . . . Twenty years on, Cassie is still tormented by nightmares. She returns to Norfolk, determined to solve the mystery.

FORTY YEARS ON THE WILD FRONTIER
Carl Breihan & W. Montgomery
Noted Western historian Carl Breihan has culled from the handwritten diaries of John Montgomery, grandfather of co-author Wayne Montgomery, new facts about Wyatt Earp, Doc Holliday, Bat Masterson and other famous and infamous men and women who gained notoriety when the Western Frontier was opened up.

TAKE NOW, PAY LATER
Joanna Dessau
This fiction based on fact is the love-turning-to-hate story of Robert Carr, Earl of Somerset, and his wife, Frances.

McLEAN AT THE GOLDEN OWL
George Goodchild

Inspector McLean has resigned from Scotland Yard's CID and has opened an office in Wimpole Street. With the help of his able assistant, Tiny, he solves many crimes, including those of kidnapping, murder and poisoning.

KATE WEATHERBY
Anne Goring

Derbyshire, 1849: The Hunter family are the arrogant, powerful masters of Clough Grange. Their feuds are sparked by a generation of guilt, despair and ill-fortune. But their passions are awakened by the arrival of nineteen-year-old Kate Weatherby.

A VENETIAN RECKONING
Donna Leon

When the body of a prominent international lawyer is found in the carriage of an intercity train, Commissario Guido Brunetti begins to dig deeper into the secret lives of the once great and good.

A TASTE FOR DEATH
Peter O'Donnell

Modesty Blaise and Willie Garvin take on impossible odds in the shape of Simon Delicata, the man with a taste for death, and Swordmaster, Wenczel, in a terrifying duel. Finally, in the Sahara desert, the intrepid pair must summon every killing skill to survive.

SEVEN DAYS FROM MIDNIGHT
Rona Randall

In the Comet Theatre, London, seven people have good reason for wanting beautiful Maxine Culver out of the way. Each one has reason to fear her blackmail. But whose shadow is it that lurks in the wings, waiting to silence her once and for all?

QUEEN OF THE ELEPHANTS
Mark Shand

Mark Shand knows about the ways of elephants, but he is no match for the tiny Parbati Barua, the daughter of India's greatest expert on the Asian elephant, the late Prince of Gauripur, who taught her everything. Shand sought out Parbati to take part in a film about the plight of the wild herds today in north-east India.

THE DARKENING LEAF
Caroline Stickland

On storm-tossed Chesil Bank in 1847, the young lovers, Philobeth and Frederick, prevent wreckers mutilating the apparent corpse of a young woman. Discovering she is still alive, Frederick takes her to his grandmother's home. But the rescue is to have violent and far-reaching effects . . .

A WOMAN'S TOUCH
Emma Stirling

When Fenn went to stay on her uncle's farm in Africa, the lovely Helena Starr seemed to resent her — especially when Dr Jason Kemp agreed to Fenn helping in his bush hospital. Though it seemed Jason saw Fenn as little more than a child, her feelings for him were those of a woman.

A DEAD GIVEAWAY
Various Authors

This book offers the perfect opportunity to sample the skills of five of the finest writers of crime fiction — Clare Curzon, Gillian Linscott, Peter Lovesey, Dorothy Simpson and Margaret Yorke.

DOUBLE INDEMNITY — MURDER FOR INSURANCE
Jad Adams

This is a collection of true cases of murderers who insured their victims then killed them — or attempted to. Each tense, compelling account tells a story of cold-blooded plotting and elaborate deception.

THE PEARLS OF COROMANDEL
By Keron Bhattacharya

John Sugden, an ambitious young Oxford graduate, joins the Indian Civil Service in the early 1920s and goes to uphold the British Raj. But he falls in love with a young Hindu girl and finds his loyalties tragically divided.

WHITE HARVEST
Louis Charbonneau

Kathy McNeely, a marine biologist, sets out for Alaska to carry out important research. But when she stumbles upon an illegal ivory poaching operation that is threatening the world's walrus population, she soon realises that she will have to survive more than the harsh elements . . .

TO THE GARDEN ALONE
Eve Ebbett
Widow Frances Morley's short, happy marriage was childless, and in a succession of borders she attempts to build a substitute relationship for the husband and family she does not have. Over all hovers the shadow of the man who terrorized her childhood.

CONTRASTS
Rowan Edwards
Julia had her life beautifully planned — she was building a thriving pottery business as well as sharing her home with her friend Pippa, and having fun owning a goat. But the goat's problems brought the new local vet, Sebastian Trent, into their lives.

MY OLD MAN AND THE SEA
David and Daniel Hays
Some fathers and sons go fishing together. David and Daniel Hays decided to sail a tiny boat seventeen thousand miles to the bottom of the world and back. Together, they weave a story of travel, adventure, and difficult, sometimes terrifying, sailing.